Linking The Threads

To order additional copies, please contact us.
BookSurge, LLC
An Amazon.com Company
www.booksurge.com
1-866-308-6235
orders@booksurge.com

HILARY
RUDICK

LINKING
THE THREADS
A Tribute To A Litvak Tailor

2005

Linking The Threads

ACKNOWLEDGEMENTS

I'd like to say a very sincere thank you to the readers who were my special friends, colleagues and researchers. They encouraged me to reach my goal,   .

My special thanks to Peggy Lucas for working under pressure with such good grace.

It gives me pleasure to pay tribute to my completely wonderful children who complained that not only did they have to *live* this life, they were now required to read it!

To my loving husband for his humour, his criticism, and his patience at being woken up at midnight to read and re- read.

We all have a story to tell. This is ours. My intention in writing this story was to paint a picture of the person Wilfred was, for Dan, who never knew him before he was ill.

In retrospect, I wanted all of us to remember who he really was, for the future generations, particularly our grandchildren.

I wanted to document why we had the left beaches and blue sky to end up living in the mulch of England.

I am grateful to my cousins and good friends who held my hand through thirty years of difficult times.

The story would not have had a happy ending without the generous caring Tzedakah of Basil Wunsh, David Rose, and Jackie Turner.

May the descendants of the Levinthal clan
inherit their innate determination.

YIDDISH

I have included Yiddish phrases in this book because it is the *Mameh loshn*, the mother tongue spoken by millions of people throughout Europe since the 11th Century.

Yiddish speaking people moved to USA, Canada, Australia, South Africa and throughout the modern world.

It is the language my generation remember and learnt by hearing it spoken around us as children. It brings back the smell of Bobbe's kitchen. The words are so expressive that they do not need translating.

Sometimes, it was the secret communication of the older generation and it is the most effective way to say something you really feel, where the idioms are picturesque and the intention hilariously funny.

While the author is not a Yiddish speaker she can definitely be described as an *"Oi Vey Yente."*

Supposing you do not understand the words, read them out loud, **with gusto,**

You will laugh at yourself. *Mazeltov* to you all for choosing to read this book.!

*This book is dedicated to the fond memory of those
who already took the journey.*

*Birth is a beginning
And Death a destination
And life is a journey.............*

*Material from the Gates of Repentance © 1978
copyright to: Central Conference of American Rabbis.*

COVER: DAN SMOLLAN

PART ONE
Zagare, Lithuania 1905

CONTENTS:

1.

DONIYEL

Gittel watched the last languid drops of blood drain down the
kashering board as she emptied a handful of rough salt onto
the pale meat of the slaughtered chicken. It imitated her heart
being drained of blood, the salt on the wound of her shredded psyche.

She knew he had to leave, She believed G-d would protect him and
somewhere there must be a better life than the measly fearful existence
they eked out from dawn to dusk in this now almost barren town on the
border of Shavli Province.

My Doniyel, *mein sheine zun*, the flesh of my flesh, he had inherited
all the good things from both sides.

His peers acknowledged his bargaining powers. With his logical
brain, he solved people's problems. His brothers had found him to be so
wise when trading in their store that sold iron and metal ware. They sold
goods found, which they repaired and re-sold. They had benefited by
Doniyel's help even at such a young age.

He could fix anything and then, *alevei,* amazingly negotiate a good
price and still remain the buyer's best friend.

His desire to study was thwarted by the laws of Alexandra III's
decree that Jews could not study medicine or law or engineering. He had
become a tailor, a much sought after trade because the artisan could work
for himself. He had learned his skills with creative diligence.

He had wonderful talented hands and a good eye. He found fabrics
in the market, bartered skillfully for them. He stored them away until
the right client came along. When a suitable buyer appeared, he would
produce the silk for suiting and the wool for a coat, and he developed
a name for himself among the well-dressed young men of Zagare and
beyond.

Late into the night, after a hard working day, he still sat with his
father Reb Shlomo Ben Zalkind studying Torah and the implications of

the texts. He learned about his heritage, which was all we, his parents, had to give him at this point

Our life had not always been this hopeless, she thought .Her parents, Of Blessed Memory, had died in the Black Plague. Her mother, renowned throughout the village shtetls for her embroidery and needlework, had taught Gittel her skill while she sat at her knee.

When Reb Shlomo Ben Zalkind's wife died, leaving him with three boys to bring up, he was grief-stricken and worried—a Rebbe without a wife was unacceptable to the community.

Shortly thereafter he had occasion to visit Linkuva, a small town near the shtetl of Zagare on the road to Ponevys.

He came upon me weaving and twilling a cover for a new Torah (five books of the law) for the Synagogue in Linkuva. The first cover had been made in 1565 when the synagogue was originally built. It was threadbare and worn. Gittel had been chosen to replace this exalted cover for the revered words, which were read and studied in the synagogue each Sabbath. She considered this a very great honor and an acknowledgement of her skilled hand work.

The Rabbi stopped to talk to her, examining her fine embroidery. After this meeting he visited the local Rabbi, on the pretext of finding talent to make his own shul in Zagare a new Parochet for their Aron Chodesh (curtain for the Ark.)

In his wisdom the local Rabbi told him that Gittel was an orphan, but he sang her praises "a Balebosta, a very accomplished young meidal," and educated, reads and writes Hebrew, a very suitable background for the wife of a Rabbi. .

For this piece of good news he received a handsome *shadchun* fee (a marriage broker) from the Rebbe's community.

Gittel was young, alone and so enchanted that this respected good looking man could envisage her as his wife, a dream she never expected to fulfill.

Under the Chuppah he spoke to her softly, his strong brown eyes gazed very directly into hers as he pronounced the words of the wedding ceremony,

"Me kodesht li ....

Behold, You are consecrated to me according to the law of Moses and Israel"

And so it came to be, that in 1882 Gittel become the Reb's wife. They lived across the pathway to the imposing brick Shul in Zagare, a strong and vibrant community. Reb Shlomo was the head of the Yeshiva, a college where young men studied Torah. He supervised the Kashrut, (the laws of keeping kosher in the community.) Over the years, as he grew older and needed more assistance, this began to fall more on her shoulders although naturally only his word could be considered as absolute.

We did have *a shochet* (a man who kills the chickens according to religious law) but for community members coming to *Kasher* their dishes or request help with their utensils she was often left to advise them, after consulting with the Rebbe.

The strict Kashrut laws (laws of kosher eating)of the community were strongly observed, it was a way of life where we knew no other, and it was considered a privilege to be witness to the local villagers coming to ensure their meat was halachically kosher (killed according to the law of Halacha and in a humane way.)

The Rebbe's wife worked hard in her new home, the young children grew to care for her although they always remained slightly distant. The Rebbe was a kind, good husband, and if she wished him to be more loving or tender it was a girlhood dream experienced in the fading memory of her father bringing her mother a bunch of field flowers with that special private smile. Gittel smiled to herself at the memory of her mother combing her hair and dropping sweet apple spice onto her apron just before he came home.

In 1885 her son Doniyel was born. He grew to be a confident little boy, sharp and eager to experience everything around him. He had a beautiful baritone singing voice and would sing loud and clear as the Rebbe sang grace at our table. The two of them enjoyed singing so much it was perhaps the only time she saw the Rebbe laugh and sing with all his heart.

He taught him all the prayers but he also taught him songs of old, songs of praise and sometimes they would sit outside and sing until the Sabbath stars came out.

Doniyel grew into an elegant young man. He loved dancing. In the winter he skated all the way across the Shventa River to school. Often I would wait, anxious as to why he was not home on time. At these times Gittel made the Rebbe walk down to the river as it was not acceptable for a woman to walk unaccompanied, and there he would find Doniyel happily practicing his turns and swirls on the ice, singing heartily to himself—oblivious of time passing.

The older brothers could sense that Doniyel was his favorite child and sometimes they were secretly mean to him, but he was of such sunny nature and clever cunning, that he always turned this to his advantage.

So, with these thoughts in mind she had to steel herself in the knowledge that she knew they had done the right thing. She knew that her son was street- wise and would find a new pathway in life. He was brave and handsome and my chest felt tightly suffocated at the thought that she might never hold him in her arms again.

Around the time of Doniyel's birth, Tzarist Russia was an unhappy place for Jews. Laws were becoming more and more stringent, taxes were levied to a point where families could not afford to eat after paying the tax, conscription was the nightmare of every parent because Jewish boys were forced to go into the army for 25 years.

They would be old and hardened men before they could be released, veterans of many wars and much hardship.

The Russo—Japanese war brought more misery, battles with the Germans coming into the villages were increasing .The conscriptees were being sent to Germany to work. This caused a negative influence in the economy of the communities and there were times when the shul was unable to pay the Rabbi his salary.

During the night hollow knocking on the kitchen door brought distraught families reporting the capture of a son. *"Avec genemen-Avec genemen"* "They took him – they took him" a frightened father would cry. *Khapers* as they were referred to, or snatchers were paid to bring in young men for conscription.

The Rebbe was forced to levy a 10 zloty tax per family as a fund raiser to hold funds towards paying ransom as the Germans and Poles captured Jews and held them for larger and larger sums of money. He never turned a family away and we all prayed for the safe return of a member of our community.

Tsar Alexander the II was replaced by a wicked wanton Tsar Alexander III.

The Principles of living the life of a religious Jew became even more hazardous as new laws were proclaimed.

The Tzar forbad Jews to dress in traditional clothing in the street and *peyos* (sidelocks) were forbidden. Police were commanded to shave the culprits publicly in the street and young men started to feel uneasy, degraded and angry. He tried to ban married woman from wearing a sheitel, a wig to cover their hair and this caused heartfelt anguish and shame on many pious women, who knew no other way.

Her blood curdled when she heard that Jews would have to fill a quota in the army. In order to fill this quota, boys of twelve would be sent into training rather than risk the community being punished.

Wealthier families could buy their way out of the quota but, as the son of the Rebbe, our children would have to be included in the count.

Rebbe Shlomo Ben Zalkind was responsible for the recording of all tax collection for the Tzar, in our area He had to record all the births, deaths and marriages.

In his quiet way, as an enlightened and educated man of the time, he encouraged me to do more than just "slach" the chickens. (This was the ritual kosher killing of the live stock according to the humane laws of Kashrut .We never ate meat that had not been halachically killed.

She had been taught by her father to read and write and this stood her in such good stead in her new life. Often the laborious recording of details took time away from his studying, so he encouraged Gittel, with her neat and careful script to help him with recording the community details. In time she took over this function. Certainly in the recording of births, she knew who had given birth more often than he did, as the woman acted as midwives for each other. Often a group of women standing outside a house could mean they were guarding the doorway lest Lilith, supposedly Adam's first wife, came by to steal the baby. This was a myth we all sincerely believed in and we went to great lengths to prevent her "evil eye" from seeing the baby.

When the time came for her to record Donyiel's birth, they had several births to record and many traumatic things were happening in the village. In her anxiety to get it all written down, she genuinely forgot to list their son's name. She lay in the dark—weeks later, when she realized what she had done. In her realization she new it meant he could not be added in the quota. Gittel prayed for forgiveness to the other babies registered. She prayed to G-d for understanding and she prayed that the Rebbe would not check up on the names and would understand her fear. In his correctness he would have felt obliged to add their sons name and *My Doniyel* was not going to waste his talent in the army of Siberia in 1884

2
GITTEL

As a poor orphan, I did not have an enviable dowry to bring to my marriage: However, my father had been a jeweler at the Tzarist court. At times he had been paid in precious stones rather than a wage. These had been hidden away once my father had proudly displayed the sparkling stones to his family, handling them with the reverence he felt for stones and explaining to me at great length why each was of value.

I came to my marriage with the Rebbe clutching my hidden bag of rubies sapphires and diamonds.

Reb Shlomo was a man of simple needs and believed within his holy nature that we served the community and our service was our wealth. He did not want to be seen as having valuables himself, or cause envy in his fellow men.

In the newness of my situation and without the confidence of a more experienced woman, he convinced me that it would be a great mitzvah (blessing) to donate the stones to the synagogue and to sew them into the new Parochet I had been invited to make for the Zagare Shul. This would bring great prestige to the decor of his shul. This grand synagogue prided itself in the handsomely carved heavy wooden Bimah (central podium), the stained glass windows that had been brought from old Prussia and the raised leather seats in the front rows.

My name would be mentioned when people admired the Parochet, and the Rebbe would feel proud of his wife, Gittel the orphan,

As hard as I prayed, I was never able to rise above my feeling of resentment at being gently forced to give my jewels away and I never came to terms with the fact that they were no longer mine.

As one of my initial important marital duties, I set about producing this revered adornment for the Aron Kodesh (the richly decorated ark built into the eastern wall of the synagogue. It is here the Torahs are kept).

First I took a plush silk velvet cloth that my mother had used in our front room and I gently washed and dried it. The next day I walked to the market down Sheduva Street. I passed the heavy wooden log houses, each neat and secure in their allocated yard in the street surrounding our parish. I returned the curious stares of the Zagare residents, each wondering why I was going to market so early in the week!

I turned cheerily down the dirt road past the Jewish orphanage, shivering at my memories of the cold hard beds. Soon I reached the *balegan*—the noisy activity of fresh food market in the central square,. I sang softly to myself, making my way around the dusty carts, knowing I was going on a happy mission. I successfully exchanged my warm home baked Ruggelach (ginger biscuits for fresh young beetroot and strong brown onions.

I boiled the beet slowly until the color was deep rose, then I added the onion skins to deepen the color and as many cups of salt as would dissolve in my potion. I held my breath, donned my oldest dress knowing I would splash onto the surrounds and dipped the grey silk velvet into the deep vat. I closed my eyes and slowly recited a *brocha* (prayer) of thanks for the privilege of being awarded this honor and then I gave thanks for the pleasure I took in making it.

I opened my eyes and there before me in the swirling warm water, lay my deep ruby velvet. Perfect! *Shterk Royt borsht*! I dried it and stretched it and the Rebbe and I spent many companionable days discussing my intended design. It warmed my heart to see him excited by the project. I wondered if I loved him and if he loved me.

Day and night I stitched and pulled the silver and gold threads, my metal thimble knocking rhythmically against the frame. I used large curved needles and thin short needles and I embroidered each stitch with love and dedication. Around the plaited border I sewed 613 loops of cable stitch. Jews are commanded to perform *613 mitvoth* (good deeds) in their religious life. These cover all the laws of "how to behave towards your fellow man" and are the basis of good Jewish behavior.

The two rampant Lions I stitched as a honey comb filler covering their bodies with hundreds of little stitches making them rich and strong. For the two tablets given to Moses with the ten commandments embroidered across them, I used petit point in a fine blue thread that I'd had in my workbox for years. It had tones ranging from light blue to royal blue and shone as if the light of laws needed to be illuminated.

The scrolls and leaves decorating the corners were my *piece de resistance*. I used all the Jacobean couching needlework skills that I had struggled to learn as a girl. This type of embroidery had become the mark of my family. Into these flowers and buds I sewed the 13 rubies of my trousseau. 13 principles of faith are set out in the Shulchan Aruch, the guide book to interpreting Judaic Law. I sewed the gold thread over and over the rubies, knotting it repeatedly to keep them bound safely into the velvet. I sewed it so tightly that it almost covered the rubies. I told the Rebbe I didn't want the curtain to be seen as being too extravagant, but secretly I didn't want anyone to know MY rubies were there.

Into the cornflowers surrounding the scrolls and leaves, I wove the 7 sapphires my father had shown me while telling me they were the color of my eyes. This signified the creation and seven days of the week.

The Crown was the most difficult part and I spent many long hours making it. Other women in the village brought their threads to me in order to have something of their own in the holy curtain.

My mother had taught me to do blackwork, an embroidery field with many complicated knots and double knots which gave a rich raised look and made you want to run your fingers over the repeated pattern to read it in its entirety. I sighed *"a Groys' n dank mammele"*, a heartfelt thank you my mother.

One cool summer morning, as I was sitting on the front porch sewing, the Rebbe approached me holding a string of pearls. I realized they were important to him and surmised they must have belonged to his late wife. He enquired gently if I'd like to use them, as he wanted to add them to the collection of jewels. I nodded without comment and after he left I pondered over it for a while.

I put my work down, clasped the warm lemon tea in my hands, and looked out over the nodding pink and purple cosmos in the field in front of me. I came to the conclusion that I had no reason not to use them, or to resent her, the poor woman was not in any way a threat to me and I must behave generously.

Into the crown, the Keter Torah (used above the two tablets to indicate the sanctity of the Torah) I sewed the tiny pearls which had been his late wife's bracelet, crowned by the diamond.

When it was finally ready on a Sunday morning, the Rebbe agreed to rise early before the morning service and come went into the shul to hang the curtain. Normally the *Shammus* (organizer) of the shul would have done this, but I wanted the Rebbe to be alone with me when he saw it completed.

He sat down slowly, looking at every inch of it with an expert studied eye. After he had scanned it extensively he paused, drew a deep breath and smiled from deep inside himself. Abruptly he stood, nodded, then turned and went back to his study.

I knew he was pleased but I only got the acknowledgment second hand from comments he made to the congregants over the years and I had to be content knowing I had brought him *nachus* and done him proud.

Doniyel came to have a look at the Parochet hung in its position. Always my supportive loving son, he gasped "A *mechieh*! superb! He hugged me with pride.

"*Shein vi di zibben velten* "he said "it's as beautiful as the seven worlds ….."

Our daily life revolved around the services of the synagogue. As we lived next door to the building, all our sons were called upon to make up the minyan (10 men necessary for any services that took place.)

After the Sabbath evening service on a Friday night it was a customary for the young yeshiva boys to escort the Rebbe safely home. As they approached our house they were always welcome to partake of the meal. By reputation, our table was often crowded with young men eager to hear the opinion of the Rebbe and, I hoped, to eat of my tasty cholent and enjoy my layered pear strudel.

I made a special effort on the eve of Shabbos. Before the dusk, I lit my candles, baked the warm sweet plaited kitke and prepared our meal for the following day, so that we did not desecrate the Sabbath by cooking. I loved setting my table in a decorative manner, using our best silver dishes and my favorite warming bowl with its engraved silver hood, another gift from the Tzar. I baked *kichel (a sweet biscuit)* to eat with the herrings, and I had a large pot of chicken soup, made from the giblets I had collected. This gave off a welcoming aroma to the returning men. Then I rushed off to the bath house where all the women were exhilarated at the approach of another *Shabbos.*

The other Levintahl family, my husband's brother, invariably joined us with their children. The Gordon family next door came over after the meal when they smelt our coffee brewing on the Shabbos warmer.

The Rabbi leaned back in his chair, chewed his sugar cube, enjoying the exchange of young ideas, then in a slow and regular ritual he always took another cube in his mouth and sipped his coffee, leaning forward in his chair, to give his considered opinion.

3
THE WARNING

At the tender age of seventeen Doniyel was already building a reputation as a tailor of merit. Men admired the fit of his suits and enquired about the name of tailor. They began to travel from Ponevys, Sheduva and Keidani to Zagare to be fitted.

Among those men was Vladimir Gelbkopf, so named "the golden head" for his golden curly hair. He was an officer in the Lithuanian cavalry. Not much older than Doniyel, he was 19 and had been in the army since he was fifteen. He obviously came from a good Lithuanian family and was well educated. He was fascinated by being in the Rebbe's house and loved to be able to look at the well-thumbed books on the shelves. Because he was 6 foot 4 inches tall, with size fourteen shoes, the regular army issue did not fit him and each year he was given a permit to commission Doniyel to make him a new uniform.

Whenever Vladimir sent word ahead that he would be coming, Doniyel was secretly pleased, although he never boasted about it. He knew the village people would all stand and *kibitz* (whisper) when the handsome horses and guards were parked outside the Rebbe s house where Doniyel had his work room.

The Rebbe had taught his children to respect people of all origins. The young officer in turn treated Doniyel and his family with equal respect and Doniyel believed he was building a friendship with him.

One Friday morning in the early spring, he arrived, hot and sweating from the long dusty journey. Doniyel did not relish the idea of measuring him up in this state.

It was the regular custom of all the Jews in the village to go to the Mikveh (ritual baths) on Friday in preparation for the Sabbath.

He invited Vladimir to accompany him, explaining they would be back in time for Doniyel to measure him up before sunset when the Sabbath came in. Vladimir was aware that the family did not work on the Sabbath and he usually took care never to arrive for a fitting on that day.

They walked into the village together with Doniyel's friend Solomon. An unlikely trio, the tall officer in his impressive uniform, Doniyel in his well cut trousers, fancy braces and polished shoes and Solomon who was plump and untidy in his traditional black coat and hat, which he usually wore lopsided. This gave him the look of someone who was a bit *ibber botel.(confused)*

The baths were crowded and buzzing with chatter. Bathers greeted the trio a bit warily but soon Vladimir was drawn into the bantering camaraderie they looked forward to a day of rest and renewal.

After the bathing, the participants of the baths parted with the shouts of familiar humor," *A gezunt in dein pupik"*—good health to you the men shouted! Returning home refreshed and cleansed, Doniyel measured the officer as meticulously as he normally did, with little Chanele, Doniyel's sister, peeping shyly at the tall soldier.

The young soldier had, as usual, brought Doniyel many extra yards of the regulation cloth. After he had completed the measurements, he knew Vladimir loved to have a coffee and taste his mother's dark sweet ruggelagh.

Finally, just before the first star appeared in the sky, he ushered him out to the waiting horses, assuring him the uniforms would be made to measure. This was an excellent commission for Doniyel and he looked forward to completing it successfully. As they were about to leave the front door, he dropped his helmet onto the porch floor, both men knelt down retrieve it, and in that one private moment, where their heads were close together he whispered hurriedly "Doniyel, you must leave here urgently, the pogroms are coming." Then he rose with a bland look on his face, shook hands warmly and mounted his horse.

At night I lay in my warm feather bed too frightened to sleep. I knew the Rebbe was awake in his bed next to mine. I longed to go and lie alongside of him but I never approached him in this way, as he would not have welcomed it.

We listened anxiously for the sound of stamping hooves. It would bring misery, death and destruction. It would come upon us suddenly like a recurring nightmare - swift and cruel.

We were powerless- we had no means of combating this action, either by bodily strength or brave desire to do so. We lived our simple lives as pious and non fanatical Jews.

I wondered if my father would have believed how much hatred and revulsion had filled the land he had so loved. Lithuanian Jews and non Jews had lived symbiotically side by side, in comfortable respect for each others cultural differences, even attending each others celebrations occasionally when people had worked together for a long time.

The landed gentry knew that the Jews on their lands were an asset in many ways, adding to the community intellectually and culturally.

The reason for this was that young boys studied Torah from an early age so they became literate much younger than their Lithuanian counterparts.

They were adroit traders and specialized craftsman. They made things of worth that added to the wealth of their neighbours and the reputation of their village.

But in the early 1900s, rumoru mongers, misunderstandings, and wicked rulers degraded all that we had established. We were living in an uncertain hell, our energy taken up by just trying to survive each wretched blow to our community, losing our credibility, even among ourselves.

That awful night, I heard the thunder coming, it intruded on the black night like a dragon breathing fire. The darrump daruump of the hooves on the cold stone cobbles.

I leapt up to take our daughter out of her cot, Doniyel ran to the front door of our house and slammed the heavy square log across the door, a protective rod he had put in place to withhold the stabs of swords and axes.

We hurried down to the cellar. Here we had blankets and a few supplies hidden under the straw, G-d forbid, we should ever need to hide out for an extended time. We cowered in the darkness. The Rebbe murmured softly in a trance- like way, swaying vigorously back and forth

"Ah klug tsu meine sonim " (will this never end!)

Glass shattered. High pitched screams.- Human screams,donkey screams mixed with the violent yells of the victors, the hooves pounded

the stones again, darump darump pervaded my eardrums, and then
……. empty silent black night.

We dared not open the door, or light the lamp. Doniyel soothed
his sister Chana, crooning a lullaby to her rocking in the chair. We sat
quietly until the sun came up and we heard loud banging on our doors.

Rebbe! Rebbe!

Tsee felt, ikh pes? Are you alright?

We dragged our fearful fatigue up the stairs and the Rebbe still in
his gatkes,donned his clothes and hat braced himself with a cold steely
look on his face. We opened the door and the Shamus came bursting
into the room. Behind him followed a motley collection of people, all in
disarray and in a state of noisy agitation. Oi gevalt!

Oi gevaltinga!!

We hurried across to the shul, and stood in open mouthed
disbelief.

Our beautiful building had been cruelly mutilated.

Walls had been smashed. The stained glass windows were lying in
the dirt imitating a rainbow of shards as if they had been grated like a
vegetable.

The leather chairs were slashed open with their stuffing exposed like
a raped cat.

The wooden fencing surrounding the bimah had been partially
knocked down, but all eyes were frozen at the sight of the Aron Chodesh
which had been heinously attacked. My feet froze as I caught sight of the
Parochet ripped from its place and lying buried beneath the rubble of
wood and stone. In full view lay our worst nightmare, the precious Torah
lying on the floor damaged.

The Shamus and Doniyel ran to gingerly pick up the Torah , they
placed it carefully on the reader desk and stood back for the Rebbe
to come closer. By now most of the shtetl dwellers had come into the
synagogue and all eyes were on him.

The Rebbe held up his hand for silence. When order was restored,he
carefully rolled the torah closed, picked up his prayer book and began
to doven (recite)the morning service amid the debris and rubble, as if

nothing had happened. To us, his kin, we could hear he was dovening more rigorously and more fervently than usual.

Immediately all the men followed suite and the house of prayer was filled with the familiar sounds of the shachrit service. (morning prayers)

While they were busy praying I pulled the velvet beaded Parochet out of the rubble and ran unnoticed to my bedroom across the way. I put a chair up against the door and examined it with a pulsating feeling in my temples. All the precious stones were intact and although it was ripped across the top, it was redeemable.

I lay on my bed and sobbed.

I sobbed for my father, I sobbed in relief and I sobbed at the injustice of the sad persecuted society we had become.

We harmed no one. We tried to live a decent honest life and yet, we were the targeted victims of so many peoples rabid contempt.

I remained in my room for many days. I hid the Parochet under my bed when anyone entered the room. The rabbi thought I was traumatised and he left me to "rest "- so he thought but, I was sewing frantically.

I sewed as fast as my fingers could move, pricking myself horribly but determined I would never give my stones back to anyone who did not insure their safety.

I turned the Parochet inside out. Over the outer side I covered it with a soft strong blanket. Just an ugly grey piece of cloth that would not attract attention. Inside I padded it with felting.

I folded it into a roll and sewed a cloth handle on one end to make it easy to carry.

It was all I had to give to Doniyel if he needed to run and it would give him wealth to trade with and warmth to sleep with.

It was his inheritance and I would not allow myself a feeling of guilt about giving it to him. I made a decision not tell him what was inside. I would just pray that it was not lost to him. I firmly believed G-d would present the stones at the right time under the right circumstances.

When I had completed my task, I emerged from my room feeling stronger more determined and more peaceful.

4
PREPARING FOR THE FLIGHT,
THE STORY OF PESACH

Gittel was tired, but felt a satisfied pride with her day's work. For weeks she had been preparing for Pesach (the festival of Passover). She had packed away her everyday dishes and cutlery and taken out her special set of Pesach crockery, which had belonged to her mother. These they kept aside during the year, using them only on Pesach so that no *chometz,*, non- pesach meal, would have touched the plates and rendered them unsuitable for use on Pesach. Most of the community did not have the luxury of two sets and had to go to great pains to make their dishes suitable for use on Pesach. She had polished the silver until it shone, first with lemon juice and then with silvering solution the way she remembered it in her mother's house. The candlesticks stood high and proud on the shelf .She had washed and pressed all her simcha tablecloths, which her mother had embroidered. These were kept for celebrations and high holy days.

The three older brothers had made large vats of Pesach wine. With their father they had periodically tested it, until the Rebbe had pronounced it ready to drink. Gittel heard a lot of laughing on these occasions, coming from the shed outside where we kept the wine. She smiled to herself. We didn't have much to laugh about. We were required to drink four glasses each so it was imperative to have enough good wine to go around. The special unleavened bread had been baked in the oven space we had hired in the village.

You could purchase matzo from the Pesach bakery set up in the village, or you could hire space in the Pesach oven to bake your own. The Rebbe preferred me to bake ours and Gittel took pleasure in the task as it was a ritual required only once a year.

Mrs Zimmler along the road had grown enough horseradish for everyone to prepare and my nostrils flared at the thought of tasting it.

We would start the meal with boiled eggs in salt water "to symbolize the tears of slavery". The family had been saving fresh eggs from the hens to cater for their very long table of guests.

The Rebbe would wear a white kittel, a garment resembling a gown to show his cleansed and pure state. This garment was commonly worn to symbolize new beginnings, the birth of a new born, or the bridegroom, so too, when we die, and begin our new from of life, we are wrapped in a white shroud.

Gittel smiled as she thought about wearing a newly-stitched two piece suit which her handsome son Doniyel had surprised her by making, without even fitting it. It was in navy serge with six decorative buttons he had found and saved for a special garment. She was the lucky recipient of that fashionably designed garment, and looked forward to showing it off in the synagogue.

It is said that Elijah visits every home on Pesach and so traditionally we leave the door open and we put out a special cup of wine for him.

Our Elijah's cup had come from the Rebbe's family, originating from Sheduva, and was made of gold and silver with vines and blossoms twirled around the stem and the lip of the cup. It was heavy and old. Gittel loved to hold it in her hand and think about her own childhood Pesach table and how she had continued to sing the four questions until she was almost grown up, before her parents died. Traditionally, the youngest child at the table would ask the four questions.

This Pesach, little Chana would just be able to do so assisted by her brothers.

"Why is this night different to all other nights" was the first question?

Gittel knew why this night would be very different to all other nights and acknowledged it to herself in dread.

Doniyel had called us both into the Rebbe's study after Vladimar's visit. He had talked about the rumors he heard in the surrounding shtetls. He told the Rebbe about the activists, the group of young Jewish men who felt they could no longer be dormant and accepting of the ill-treatment and unfair laws of the Tzar.

Many had been beaten and thrown in prisons, never to be heard of again. Young men were being used as slave labor to build the new railway and men traveling along the road trying to do their regular business, were being attacked and robbed by soldiers and then left at the side of the road often too injured by the attack to seek help.

The Jewish Bund, a socialist labor group, was formed in secret. People talked of a Jewish State but we in Lithuania could not imagine such a wonderful dream surrounded by the awful reality of our lives These Bund members were in great danger if they were identified and the Rebbe was worried about Doniyel's possible involvement in this movement, sensing his anger and growing restlessness, and his need to express himself.

We had the added problem of him not being registered when he was a baby. Now at the army service age, this was a major problem and the only possible answer was for Doniyel to go away. *Khapers,* kidnappers were becoming desperate to fill quotas and save their own skins.

Doniyel was confused. Part of him wanted the adventure, the promise of a better life and the curiosity of unknown lands. But part of him was aghast at the thought of leaving his family, his homeland and established life however fraught it was. How would he know if they were safe, how would his mother cope with the horse and cart and the beloved unruly donkey on her own? Where would he go to and how would he get there?

He told us he had saved a small amount of Zlotys but resolved to leave half of it for us in case we needed it. He would make a plan to earn money as he traveled He thought he might be able to go to Riga and find work there.

I tried not to think about these things as I baked the last coconut cake for Pesach. Instead of the flour which we could not use at Pesach, we substituted almonds, coconut and matzoh flour. These cakes tended to be very bland and sometimes quite heavy. My family were always very complimentary about my Pesach cakes as I spiced them up with orange rind, honey and cinnamon and many whipped eggs in order to taste a little better.

This year I made a mammoth effort. Baking eased my pain, but the constant tasting added to my waist. I made crispy biscuits filled with dates. I made raisin kugel with brandied sugar and soft fresh cheese with the sour milk. I had hung it in a open weave cloth in our kitchen window. I made a special batch of imberlach (carrot sweets) because I rationalized that if I sent them with Doniyel, the carrots were nutritious, the sugar would give him energy, and the ginger would stop his tummy from rumbling on the long cold nights ahead. I made pletzlach (prune sweets) and almond biscuits, I made pickles and peppers to put away. Whatever I baked, I put a little aside, mentally preparing for his departure. Who knew if he would have enough food and where he would find a kosher *nosh* (snack) without his mother to provide?

"Nu Gittel, the *tzimmes* is burning" called the Rebbe from his study.

My carrots and prunes were ruined while I sat thinking about my Doniyel.

She tried to salvage them by pouring more honey over them, burying them under another layer of carrots. Burnt offerings made her shudder. She placed all the food she had set aside for Doniyel in the Pesach cupboard lest it should be mixed with the chometz, the non- pesach goods, She made sure his clothes were washed and ironed, not that he needed her to prepare his clothes, he was much better at it than she was, she thought, but it gave her some small comfort.

She carefully placed her potato kugel in the oven to keep it crisp, and cast her eye over the long, handsomely decked table to ensure she had not forgotten anything that was needed for this elaborate meal. Then she crept off to her room to unfold the blanket roll and look at it one more time. She lovingly re-folded it tightly, making the *brocha* "to be said at the sight of the rainbow" a wish for her son Doniyel to see a rainbow soon
....

Blessed art thou, King of the Universe, who rememberest the covenant, art faithful to thy covenant, and keepest his promise.

5
THE SEDER

The Passover Seder was enacted to re-tell the story of the Jews exodus from Egypt under Pharoah's cruel laws.

Its central theme is Liberation. We enact and attempt to re-experience the exodus from Egypt, but it included thoughts of the renewal of our Jewish identity. At this time we included a celebration in honor of the return of spring.

Many people in the shtetl made new curtains and white washed their walls to achieve a feeling of freshness and renovation.

It is said," We are commanded to remember the past while slaves in Egypt," and in doing so, we look to the present and future.

Each year the family joins together to re-tell the story of the exodus. This involves all the family members, anyone can conduct the service, and everyone plays their part. Innovation is essential to keep it interesting although we enjoy all the old familiar songs we sing each year.

The Seder begins with the injunction to "Tell it to your children."

The social integration of all invited to your Seder table becomes a binding factor in the meal of intimacy, the story you share together, young and old. You are asked to express your thoughts and hopes for the future.

The Seder always ended with the words, "Next year in Jerusalem."

As we sat in Zagare, it was a wish we all harbored and mouthed, but an ethereal one at that. Jerusalem was too far away from us in 1905. Tonight, the young men spoke of making a pilgrimage more eagerly than they had before.

This year the relevance of the story to our current situation was uniquely realistic to all our guests around the table. We explored the meaning of our Jewish existence. We talked about G-d's presence in the world, and the historical and mythical elements. This made for a magical evening which children remember all their lives.

On his return from Shul, the Rebbe had called Doniyel into his study, placed his Kittel over his shoulders and told him he would have the honor of conducting the Pesach Seder tonight.

"This will be an evening you will remember, wherever you live your life and however you conduct your home. Always remember that the repeat of the Pesach tale reminds the young people of their obligations and renews their belief in Judaism. "It will be my privilege to listen to you tonight."

In his heart the Rebbe thought to himself, "I will have the freedom to just sit and listen to you, my son, to enjoy the sound of your voice and experience my own nachos, contentment and pride in your knowledge, and to hold this memory of you dear in my heart".

The Rebbe sat back. He listened intently to the talk of pogroms, stories repeated with fear and dread from surrounding towns. Although we were at the far end of the country, the horror was creeping nearer. News of the forced conscription had been posted up around the shtetl, and any day now, soldiers could be expected to round up young men. Incidents of anti-semitism were increasing and the Rebbe had been called upon to counsel several people on the unhealthy situations of late.

In the words of the Haggadah, the printed story of the Pesach Seder, it reads *"Behold we are ready to fulfill your commandment .And you shall live by them and not die by them. Therefor, our prayer to You is that You may keep us alive and save us, rescue us speedily so that we may observe Your commandment and do Your will and serve You with a perfect Heart."*

We all took part in reading the story, going round the table listening again to the age old tale as it is told in the Haggadah (the Pesach book) and little Chana had stood on her chair and proudly asked her four questions. In between, the children kept nagging "can we eat now, can we eat yet?" It was a long haul for them, but the waiting was part of Pesach.

This brought us to the second part of the seder. We began some of the other rituals.

In the middle of the table stood a magnificent three-layered silver matzoh dish. It held three pieces of matzoh. The matzoh is meant to be a symbol of freedom. Its simplicity and tastelessness can still be appreciated. It was the first food the Jews ate in the desert. It must have tasted wonderful after fleeing their homes in such haste, as it does to the first born who subsequently fast to commemorate all this. It also symbolizes the Trust they put in G-d when leaving Egypt in such a hurry, that they were not able to prepare bread for their journey,

It is customary to break the middle of the three matzot in half during the ceremony. This was to emphasize that life on earth is not perfect and to remember that there are still Jews today who are not free. In each country this had a different significance. We had long heard of our Soviet counterparts and how they were suffering, and now here in Zagare we were to witness this happening in our very community.

At this point in the evening the Rebbe took over from Doniyel who was leading the seder. Without looking at anyone in particular, although Doniyel sensed his father's words were directed at him, the Rebbe re-told part of the story illustrating how we can never allow ourselves to be enslaved again and if your trust in G-d is strong enough, he will lead you forward, and provide a solution. He pointed out the fragility of the matzoh and how the same ingredients, the flour and water, made bread, but could be altered to make matzoh and serve the purpose.

"In the same way, you young men here, can change the direction of your lives using the same tools—just use them innovatively and have faith." he said, in his quiet learned wisdom.

The other half of the broken matzoh, called the Afikamen, is hidden away It is meant to refer to the hidden meaning, the Messiah we all wait for, the unknown, It is the last thing we eat at the end of the meal so that the taste of the matzoh can linger on our tongue all year long.

As the meal ends, all the children run around excitedly looking for the Afikamen, knowing there is usually a silver piece for the one who finds it.

Doniyel then proceeded with the long practiced customs We dipped our *Karpas* (parsley) into salt water and ate it to symbolize the new spring season and rebirth. Next, we dipped the *Maror* into the *Haroset* (Maror are bitter herbs as in lettuce, to symbolize the bitterness of the slaves, the Haroseth, made from nuts wine and crushed apples, is to symbolize the bricks and mortar they were forced to make as slaves). In our family it was customary to make it with nutmeg but in the Rebbe's family they made it with cinnamon. This year we had both, as our little compromise to our own memories. The roasted egg on the Pesach plate symbolized a burnt offering for the temple in Jerusalem and the roasted bone that of the sacrificial lamb. The meal was long and sumptuous, never hurried and full of mirth.

It was *Ess and Fress!!*

In between, we sang songs and ate more food. On this night more than on any other night the poor and the needy were always welcomed to the table and we had many extras, secretly called *nog shleppers*, hangers-on, by the children, who waited excitedly to see each year who would arrive. We were happy to have them and privileged to host them. There was Haim Zakinov the grave digger. All the children avoided sitting next to him for fear of getting soil from the grave on their shoes! There was Malka Simkomowitz, they called her the *kvetzer,*the complainer, because she spent all evening telling whoever sat next to her all her *tzoris* (troubles) but, she did bring us homemade fudge and there was kindly old Nessa Ponevshka the cheesemaker, who smelt of sour milk. The mischievous Gordon boys pulled up their noses and ran away laughing. By the end of the evening we were all very merry.

Even I had drunk the required four cups of wine and as the last guest left, the Rebbe, his mood lightened by the wine, took my hand and thanked me for the wonderful meal We sat outside on our now quiet porch in the dark of the night, alone together, in stoic silence. We felt a great umbrella of sadness open up above us.

6
DEPARTING FROM ZAGARE, LITHUANIA

In the weeks that preceded Pesach, the unrest had increased alarmingly. The news that Zemach the tailor had been shot made us face up to the reality: the time had come to make a definite decision.

A year before, in 1903, the massacre of 49 Jews in Bessarabia had left the communities in fear of reprisals from the marauding bands of Cossacks and Lithuanian law keepers who were abandoning all sense of reason in their wild and violent behavior towards the Jews.

In recent months the "Union for the attainment of complete emancipation for the Jews of Russia" had been formed. Doniyel had gone along to some of the meetings with Solly, until the Rebbe cautioned him quietly, *"Mein Zohn,* do not make yourself visible, lest you are arrested and your identity papers sought! Our lack of records would reflect on the whole family and this will reflect on the community and could cause them to be punished."

This factor had also made Doniyel wary of playing an active role in the young Jewish Bund, and Jewish youths were being arrested every day.

The previous month, the march for freedom of speech in Vilnius had been followed by more strident voices calling for a Republic of Zagare. Jews and their non-Jewish neighbors were fighting for political recognition and better governance. Within the Jewish community or *Kehillah,* the religious laws and the lawgivers were so strong and well respected that their jurisdiction – and the idea of abiding by the law – was more readily accepted by Jews than by the wider community.

Zagare was regarded by the larger Jewish community of Lithuania as "the City of Torah".

Doniyel heard headstrong young men stand up at secret meetings held in blacked-out barns to avoid detection. "Rise up, Chochmanim of Zagare, wise men of Zagare, come forward and present a strong educated voice!" they shouted. "We can no longer live as if we are third-class citizens – unable to pray as we choose, unable to protect our womenfolk and to earn a reasonable living in a field of our choice. We demand the freedom to use our capabilities fully."

As the town became more impoverished the ranks of the empty-bellied grew, as did their fervour. Late one night an angry and belligerent crowd marched recklessly through the town, calling for the fall of the Tsar. Doniyel and Solly hid in the darkness under a sycamore tree. When the *tummel* and commotion of the angry voices had faded into the distance, they lay back on a cushion of fragrant leaves and resolved to leave their childhood home. They exchanged long draws on the forbidden cigarette they had found, breathing out more than in, inexperienced at smoking.

"I have sewn a coat in the heavy grey serge left over from Geldkopf's uniform, the color most armies wear around here, but without epaulettes or trim so I can pass in a crowd if no one looks for my rank, " Doniyel said to Solly. "The coat has three layers – the outer layer is heavy and will protect me from cold. The lining is strong and you will not see any pockets except for the regular breast pocket across the chest. "Between these two, is a light layer of strong waterproof material which you can only access from inverted pleats in the visible outer lining. The invisible pleats act as a barrier without zips or clips. Only I can slide my hand into the deep vertical spaces into which I shall pack the papers of my life. In here I will place my *zlotys*, and the tiny *chumash* prayer book, given to me by my late Zaide. My *tefillin*, the phylacteries and maybe the photographs of my family could be hidden in the deepest pocket which I can feel near the hem of my coat."

"Would it be safe to take my photographs?" Doniyel speculated "I could not bear the thought of not being able to look at them, yet maybe it would be best to keep them in my mind's eye forever. No, I cannot leave them behind. I need to look at them."

"The tools of my trade – especially my left-handed scissors – can go into my shoulder bag and this I would carry with my food parcel from Gittel as if I were a regular smouse, traveling along the road."

"We must travel separately," suggested Solly. "Give me the address of the Rabbi in Riga and I will meet you there within a week."

"I'll don the *schmattes* of a coalman, blacken my face and hands and I'll beg for lifts along the road, walking and hiding where necessary as we agreed.

"*Zei gesund*—keep well". We shook hands and looked into each other's eyes, taking in the other's trepidation and realizing we were making a life-altering decision.

"*Mit mazel, mit mazel,*" he hugged me. "I will see you in Riga, G-d willing – *Baruch hashem.*" He then turned towards home and we went our separate ways.

Doniyel trod the familiar path to his house, absorbing the shapes he had known all his 18 years. He stopped at the old Zagare cemetery and knew that parting would be a great hardship. He picked his way among the familiar names, pausing to place a stone on Bobba's tombstone, his eyes filled with tears as he remembered how she would croon to him when he was very little, and how he used to help her roll the dough, proud to be allowed to break off the small piece of dough one was commanded to give to charity when making the Shabbat *challah* bread.

Without warning, he suddenly felt filled with rage, great billowing anger and resentment. He wondered why a people who revered Hashem, who practised *tzedakah,* kindness and goodness as part of their daily lives, who tried to live life by the 613 commandments, should be treated so badly and made to leave their home, their parents, their loved ones.

"Cast out like animals to fend in the wild unknown. I would be leaving with *kadoches*—*kadoches*—nothing, but a few stones in my pocket." (Little did I know that those stones would be my passport to better days).

"Verstunkende khazery!" he muttered angrily, kicking a pine cone into the water, with an image of the smelly pigs in the market in his mind. At that moment all he wanted was to live in *der heim,* to enjoy his family home, find his *shidduch,* his match, and accept contentment in the way of his people. As soon as he formulated that thought in his mind , he had to acknowledge to himself that he did want something more – much more than just being a Litvak Jew, rejected and complacent. A sad place to be!

He cast his thoughts back to the Rebbe's words of yesterday:

"Doniyel, the Shabbat has kept the Jews together as a nation since the beginning of time. Try to remember the Sabbath and keep it holy. Above all else, be true to yourself and do only what you believe in. We learn throughout the Torah that preservation of life is paramount in Judaism, even over and above the Shabbos.

"You can maintain your Jewish beliefs in your head and your heart, privately holding them as your lifeline, until you can practice them openly and proudly in your new place, wherever that may be."

He sighed softly, my Rebbe, my father, my teacher. He patted my shoulder, looking up at me with pain and anguish, and with a love in his eyes that he didn't often show.

"Take my life's teaching with you and you will pass it on to your children, and your children's children."

Then he recited the blessing for children over my head, as he had done all my life, and handed me a tiny piece of card, the prayer for travelers that he had written in his own careful hand. I placed it in the pocket near my heart.

As a young man of curious spirit, Doniyel's tension at the traumatic goodbye to his home soon gave way to excitement. He admired his parents for not begging him to stay, to write, to make contact. His father had whispered to Gittel, *"Macht nicht kein tzimmes"* (Don't make a great pudding out of it!) He felt they firmly believed G-d would take care of Doniyel. This acceptance was part of the harsh life in Lithuania in 1905.

It was three-thirty in the morning. He wondered if Solly would fare as well as he had, on his hazardous night flight. He began making a mental note of how they would manage with the five days of Pesach still remaining. This meant they could not eat bread or food that was not "Kosher le Pesach" and unless they found a kosher place to eat and to hide, they would be wholly dependent on their packages from Gittel.

It was ominously dark, the stars had their eyes shut, and the wind whined through the trees making the steely sound of a siren.

He wheeled his bicycle out of the storeroom, ensuring he did not click the lock for fear of alerting the neighbors. This bike had been given to him by his brothers as his barmitzvah gift. It was the envy of his friends. Today it would be the escape vehicle to his new life as far as he could ride safely. It was too risky to take the train and he must be out of Lithuania by the light of day.

Stealthily, balancing on the balls of his shoes, he wheeled the bike into the lane, passing the shul with a lump in his throat. He crept past Uncle Isaac's house. He passed the steps of the Gordon front door, where he had fallen and knocked out his first tooth, not a lit candle in sight.

He turned towards the river and rode swiftly and silently through the trees alongside the Alte Zagare cemetary. He kept off the road and took little known stone paths till he reached the "Pot man's" house. As kids they had thrown stones at the man who sold pots, fascinated by his weirdness. As innocent children, we were not aware of the reason for his "oddness" in this simple society and laughed at his rooftop covered in iron pots and pot lids.

As he reached Gediminio, the street was deserted. He could make good headway along this well known thoroughfare and then back to the little known sand roads. He climbed onto his bike and rode like hell through the used debris of the "alte" market. The smell of the scattered and rotting cabbage leaves, the discarded sacks and the donkey droppings wove a triage of warm familiarity past his nostrils, a smell that had come to mean all the extras that market day brought to his young life. Gittel coming home with some little treat for him.

He rode past the fireman's house and Dr Mendelson's clinic. In his mind he pictured his pretty daughter, pondered who her *shiddach,* her match, would be. He had tailored Mrs Mendelson a suit and Rivka had been sent to collect it. Perhaps ....he'd wondered—too late now.

Down the muddy Zydu Lane he crossed the river and rode into Neue Zhagare. He decided to dismount, no need to take chances. If anyone was watching behind their dark wooden windows, he must not look as if he was fleeing.

He pushed the bike now, doing fast walking, carrying Gittel's package and his blanket roll on his back, stumbling in his hurry to get across the fields and into the security of the woods again.

Half an hour later he was out of town headed towards the border of Latvia and Lithuania He hoped he remembered the route that the coachman, whom he had traveled with most recently, had driven the horses. He kept his ear to the ground for any signs of life apart from donkeys neighing.

The moon was dull and blurred. His heart beat loudly in the quiet of the Lithuanian night.

Despite the chill, his loaded coat made him sweat. He was carrying his whole life in those hidden pockets. He had doubled back past the sign to Linkuva, as the road was more protected, turned left and mounted the bike again, trying to make up time.

Normally it would take 8 hours to ride to Riga. Libau, the port, was four hours further but he had to make it in a shorter time.

Out on the open road now, he pedaled furiously, suddenly overcome with heartache at the reality of what he was being coerced to do. Tears poured down his face and he sobbed out loudly to the relentless friendless black sky.

Pushing himself harder he rode on, sniffing grossly to avoid taking a hand off the handlebars.

The house of a well known *khaper* (snatcher) was just ahead of him. He rode by nervously and as he passed he saw the light switch come on suddenly in the house. He slid off his bike and slithered into the bushes—his temples were "bombing." *Oy Vey, oy Shleght* "he whispered to himself. Not now, not after all his planning, and not after surviving eighteen years in the back row. "Please, please", he prayed, "make me invisible and without odor."

He almost held his breath. He lay as still as a stone in the graveyard.

The door opened and a dog flew out. The dog lifted its leg, sniffed under a bush, hesitated for an endless moment, turned his head towards Doniyel, and then, with a whimper, it ran back inside the house and the light faded. Doniyel leapt onto his bike and whistled off thankful he was fit and tall and could pedal strongly despite his shaking knees.

The flatness of the Lithuanian landscape turned uphill. Doniyel recognized that he was headed in the right direction for Riga, but time was not on his side. He could not rest despite the ache in his lower back. He kept going, fuelled by fear of discovery and the determination to succeed. He fled past wheat sheaf and apple tree, past the long grass and along the curving road that seemed to have no end.

Within a few short hours he reached the border and turned off the road. He had arranged with his brothers that he would leave his bike in the woods under an oak tree, so that if they had the opportunity to come and collect it, they would know in which area to look. He covered the bike with fresh branches. In the tree above he hung his blue handkerchief.

He allowed himself a long drink from his flask. Then he took out his Chumash, his little prayer book. He tied his Tefillin box and straps to his head and arm to do his morning prayers under the trees. He concentrated hard, trying to abolish the thoughts swirling round his head. It gave him strength and boldness. It re-fired his determination. He packed his pockets, stretched well and picked up his Ruggelach, his Imberlach and set off again. Now it was essential to keep his wits about him.

He picked his way through the wet morning grass keeping under cover of the forests. He ran wherever he could, walking in between. He crept under the natural pass of the old stone wall, until finally he believed he had by-passed the border point parallel to the woods between Lithuania and Latvia, at least that was where he hoped he was.

Cautiously he ventured towards the road. Yes—he recognized the area. The roads were wider and the land ahead more steep. He had done it! He'd slipped by the border guard, and shortly he'd be well onto the other side of the Latvian border.

Hurrying to make up time, but trying to not to look as if he was running away, he marveled at how Hashem had protected him and he had not passed a single coach, horseman or winter fox. It was an hour before sunrise and he had to get into the Riga so he could hide among the residents and daily life. He was grateful he spoke fluent Latvian as well as German and could pass as one of the locals.

The Rebbe had told him to count three streets, turn left into an alley way to take a short cut to the Rabbi's house in Riga. He hoped they would take him in without questions and hide him in the cellar until he could take advice on what to do next.

He found the alleyway but there were so many barking dogs he decided to keep to the main road. Pushing himself to the limit he began to puff and cough but still he propelled his body forward and onward, concentrating on moving his feet and holding his parcels over his shoulder. The sky began to wash soft milky pink clouds over the horizon a suggestion of dawn began to show. His night time cover was running out.

He heard a horseman behind him. He walked slower, relaxed his shoulders not wanting to look round. He sauntered a bit, the horse came nearer, he held his breath and then he glanced up. It was the just the water carrier. He was on his pre-dawn delivery. He waved and passed by. By now Doniyel was so weary and so tense he could not escalate his body back to his former pace. He plodded on until he knew he was in the Rabbi's street. He passed the synagogue and looked warily around.

Ordinary passers by were beginning to surface as he tentatively knocked on the back door. The Rabbi's son opened the door and looked at him enquiringly. He called back to the Rabbi to the door realizing the stranger was near collapse.

Rabbi Klevansky looked at me blankly until I said! "I am Reb Shlomo Ben Zalkind's son, Doniyel." He put his arms out and held me warmly. I clutched him for fear of sliding to the floor, realizing that he had only seen me as a bar mitzvah boy and not as a tall young man.

They closed the door quickly, and took me down to the cellar

His son Meir brought me water to wash and a glass of good Pesach wine to drink, although it was barely 6 a.m. in the morning. I absorbed it down my throat as if I were a sponge, feeling it flood through my pores with rich harsh warmth. I broke the fresh matzo and nibbled it weakly.

On the straw in the cellar, I laid my head on my blanket roll, clutching it and wishing for my mother. I vaguely heard their cow moo vociferously in disenchantment at my sharing her space, but before I could mutter the relevant prayer I was asleep.

In what seemed like a moment later, I remember awakening to the sounds of the shtetl coming through the wooden slats of the house. It took me time to acclimatize and to realize that it was twenty-four hours later.

My muscles felt like marshmallow. I was weak with fatigue and tension. I tried to get my head around the fact that I was out of Lithuania, but a long way from safety yet.

8
A LEBBERDIKKE VELD

Riga was a *lebberdikke veld,* a place zinging with culture, some regarded it as the "Paris of Eastern Europe." It was the home of music and fashion, theatre, art and architecture. Incredible churches with towering spires and carved concrete that curled atop the belfry buildings. He had never visited Riga on his own, but had heard his elders talk of gaiety and the frivolous pursuits that a shtetl town like Zagare did not play host to.

Perhaps he would find a better life here and he'd be able to build something for himself. Then he might move his family away from Lithuania.

Rabbi Moshe Klevansky and his family included me in their daily life. They were supportive and kind, and generously shared the little food they had with me. As we sat at their table in the kitchen with the curtains drawn and the fire cold and empty, I sensed their nervous tension. Each time a loud voice or a passing cart rumbled by the window they seemed to hold their breath, glancing about nervously.

I asked about the situation in Latvia and began to realize that for Jews, it was not much different to being in Zagare. My heart felt heavy as I came to realize that this place may not be the end of the journey.

It seemed that other Lithuanians had tried to cross the border and loud-hailing uniformed soldiers on horseback had warned of harboring aliens, promising threats too horrible to contemplate.

Despite the fearful atmosphere, I felt I needed to go out and see Riga. I took off my heavily loaded coat and wore my host's long winter coat with high collar and a hat low over my face. I spoke fluent Latvian but decided to speak only German if I was approached. I walked down the wide streets up the hill to the town square.

The Daugava River flowed broadly through the town. I walked along the bridge dreaming that I could throw a coin into the water and my wish would change the world.

The Valdemare Iela, was a broad street, filled with activity, music and woman clad in fur coats and high heels that clacked on the cobbles like the beat of an ominous drum. The sound of the heels became a quickstep, prancing along the roads, and posing as players in the script of the rumored Latvian life style that I had imagined I was going to experience.

I came to a brightly lit house where music was filtering loudly through the windows. A beautiful girl with electric blonde curls smiled welcomingly at me. I stopped in total shock, I looked around. Yes, it *was* me she was smiling at, and my body felt warm and full of wonder. Instantly I remembered who I was, a runaway Litvak with no papers, no name—no money and no home to go to. I dare not get into a conversation with any stranger, let alone a female to whom I had not been introduced, or of whose origin I had no clue. For a fleeting moment it felt like a delicious unconscious wish, one beyond my wildest comprehension.

I turned into the Raina Boulevard. The paved square had benches under the trees and a carved fountain spewing water into a pond where couples sat talking intimately, enjoying the night. A violinist played music that I was not familiar with, but it had a lilting softness that I could enjoy. A fire brewed coffee in a large crude samovar on the pavement and I longed to feel the warmth in my middle. I could picture dipping Gittel's ruggelach into it for sweet comfort. I purchased two bags of smoldering chestnuts and kept my hands in my pockets to hold onto the warmth.

I walked along the outskirts, staying out of the light and watching this parable of a life, so foreign to me.

Eventually I came to an area where I had heard there must be a synagogue. Just as I was searching for a familiar doorway, a mezzuzah or a Magen David to indicate something I recognized, I heard the gallop of horses behind me. In the ingrained dread that the sound brought to me, I smelt trouble. Ahead of me I became aware of an elderly Rabbi holding the hand of a small boy.

The soldiers on horseback rode up to him, shouted some words I could not make out in Prussian, the soldier leant down, grabbed hold of the old man by his coat and pulled him up roughly to spit in his face while galloping off. They held him in such a position that the front legs of the horse kicked him at every gallop. At thirty yards away I heard the crack of his ribs but much worse, I heard the silence of his suffering.

My immediate instinct was to run out and try to rescue him but my senses told me I could not reach up to him. The horses were way above my head and more importantly I carried no identification. It would have been reckless and to no avail. As they high-stepped off down the street, they dropped him to the ground where he lay in bundled heap on the cobbled street. People did not stop. It was such a regular occurrence, no one approached him.

When I thought the coast was clear I strode quickly towards the boy. He stood quietly, confused and fearful. I gently took his hand and walked into the shadows. I held him close, trying to reassure him without speaking, not knowing what language he spoke or what the consequences could be. He was like a stone, rigid and blank, as if this was not a new experience and he was protecting himself from shock.

It was one thing to listen to the Bund reporting these incidents as I had done over the last few years. It was quite another to actually be part of the incident and witness to a man who could have been my father being crushed for no reason except that he was a Jew.

My despair knew no bounds.

All the anguish of leaving my family, the trauma of the long night, of my muddled thoughts and my vision of hope and future, my feeling of utter emptiness became a trough of bleeding pain. I could not weep and I dare not feel.

At that moment an elderly woman came tentatively forward and beckoned the boy. I asked her in Yiddish if there was a shul nearby and she nodded. I followed her quickly round the corner and we entered the darkened door of a Beit Midrash, a house of learning.

As my eyes became accustomed to the light of the single candle set behind a heavy wooden screen so that no light could be seen from the street, I saw a group of bearded men huddled together—old and young, that same face of fear and anguish – the hopelessness that I thought I had left behind me.

We hurried out to where the Rabbi lay and carried him into the room, laying him down gently on a blanket. He opened his eyes and held his hand out to the little boy. I was doubly grateful he did not die in the incident as this would have left his grandson with much more memorable trauma.

While one of the men went in search of a doctor, I sat down with a mug of soup. I listened quietly to their talk, wary of saying who I was. In this day of uncertainty, the terror of being forced to report your fellow Jew existed everywhere.

"How can we change our lives" they asked each other? "How can we escape this inevitable degradation -the beatings—the untimely death?" Eventually we became overwhelmed by the awful feeling of being a despicable person, "Dirty Zid" was shouted so often you began to forget who you really were. It grew to become your label. It stuck to the image you carried of yourself.

They were talking in hushed voices, saying "The street is paved with gold. We hear that you can earn a good living and the land is fertile"

I pricked up my ears.

"They say you can travel freely and *doven* and pray without hesitation. The fruit is tropical and exotic and the vegetables are of such variety one could eat a different vegetable each day of the week. Children play in the streets and men can walk tall even when you are Jewish."

Shipping companies were offering cheaper tickets to fill the ships and by filling the ships, make it a viable possibility for them. "*Mein zun*" the elder man said, "if you travel to Libau you will get a boat to Southampton or London and from there you will get papers and a place on the ship."

I had never envisaged going to Africa, but suddenly the idea sounded like a marvelous adventure. It had the sense of opportunity, and a totally unknown excitement about it. I wanted to run home and discuss it with my father, the Rebbe but, sadly, that was out of the question. I was nearly eighteen, alone, and I had to make a decision on my life and I had to make it soon.

9
THE GALEKA

I stood in awe at the size of the boat. I clutched my blanket roll and last few ginger ruggelagh tightly as I nervously climbed the gangplank to the deck. It all seemed so surreal—was I a pirate going to sea? Was I an officer boarding my ship? Who was I and where was I headed? I had no picture in my mind and I recognized no one else boarding.

People from all walks of life were traipsing up the rope gangplank, some faster than others.

At the top of the steps we were directed down a long windowless passage and then single file down very steep narrow stairs into the hold.

I'd heard that traveling third class was like living in a hellhole and hoped I would be early enough to claim a spot near some air. The hold smelt dank and decaying. *Oi Vey,* was this boat sea worthy?

Being so young, one had to use one's *saichel*, one's sense, and while not looking too pushy to others, still make the best plan for yourself.

I spied a shelf, a triangle of broad wooden bolster in the corner of the hold quite high up and near an air vent. I hurried towards it, climbing over horizontal bodies and bags, hauled myself up and plonked my bag down.

Yes! It was dry. It was relatively airy and I could separate myself partially from the increasingly solid line of persons coming down the stairs. I squatted down to watch the people below and to guard my space.

Part of me felt absolutely terrified at the decision I had made. Part of me felt quite chuffed with myself at just "going out to do it!" I had risked spending all my available money and leaving Solly behind. I'd waited three days longer and he had not arrived. My ticket had cost all of eleven guineas. That would take me to Algoa Bay, in South Africa.

The "Cape of Good Hope", as it was called, created a picture of warmth and welcome that I felt was worth the risk. As we came on board we were welcomed with a cloth purse bearing the ship's name printed on it. Into this, one was supposed to place all one's valuables, but I preferred to keep them hidden deep in my coat pockets.

I had tried to send a note to my father, not knowing if it would reach him. I had also sent a little kerchief to my mother, wrapped a tiny Latvian cake into the kerchief for Chana, and included the name of my ship and date of departure so at least in the short term they would know what had happened to me. Perhaps when we docked for a short time at Southhampton,I would find a messenger and attempt to send a second letter.

The ship's bell clanged loudly, the captain's voice boomed out, commanding all passengers to come onto the decks. The chimneys spewed smoke into the sky and the ancient engines groaned into action.

I felt devastated—frightened – exhilarated—keyed up, wondering what the next phase of my long journey to "somewhere" would be like.

The Galeka lurched. The body of human forms lurched with it and then it settled into the rhythm of the waves and we sailed out to sea, dancing along the white tip of the swells, to the music of gulls and the salty sting of great sadness. I couldn't bear to watch the line that was the land of my birth receding.

I left the deck and climbed onto my little shelf.

I took out my traveller's prayer, written in my father's hand.

"May it be your will, to lead us in safety, to guide our steps so that we arrive at our destination alive happy and in peace."

I held the little card in my hand and thought that the Rebbe, in his wisdom, had known my journey was going to be a long one, but "Drom Africa", he could not have imagined that!

I lay back on my pedestal imagining I was Lord of the third class passengers, elevated by my thoughts rather than my luck at finding this private little shelf. From memory, I chanted the words of my favorite piece from the siddur, my study book, feeling great wonder at the relevance and comfort of the words.

"Birth is a beginning
And death is a destination
and life is a journey:
from childhood to maturity

and youth to age : from innocence to awareness
and ignorance to knowing."

I was certainly on my journey of life, swelling high and low as the sea took us south, into waters unknown and life style untried.

Would I find Jewish *menschen* who would accept me? Would I be able to communicate with them? I didn't want to be a foreigner, a *greener* in my new land.

The bell rang for a meal. The upper classes ate in a dining room but there were so many people below deck, the food was brought down in large cases and hungry anxious hands grabbed it without any thoughtfulness to others. I climbed down and noticed some men placing wooden crates in a circle as they prepared to eat their meal together.

I collected my watery potatoes in greyish cabbage druel and indicated to them that I wanted to sit with them. They nodded welcomingly and asked me a question, which I gathered was "What is your name?" "Doniyel", I replied, pulling up a box to sit on. I listened carefully to their conversation, missing most of the gist of what they were saying. *"Spreken zi Deutch?"* I asked. One man nodded and we struck up a conversation. His name was Rudolph, he looked about 25 and he came from Breslau. He spoke English as well and I asked him if he would teach me to converse. The White South Africans spoke two languages, English and Afrikaans.

I knew it was imperative for me to speak English or I could not get by with people. Rudolph was well- dressed and well fed, but congenial and polite, and I resolved to slowly ascertain if he was Jewish. I certainly could not ask him.

10
FIRST SHABBAT IN DROM AFRICA

It had been a strange week with many unpredictable experiences, most of them pleasant. As the week drew to a close my thoughts always drifted towards Shabbat preparation in Zagare. I wondered what they would think of a house with its own private bathroom and steaming hot water running freely out of the tap. I worried about Gittel managing the donkey and wondered how little Chana was progressing. I didn't allow myself to think of what life could be like as we did not hear any political news.

I was looking forward to the familiarity of Shabbat rituals. In the face of my African experience so far, it was hard to imagine being Jewish in this colonial seaside town where no obvious preparation for Shabbat was visible to me.

I dressed carefully for Shul, not having too much to choose from, but being sure to be well-pressed with what I did have! My handmade trousers were superbly fitted and shoes gleamed.

I was grateful for the Shabbat invitation which, as I had gathered at the barber shop, was quite an honour. Mrs Dorah Nurek was the chairlady of the synagogue, a real *balebusta*, "a doer" as they say in town. To add spice to this rumored advantage, it was said that they had many daughters!

Mr Nurek had told me how to get to his home and to be there for 7 p.m. to make a timely arrival before the first evening star of the Shabbat came out.

I walked very slowly up the steep hill to Russell Road, taking in the trams, the busy scurrying bodies, laden with weekend shopping. I sat down at a bus stop to watch the African men and women making their way home for the weekend after their work where they slept in the backrooms of their employer's homes. I had learnt that they lived on the outskirts of town. Listening to them speak in their different tongues, it sounded to me like they spoke very fast and everyone spoke at once, making their points very loudly, but I understood that it was not a belligerent attitude, it was just the way they expressed themselves.

I glanced up to the sky as I reached the home of the Nureks to ensure that the first star was not out in the sky yet.

Knocking tentatively on the door, I paused. I was about to knock a little louder when, before my second attempt, the door was flung open by "The Chairlady" herself. She stood there stolid in her navy high heel shoes, with a leather bow as big as her feet on each shoe.

A small but very imposing figure with a sergeant major's face and the demeanor of Captain Hook! *"Gut Shabbos"* she said, seeming to be most welcoming, all the while checking me over very thoroughly. I stepped inside and immediately felt the warmth of home.

I smelt the soup and I saw the home-baked kitke, the plaited bread my mother would make each week. The table napkins were crisp white and the silver candlesticks shone like my shoes, lit to welcome in the Sabbath. I stared at the salt cellars shaped like carved elephants and presumed they must be an African thing, but I learnt afterwards that Morris Nurek had bought them off an Indian trader.

I felt a sense of quiet holiness infuse my being. Maybe one could celebrate Shabbat under this African sun so far away from home.

I washed my hands, murmuring the prayer for washing hands quietly to myself. I lulled myself into Sabbath peacefulness.

When I had finished this familiar task, I was introduced to two gentlemen already present in the room At this point Miss Nurek, their daughter Tuvia, came in bearing the herring for the table. Dorah quickly introduced her and her younger sister Sorah and then summoned them purposefully back to the kitchen.

I accepted the drink from Mr Nurek and sat back.

At that, there was a knock on the door. I turned to see the new comer. A vision moved into my focus. My gut lurched, my chest grew too tight for my heart, my eyes took in the inimitable shape of Solly Trompaitzky, accompanied by what could only be, I was convinced, the ghost of Zagare—old Bobba Trompaitzky!

I thought it must be the whiskey on an empty stomach but he ran towards me and covered me with a weeping bear hug as only a person of Solly's size can do. I had to steady my legs and I could not utter a sound!

The participants of the room watched us in breathless anticipation. This was a dream I was experiencing, it could not be reality.

"Doniyel, Doniyel, I never thought I would ever see you again", he said in emotional Yiddish.

"Solly what happened?" I cried.

At this, Mrs Trompaitzky recovered from her surprise and composure and came forward to kiss me good shabbos. "*I am wot heppened*", she said in broken English "my zun, my zun, he had to take me too. I came to look after you two *boychicks*,- to see you keep kosher."

The whole room laughed, and rejoiced in the unbelievable miracle and joy of our reunion, something I never envisaged on my foreign horizon.

"It's a long story Doniyel, I will tell you later," he said, still holding onto me. I could not grasp the concept. We had made it together, in the same town, at the same shabbat table, singing *Shalom Aleichem* together!

Much later that night, we sat under the stars to talk. He told me that when the time came to say goodbye, unlike my parents, she had wailed so loudly half the village were disturbed and he could not leave. After three days she was still wailing. He was an only child and his father had died when he was young.

But, in the streets, the Tzar's army was routing out young men daily and eventually he came to the conclusion it was the lesser of the two evils to take her with him, however far away they could manage to get.

"Doniyel" he said, "I will never be concerned by her *nudging and groaning* about her aches and pains again. She slept in ditches and walked as fast as I did. She talked to me all the way. When I would not listen she talked to herself, but she was brave and resilient, much stronger than I ever imagined. An old woman and a boy were less conspicuous along the road, and we were able to move fast. Then, heaven blessed me for my mitzvah,—that good deed of *shlepping* my mother!! We were in luck, we found a milk cart from Linkuva who was making an escape himself and he drove all three of us to the coast where we picked up a boat immediately. I felt so miserable and uncomfortable that I had let you down and I didn't know how to find you my friend, but—it was survive, escape and take the only choice we had!"

Doniyel was so grateful for a landsman, someone from home and someone to relate to. "I was so mind- boggled by Solly's arrival" he said to himself later," I scarcely took any notice of Tuvia that evening."

I fell asleep remembering her sweet-natured laugh and I resolved to call again despite being aware that "The Chairlady" seemed well disposed to the other gentleman present. They were very well dressed and obviously 'well to do'! At this point I was a new immigrant with no future and no past, not a great *"gap"*, a catch, for any mother with daughters!

Solly and I talked for days. He, too, had been put up with a local Jewish family and we were unsure of what to do next. We could teach Hebrew, not an option either of us relished. We could become smouse and travel to the country towns, but you needed initial capital to buy goods and a cart and we didn't want to borrow. How to begin to earn a living? I could only go on accepting the kind hospitality for a few more weeks.

The following Sunday I dressed in my only other shirt and made my way back to the Nurek's house, taking Dorah a large bunch of flowers I had picked in the park. Tuvia opened the door and again I enjoyed the essence of her gentle prettiness. She looked surprised to see me and when I said I'd come to say thank you for dinner, she invited me in for a cup of tea.

Dorah was at a shul meeting so we sat in the front room with Morris, a pleasant innocuous man who listened more than he spoke .She poured me a cup of tea from the very same large brass samovar we had in our drawing room in Zagare I fingered it lovingly. It held 20 cups of tea and the brass had been buffed to glow in its gracious curves. I explained to Morris that we had one similar at home. He kindly enquired about my home and I was grateful for the opportunity to talk about my family. I told him about my father Reb Shlomo ben Zalkind, about the pogroms and about all the violent change that was taking place.

Tuvia sat down to listen and offered me a plate of biscuits. My nose twitched at the aroma of ginger Ruggelach. Of course they could never be the same as Gittels, I said to myself, but they were certainly a close second and I reveled in their taste, repeatedly telling Tuvia how good they were.

"I made them only this morning" she said shyly. If that wasn't a recommendation for a girl, what was!

A loud bang of the front door heralded Dorah's arrival home. She glanced at me with her *kvelling* look, while trying to effectively be polite and I realized she didn't fancy Tuvia falling for me. I took my leave shortly thereafter and sweet Tuvia saw me to the door and expertly slipped me a little bag of Ruggelach.

I was sold.

11.
GITTEL'S REVELATION

I sat on the *stoep,* as the verandah was called in Africa, a spacious covered area with red stone polished floor and Doric columns holding up the roof to keep the hot African sun from frazzling the nose of the sitter.

How on earth should I direct my life now? To work in a sweat-shop among many other tailors doing *"piece work"* as the cut, make and trim business called it, was an horrendous thought to someone who had been in their own tailoring business. Considering the standard of work I was used to producing, this was definitely not for me.

To work in the loud and dirty fruit and vegetable market seemed a waste of career time. I felt I was superior to this kind of job. But, maybe my downfall would come from this attitude and I should take anything offered? I needed new shoes, although I was not ungrateful for the shoes donated to me by the community, but they did not fit me and I felt as if I was walking like a *kaptzin*......a clown.

"Oh My Rebbe—Oh Mamele" how would you have guided me?" I was just eighteen years old but felt like I was going on 35. Life experience had matured me, and made me strong, but tonight I longed to be 'just a boy,' and for someone to tell me what I should do with my life from here on.

I went inside to lie down, exhausted from the stress of decision making, but sleep did not come to me. I tossed and turned, squashed and crunched my blanket roll from a hump to flat square. Whatever I attempted to do I could not make myself comfortable.

Gittel must have made my blanket roll in such a hurry she ended up with lumps in the lining. I had borne the discomfort all through the ship's journey and the only way I was going to get some much needed sleep was to get rid of the bumps. I sat up and lit the bedside lamp. I took out my tailor's unpicking hook and very carefully began to clip the precious stitches my mother had sewn into my blanket roll. The house was dark and quiet. Outside, only the generator conversed with the moon.

Each stitch unpicked was like a kiss on my head from Gittel. Soon I had made an open space in the left side of the blanket roll large enough to put my hand into the roll. I smoothed the bedclothes and laid the blanket out flat.

I knelt down and slid my hand slowly into the side of the roll, expecting to find the vagrant knots in the rough felt lining. To my surprise I felt warm soft velvet. The further in I reached, the more surprised I became. I could feel hard lumps and ridges. In the night light I blushed at my own thoughts. My hand was exploring a warm soft woman, smooth with secret ridges and curves. My forbidden scuffling on board the ship re-lived! I felt a bizarre mounting disquiet, I could not imagine what was inside my blanket roll.

I moved to switch on the larger lamp overhead. Then I proceeded to cut open the blanket even more carefully and turned the inside out to reveal ...."*Oi Vey iz meer*" *Baruch Hashem* – Please, Lord, could it be? Before me I saw a *Mecheia*, a vision—what could only be described as a gift from heaven. I felt dizzy, weak – mystified, and then I laughed out loud in utter amazement at what I saw and my body began to tremble. I felt irrational and volatile, I began to rock with uncontrollable emotion. "*Gittele oi Mamele*". You knew I would be penniless, you always said "These jewels should have become Doniyel's jewels". I ran my fingers over her handiwork, her stitches of love and devotion. I imagined her state of mind as she secretly made up my blanket roll and I remembered the trauma and *tummel* in the shul when they realized the Parochet, the precious curtain covering the Ark had been damaged in the pogrom and a new one would have to be made.

I pictured her stoic silent commitment to making another one while the ladies in the community admired and thanked her for doing the job all over again with such good natured intent. Normally she might have *kvetched* about the job but I remembered that she did not. No one had asked what happened to the original?

"Gittele, oy Mama, "What would the Rebbe have thought!"

I carefully cut the Parochet free of the blanket. I would re- stitch it tomorrow. I was trembling with heady excitement now. I counted the jewels that I had known so well as a child. They were all there. Oh *Gittele oh Mama*, with your wisdom and bravery I could have a choice of careers ….. I could buy a property and find a wife ….. I could make a life and bring my parents out to live in the sun, they could sit on the stoep and she would bake fresh Ruggelach.

The cock crowed triumphantly in the yard, "doodle do doodle do". The dawn was breaking on my new life, about to unfold.

I took out my tefillin, my prayer straps seemed to bind themselves to my arm this happy wondrous morning. I placed the prayer box on my head and near my heart and I gave thanks to the Lord—to my Mama, to opportunity, and to life itself. "Le Chaim. Le Chaim. Le Chaim!"

12
THE LINKUVA JEWELS

I took several of the stones out carefully, laid them in a soft cloth and bound them up tightly. I pushed them deep into my purse and them grabbed my jacket and ran out. I galloped all the way to the main road as if I was a knight on horseback.

As the tram drew up, I stepped onto the platform feeling like a very tall man. The short journey downtown to the diamond exchange was as if I were in a dream.

I rushed through the front doors only to be confronted with men in jackets and morning coats, smoking cigars and talking somberly in undertones. They all looked up as I entered and I realized with embarrassment that I must look like a *greener from* Y*ahoupitz*....a nobody from nowhere!

I turned round and ran out again.

I sat at the bus stop to think. My heart was still pounding. My head still spinning at Gittel's planned *chutzpah,* her brave and outrageous cheek. This was one deal I had to get right the first time and I needed educated help. The only place I could think of going to was the Raleigh Street Shul.

I made my way up to the synagogue and decided to go for the topdog. I asked to see the Gabbai of the shul, and explained that if he helped me make the right decisions I would be in a position to make a suitable donation to the synagogue. "You are just beginning young man," he said "time enough for your donations."

He listened to my story with a wry chuckle, and then he accompanied me back to the exchange and he duly arranged to see a dealer whose name he knew from the shul membership.

Two hours later, I was astonished at the amount of money I could raise from only half the stones I had. The Gabbai warned me to sell them as quickly as possible as the daily trading values could change and people would hear of my luck. Attitudes might change. He assured me he himself would tell no one. I smiled to myself at the thought of Dorah Nurek hearing the news …That should put smoke in her pipe. I would sell only the smaller rubies and the sapphires.

By the next day I had my first bank account in my own name. I existed officially for the first time and this was a very weird feeling. I had to link the anonymous Litvak with this new image before me and if I might say so myself, "a handsome young South African man was evolving!"

I went to see Solly that afternoon and he could not believe how fortuitous Gittel had made the insidious attack on our shul. Together we set out to look at property.

Times were hard in 1906, this factor provided a broad choice of houses right near to Raleigh Street, the area where most of the Litvaks had settled.

The first one I liked had an impressive roomy bathroom with green stone floor, a wide old bath with clawed feet and a storage seat to sit on to dry your toes. The sunny old kitchen was rusty and used, but in time I would renovate it with all the skills my brothers had taught me. It had a large back yard with a sloping lawn and I reckoned I would have enough money to build a second cottage on the lawn.

My temples began pulsating with the idea that I, Doniyel Levintahl, of no known name and no previous address would soon own a home of my own.

I looked at the agent, who was tired and worn. His hangdog look of defeat turned to cheerful charm. I had made his day when it took me thirty minutes flat to buy a house for cash at almost the asking price.

Solly and I rushed to the bank, withdrew the money and the next day we went off to see to the legal papers.

A week later I received the keys to my first home. No 13. Mackay Street How I wished I could thank Gittel, and resolved that one day, I would show her this house after I had got it up to scratch.

Solly, Bobba Trompaitsky and I moved our three simple bundles into the house.

On the first evening, Solly and I celebrated with a large chilled bottle of vodka which we downed in record time. We sang old songs and Bobba baked us black bread and smiled at our antics as we filled the kitchen with our mirth. I felt that maybe, just maybe, I could survive leaving my family, my home and my hidden identity and grow into my new persona, a Litvak landowner with official papers and hope for the future.

Next, I set out to find myself a Singer sewing machine, a presser and a work table. I believed that if I could russle up some customers they would appreciate the quality of my work. I sat down on that first morning in my simple home, just treadling away happily, with the sun shining through my window, and the kettle boiling on the old coal stove we had found in the back room.

I tailored myself a three piece pinstripe suit and, for Solly, I made up a navy double breasted blazer. For Bobba Trompaitsky, I made a grey coatdress in worsted twill with a large white collar to cover her ample bosom.

The following Shabbat we donned our new finery and set off for shul. We slipped quietly into the back row and as I raised my eyes across the shul I looked straight at Dorah and Tuvia. Dorah's mouth was gaping, it seemed to be wedged open and Tuvia had hidden her smile by looking down into her prayer book. It was a noisy and relaxed atmosphere with the *davening,* the prayers and the songs being sung by the leaders of the service undulating through the lovely old building.

In a Litvak community it is commonplace for participants to shout out corrections to the service and contrary opinions to the goings on. Men walked about talking to each other and shaking hands, greeting each other in a comradely fashion.

At the conclusion of the service, people made their way into the back hall for a *Kiddush, a* cup of wine. We had herring and kichel, the sweet thin cracker like biscuit that we customarily ate with the herring.

Morris greeted me warmly, but Mrs Dorah Nurek made a point of coming across the room to wish me a "Gutten Shabbos." She was most colloquial and asked Bobba Tromp where she had purchased such a fine coat. "Ah", she murmured coyly, "Doniyel made it for me this week." If Dorah could have turned green, she might have sprouted leaves ….. *"Tucker"*……. she said, meaning "really!" "I should have such luck", glancing over at me with renewed interest.

I couldn't see Tuvia anywhere in the crowded room so I concentrated on my most important ally. "I have opened a tailoring room Mrs Nurek," I said.

"Where is this tailoring room?" she asked me.

"In my home" I took pleasure in saying.

"And where is this home?" she asked.

I gave her the address and her eyes opened wide. "I will come to see you" she nodded, and "Donyiel", she added "will you join us for Rosh Hashana to celebrate New Year next month?"

I was excited and pleased, another chance to see Tuvia and perhaps, did I detect a note of possible approval?

We took a slow stroll home after shul. Bobba was pleased with the effect she had created and I felt very satisfied at the direction things were taking. We spent the afternoon talking about what Solly could do to begin his career.

At the top of the hill just around Whites Road we had passed a derelict bakery. We cupped our hands to look through the dusty window and Solly sighed. "I'd love to have a cake shop, to make fresh kitke and to make you Ruggelach for yomtov" he said.

"Thank you", I retorted laughing, "I already have a supply". But the idea struck me as a good one and later that night I took out my remaining stones and had a good hard think.

I would feel happy to perform a mitzvah in loaning Solly the money to open a business and felt sure in time he would pay it back to me, and if Tuvia didn't come up with the goods, I'd have ruggelach into the bargain.

We sought out the owner of the bakery. All the ovens were still there and he had gone *mechullah,* insolvent.

It would be fairly easy to purchase the bakery.

Within a fortnight I had sold the additional stones, although I kept the diamond. I came to a satisfactory agreement with Benny and Bobba. They would pay me back as soon as they began making a profit and if we could get the bakery going by Rosh Hashana, the Jewish New Year, the profit, I felt sure, would return to us soon.

I couldn't help noticing the astonishing change in Bobba T. Perhaps the fresh food, the sunshine and a little assistance from Nona, the house maid, had made her seem healthier and stronger. She seemed younger than I had always imagined her in Zagare. She was raring to go and scrubbed and polished that bakery till you could eat off the floor.

Solly and I painted a brand new name on the front, and four days before Rosh Hashana, Trumps Bakery was launched.

We opened quietly with honey cakes for the high holy days and took orders for round sweet raisin kitke, as the chollah bread was called in Africa. Bobba made her apple kringle and the finest thinnest kichel in town.

On the first day, everything was sold out by noon. The next day Solly rose early to light the ovens and they baked double quantities. This, too, was insufficient, and I found myself helping behind the counter as Solly dashed into the back to bake more bread.

One of the first customers was Mrs Polansky. I wasn't to know she was Morris's cousin. She questioned us both about how and who and where, and from this we gathered she must have a daughter!

We were fast becoming the most sought after bachelors in town!!

The following Shabbat, Mrs Polansky invited us to dinner on Friday night.

As soon as Dorah got wind of this news she called around to the shop to invite us for Shabbos lunch. Solly and I had a good laugh. If we kept this up we would be well fed for months.

As things turned out, Solly was too exhausted to make it to lunch, so I went alone.

I felt very comfortable at the Nureks. Tuvia was more relaxed with me, although young Mendel, aged eight and Rosele, aged six, never left us alone for a moment. We ate wonderful gefilte fish and Dorah insisted I take a plate home for Solly when I left.

After lunch Tuvia and I walked to the park and I asked her who had made her exceptionally well cut suit. She smiled at me and said "I don't have a bespoke tailor. I make my own clothes."

Oi vey! This girl was beshiert for me. We had so many things in common. Home values, Litvak cooking, and we could stay home together and sew. I resolved to think about this with a clear head.

I was only nineteen but without papers I could maintain I was twenty-one. The rabbi would have to make me of an age to marry, and get a civil license.

I sat down and wrote my family a long letter telling them all the exciting things that had happened to me, carefully wording where I had got the money so that Gittel might understand I had found her intended . . . . gift. I wished them all a safe Rosh Hashana and hoped to see them one day. I sent the letter to the kind Rabbi in Riga who might send a carriage to Zagare to hand deliver my letter with a South African postmark, and ensure it was not too obvious that it came from me in Africa. If this reached them, then I could find a way to send them money and ensure it would not fall into the wrong hands.

As I walked along, I picked up a lucky beetle, a little red lady bird that Africans felt was a sign of luck. Yes, I told the little creature, my mazel was changing.

13
ROSH HASHANA

I had begun to deal with my unconscious judgmental fear that the Kashrut would be less real in Africa than it had been in Lithuania. It had never occurred to me that Jews all over the world celebrating the High Holy days were doing so in different seasons. Here it was almost summer while in Lithuania they would be gathering wood for the winter.

I saw how the community adjusted to the climatic conditions for Shabbat, and enjoyed their casual approach when conducting religious affairs, although it seemed no less correct.

Solly, Bobba and I got "*opgepatchedt,* all dressed up in our new year outfits. Although this festival was known as the "Days of Awe" when one was to seriously consider one's moral responsibilities in life, it was customary to wear new festive clothes and make an effort. This reminded us of the respect and of the importance of the holiday.

I hadn't had much sewing time but I made myself pair of linen trousers, realizing it would be spring and quite warm. I had grown a moustache over the past few weeks and kept looking in the newly acquired mirror in my sewing room at this interesting strange young man called Doniyel Levintahl, almost forgetting the bearded *peyos,* my sideburns and pale face that I had left home wearing not so long ago.

We walked to shul for Shlichot, the midnight service before Rosh Hashana.

Midnight Shlichot begins on the days before Rosh Hashana. In our village in Zagare, the beadle used to go about with his lamp and knock on people's windows reminding them to come to the service as it was pitch dark. It was customary to go to the public baths at home but here we had our own bathrooms and so the religious preserve of bathing before the high holy days was something the Jews in Drom Africa took for granted. I looked forward to the day when I could run Gittel a warm bath with sizzling Epsom salts and allow her the privacy and freedom of the dreaming time I loved so much in the moist air of the bathroom.

I wondered if Tuvia would be there as, for once, men and woman sat together. Normally we were separated in the synagogue.

I caught a glimpse of her across the room, but she was with her five sisters, Annie, Gertie, Milly, Sorah and Rosele. They were sitting in a row together.

The service was a beautiful, slow melodious chanting. Candles were lit around the room and mellow dreamy crooning of the old tunes made one remember the lullabies one's mother had sung. People were looking forward to Rosh Hashana and were beginning to feel prepared for the High Holy Days.

I could picture the Rebbe swaying in my head. I ached for his twinkly eyes which said all the things he had never verbalized to me on Yomtov.

After the Service, as it was a warm evening, we walked home enjoying the Algoa Bay breeze and talked about Zagare, Linkuva—Babkes and Bulkas.

I wanted to make Tuvia a special gift for Rosh Hashana, but was not sure what would be appropriate. I asked Bobba's advice, and she suggested a book of poems.

"Where will I find a book of Yiddish poems?" I cried.

"No Doniyel, she reads English—we are here in Drom Africa". True, I nodded, smiling at her. She always used her *saichel*—her sense!

I scoured the bookshops and found a well-printed old copy of poems by Shelley. I wrapped it up carefully and stitched her name on a strip of muslin. This I placed in my favorite page, a poem of sweet hope. She would probably think I was a *schlemiel,* but I was going to risk it anyway.

My first Rosh Hashana service in Africa was strange but exciting. The synagogue was completely full. Children and non-regulars filled the back rows. Little boys in their Tzitzit's ran up and down the rows being "*shushed*" by the elders. I savor the richness of the service at this time of the year with holy songs Malchiyos—Shoforos. These familiar songs filled my heart and the longing I felt for home seemed easier knowing I would be with a family I was growing fond of.

At the end of the service everyone waited with bated breath to hear the Shofar blown

KI YOR, KI YOR, the familiar happy sound brings in the New Year.

The ram's horn is a musical instrument, a natural wind instrument and one of the oldest known to mankind used, in general, to make proclamations to the people. It is said that Moses ascended Mount Sinai for the second time and blew the Shofar to remind the Jewish people not to err a second time and not to worship idols again.

We arrived at the Nurek's feeling quite excited. The table looked splendidly pristine, a fitting tribute to the solemnity of the high holy days of New Year. All her crystal was filled with sweet fruits and nuts. Her cut glass shimmered in the flickering candlelight and her two splendid round loaves from Trumps Bakery had pride of place under the white kitke cover, which had been embroidered by Tuvia.

We dipped apple in honey for a sweet year. As I dipped mine, I caught Tuvia's eye and we connected. My heart gave a blip and I took a *gezunt* nervous gulp of wine

The Nurek children, all well-scrubbed and well-behaved, sat round the table. The meal began with the brachot we sang with great warmth and feeling. I marveled again at how we all knew the same tunes and prayers, reminding me of our roots in Lithuania. We laughed and drank, the atmosphere was *lebedike.* Eventually, we sat down to eat our fill of heimishe Lithuanian food, a real *shtup,* and my belly felt warm and round.

I had to admit the soft aromatic kneidal in the soup could come close to Gittel's, the chicken soup was delicate and the giblets were skillfully and unobtrusively awarded to me. I felt I was becoming Dorah's "alrightnik"!! The carrot *tzimmes* was sweet and soft, and the potato *kugel* was crisp on top and soft and scrumptious inside.

Bobba and Dorah began to tell stories and the younger people at the table could only laugh at their accents.

I had been lucky on the boat over to South Africa as Mr. Rudolph had spoken fluent English without an accent. My English was clear and well pronounced, without accent. Solly was not so adept at English yet, but he could make himself easily understood. In days to come, Dorah would find my well spoken English very useful and often asked me to speak on her behalf when necessary.

After the meal, to my delight, Morris asked me to recite the *benching,* a prayer of thanksgiving for the meal. In my mind, I thanked the Rebbe for his years of perseverance in teaching me. I gave a hearty rendering with a proud voice and quietly sent my thoughts all the way to Zagare as I knew they would be wondering about my celebration.

Tea was served in the Samovar and I helped Tuvia pass the tea cups around. I was beginning to feel quite comfortable in their home. She thanked me for the book and asked me to stay after lunch tomorrow so we could read it together.

I tripped like a gazelle along the road to shul next morning, davening heartily amongst the men, listening to the choir and trying very hard to keep my thoughts as pure as you were meant to be on Rosh Hashana, which was about renewal and repentance but inside my Litvak heart, I felt a happiness I hadn't expected.

The ten days until Yom Kippur were extremely busy in the bakery. Solly was doing so well and shoppers were coming from across town to buy his bread and cakes. Bobba's cheesecake was a talking- point in the women's gallery and Dorah had invited Bobba to join the women's league.

Mrs Trompaitzky had almost forgotten how to kvetch!

On the solemn night of Yom Kippur we dressed in white. It was customary to wear canvas shoes instead of leather in deference to the idea of not killing animals made by G-d.

Kol Nidrei is a time when one thinks about asking forgiveness to people you may have hurt and making up to people you may have neglected.

While walking towards the Kol Nidrei service, Solly told me that he believed they could begin to pay me back quite soon. I'd thought about this and, while I admired Bobba's strength, I was beginning to find living with her on a daily basis a "*bittere gelegte,* "a drag".

I suggested to Solly that the little house we had seen down the road from the bakery should be our next investment and we should purchase it together. He and Bobba could live there. He looked at me slyly. "Are you thinking of taking a wife?" he asked.

"Do you think her father would accept me?" I asked him tenuously.

He slapped me on the back and laughed........."Doniyel, if you don't ask him soon he might ask you!"

"When do you think I should ask him, Solly?"

"Well, perhaps you should ask Tuvia first." In the old country this would have been unheard of, but here we were in Africa, trying not to appear as *greeners,* and maybe Solly was correct.

14
THE SUCCAH

As soon as I had heard the "t'ki -oh, t'ru -oh, t'ki-oh" of the shofar, the ram's horn blown at the end of Yom Kippur, I knew with peaceful certainty that I wanted to make sweet Tuvia my wife.

The very next day Solly and I caught the tram to the lumber yard. We managed to talk the proprietor into letting us have some second grade timber to build our Tabernacle for the festival of Succot, and he'd be kind enough to deliver it. After this we treated ourselves to a walk along the beach front.

"Sol, I am so nervous" I said . "Do I ask Morris Nurek for Tuvia's hand in marriage first, or do I ask Tuvia first?"

"Well", said Solly always practical," what if Morris agrees and Tuvia declines?"

"Oi vey, don't alert the evil eye", shrieks Doniyel.

Solly laughs. "Then you will have a problem, but… if Tuvia accepts and Morris declines, well he' d have to have a good reason. However, you could probably set that obstacle right, whatever it might be."

"Yes," mused Doniyel, "I suppose you are right, what will be, will be. But when will I ever get the opportunity to ask her?"

For a clever boychik, Doniyel's nerves were getting the better of him, thought Solly.

"We'll ask her to help us build the Succah and then I'll have to go to the store and I'll take Bobba with me", schemed Solly.

"A Yiddische kop" shouted Doniyel, "Nu, let's go home and get started. "I am on *spilkes,* all nerves, with this *Meidel* "

Together they begia to clear a space in the yard for the Tabernacle called a Succah.

Bobba got busy baking and making jam. She wanted this first social occasion in their home to be *yontifdik,* celebratory and impressive. She is making her date rolls and orange pletzlach—jellied sweetmeats made from orange peel and sugar. "I am sure they must long for them from 'de Heim'", she muses to herself.

Meanwhile, Solly and Doniyel are plotting while hammering the wooden succah frame.

By noon they have placed the wooden supports for the three walls and secured the hessian covering hanging from the frame. Doniyel feels really exhilarated. The Succah is supposed to represent the intransience of our dwellings and of everything concrete, except our beliefs. In contrast, he is aware that for the first time he will have a permanent home, a thing of strong brick and stone where he hopes to live in peace and good health and maybe start a family of his own. He feels a great warmth come over him at the thought.

Tuvia has agreed to come over to their new home and walk with Doniyel to neighbors who may have some *Shach,* branches of Myrtle, that he did not need himself. This is placed over the top of the tabernacle.

At three o clock Tuvia arrives with her brother Mickey in tow. *"Oi Vey"* What now!

But Bobba, in with the plan, immediately invites him to help her with the icing and he is soon engrossed in the kitchen.

Doniyel and Tuvia walk off down the road. She is impressed to see his new home and his yard. She notices how handy he is. Morris is all thumbs and mostly it is Dorah who ends up doing the *shlepping and klapping* around the house.

They ring the doorbell of Mr Bernstein s house.

"Come in, come in Dorah", he says, looking at Doniyel with a question mark.

"This is my friend Doniyel Levintahl, your new neighbour Mr Bernstein. He is looking for Shach."

"Aha!" says Mister Bernstein, thinking it over as if it was a big deal. "Well, I just have a few branches over from our succah, and you're welcome to it.

"Where are you from, Meester Levintawl?" he enquires with a heavy accent.

"From Lithuania", I reply cautiously, glancing at Tuvia.

"Yes yes", he laughs, "but which shtetl?"

"Zagare,"I reply. "Are you a Litvak, Mr Bernstein?"

Shyly he nods."From Kovno. We came almost ten years ago", he says with a far-away look in his eyes for a few moments.

Tuvia and I drag *the shach* back to our house, laughing happily at our find.

We are greeted by Solly and Bobba who have secret question marks on their faces. I avoid their eyes and we pull the branches into the Succah.

Bobba appears agitated. "*Vos tut zich,* Bobba?" Doniyel asks. "What's cooking?"

"Vel", she says slowly, wringing her hands in her newly acquired "Yinglish", "*ve got no cups*!"

"That's true", acknowledged Doniyel. Up to now they had eaten out of the three mugs with which they had traveled and not worried too much about domestic finery. They hadn't thought about entertaining.

"I have an idea", said Tuvia quietly. "Why don't we walk down the road to the pawnbroker and see if he has any cups for sale?"

Another chance to talk to her! Doniyel leapt over anxiously at the chance, while Bobba and Solly vocally supported the idea. *Oi vey*—we were like *shlemuzels* in a play and she might smell a rat.

We donned our hats and went in search of cups. Tuvia led me to the pawnbroker's shop. I was entranced. A wealth of weird and wonderful things from leather saddles to copper pots filled the shop from floor to ceiling. The proprietor, a little bald man in a navy waistcoat, was wearing ill-fitting trousers, which of course I, as the eternal tailor, always noted. His high collar was taut around his neck and made him look as if he was being strangled. He came out of the dusty back room to enquire what we were looking for.

"Do you have a tea set?" I asked. He looked us over as if he were assessing what level of goods we could afford.

"I might have", he mumbled. "Come with me"

We walked gingerly into the back room and waited while he moved many boxes and cases too and fro. The dust rose around us as we glanced silently at each other. I longed to hold her hand. Eventually, he exclaimed with excitement and opened a carton to take out a very elegant tea cup. I had never bought a tea set before and I was unsure of what to say, but Tuvia saved the day by asking him if we might see the whole tea set.

Grudgingly he set it all out on the table. Despite my being a nebbish and ignoramus in terms of teacups, I could see this was no ordinary tea set.

15
THE TEA SET

The tea set sat proudly on the dusty back table.

It was a splendid porcelain array of twelve perfect cups and saucers, each covered in little purple and yellow pansies, with a lip scalloped with gold leaf. The milk and sugar bowl were square-ish and the teapot full and curved. The coffee pot was tall and elegant. To Tuvia's delight, it had a matching cake plate and an unusual spoon dish. She was so captivated by the tea set I knew it must be special.

When we heard the price he was asking, I nearly *platzed,* but I tried to act nonchalantly. I told him we'd think it over and be back. We walked out of the shop and I imagined that Tuvia looked at me with tenderness.

"It is very costly", she nodded," but I have a feeling it is a collector's piece."

"How can we find out?" I asked.

"We could go down Whites Road to the Public Library and look it up", she replied.

"How far away is it?" I asked, not wanting to be away too long in case the Nureks came looking for her.

"Let us catch the tram and walk quickly", she suggested.

So, in an atmosphere of playing truant, we rushed off to the library and there we found a reference to show us that this was indeed, a limited edition of a Queen Mary Tea Set.

By now we were hungry and thirsty but we knew of no coffee shop where we could get a kosher meal, so we stopped in at a tea house and ordered a glass of lemon tea. I felt like a real gentleman. I'd never sat in a tea house before and here I was sitting in South Africa, a land owner taking tea with a beautiful young lady. It felt surreal.

Tuvia could not stop talking about the tea set, and I was so nervous I dropped my teaspoon onto the floor. In the old country, if you dropped your spoon, it was said you were going to get lucky—Alevei!

Something magical happened to me -

As I knelt down to retrieve my teaspoon, suspended on one knee, I heard myself saying, "Tuvia, if you would do me the honor of being my wife, the tea set would be ours to remember this wonderful day."

Oi what a *szhlok*, a nincompoop. It sounded like I was offering the tea set as a bribe. What have I done? What did I say? I could not look at her.

I heaved myself onto the chair again. She leaned over and took my hand. It felt velvety and warm. She looked into my eyes and she said calmly "Doniyel, I'd be proud to be your wife even without the tea set, but", she smiled charmingly "we *could* have wonderful tea parties ".

I was rigid. I had done it. *Oi vevoy*! Yoi yoi, yoi. I was going to be betrothed!

"I will have to speak to your father tonight" I said.

She nodded. "And I will say nothing to anyone until you have spoken to him."

"What do you think Dorah will say?" enquired Doniyel nervously.

"I think she will '*clib nachos*', she'll be very excited", Tuvia laughed.

We hurried back to the pawnbroker. I closed my eyes and paid for the tea set. He packed it up and we carried it home very gingerly. We found Mickey still dipping his fingers into the icing bowl. Bobba had encouraged him to draw us some wonderful brightly colored pictures to decorate the Succah. Both Bobba and Solly were getting a little "antsy" at our dawdling.

We told them the story of our tea set while unpacking it onto the table. Bobba was as thrilled with it as Tuvia was. I knew I'd made a good buy.

Tuvia caught my eye, but we both said nothing and Solly and Bobba would never ask.

I saw Tuvia and Mickey to the door, knowing they would be back the next day to enjoy our Succah with the whole family.

As soon as I closed the door I raced back to the kitchen, caught Solly's hands, and did a jig around the table with the tea set. "I'm to be a *chosen*, a groom. I have found *a kallah ,a kallah a kallah*—my bride." I sang at the top of my voice as we danced around the table.

They both gave great hoops of joy and we all fell about hugging. "Don't count your chickens before they hatch *Mister Chosen*", said Bobba "you still have to ask the Father!"

"Yes", I nodded sobering up, "but I'm confident that when Dorah drinks out of my Queen Mary cups, she'll be convinced I'm the perfect match for Tuvia!"

We all laughed. What a happy night we spent decorating the Succah

In South Africa we could have a choice of the most wonderful fresh fruits as Succot fell in spring

Bobba had splashed out on yellow cling peaches from the Cape, large and juicy. We had never seen anything like them before coming here, yellow plums and red plums, large green grapes still on the vine.

We'd hung up 'naartjies'. These were mini oranges, very sweet, with a loose peel. Through the shach, the branches above us, we could see clear blue sky, something we were not blessed with on Succot in Zagare. We hung up Mickey's pictures of all seven of the species which we refer to on Succot as the harvesting holiday. Bobba had placed her best crochet cloth on the table and arranged the tea set with loving care. I placed the silver candlesticks I had carried with me from Zagare on the table. I put out the miniature kiddush cup that Solly had given me as a barmitzvah present back home. Who would have *ever* have thought we'd be using it in Drom Africa in our own home, on Succot!

'Solly the Baker'. I could always rely on a surprise.He'd made little crispy biscuits iced in yellow and purple to complement the tea set. On our new cake plate it looked spectacular.

16
THE BETROTHAL

I had arranged to collect the Nurek family and walk back to the house with them. I had no *zitz vleis,* I was restless. Until I knew what Morris's answer would be, I could not concentrate.

Tuvia and I had a special secret and I couldn't imagine pretending throughout the whole evening. I knew I had to speak to Morris Nurek beforehand.

I found him in the sitting room checking out the Lulov, the four species of branches we waved at the time of Succot. He intended giving it to us as a gift to use in our Succah.

I hoped Tuvia was keeping her part of the bargain by asking Dorah for help with her hair. I was grossly unsure of myself. I felt that if Dorah was present when I asked for his permission, I'd be stuttering and stammering. As it was, I was *shvitzing* on a cool evening.

"Mr Nurek," I said, going in for the thrust before I lost my nerve. "May I beg you for the honour of your daughter Tuvia's hand in marriage? I do not have much to offer her in material goods but I will look after her as it is G-d's will", I said, standing to attention.

"Sit down Doniyel" he said kindly. "I know Tuvia is very fond of you." He paused. My throat closed, but what ….. "and", he continued slowly "Dorah calls you a *chochem,* a wise Man. It will be a good *Shidduch,* a match made in heaven."

I felt sure Dorah was listening at the keyhole.We couldn't have been speaking too loudly "Shidduch, what shidduch?" she demanded, rushing in like a South Easter wind, with her suit half buttoned up and no shoes on her bunioned feet.

Morris rose and placed his arm around me and Dorah tried to act surprised, but her faced was filled with glee. She came over to give me a *gezunte* hug.

"Boruch Hashem", a blessing to G-d, she shouted.

"Tuvia, Tuvia *give a kuk*, come and look at your shidduch!"

My sweet Tuvia came shyly into the room beaming from ear to ear. She stood next to her father demurely and looked at me as if she was seeing me for the first time.

We collected ourselves and walked back to my new house around the corner.

We were greeted by Bobba who intuitively saw by our expressions that the news was good. "Mazeltov, mazeltov". She hugged Dorah and everyone shook my hand with joy.

We took our places at the table laid in the Succah. The Nureks complimented us on a Succah where even the women folk could fit in and we could all sit round the table together. Mickey was proud to see the result of his hard work decorating the walls. We got him to make the brocha, the prayer over the wine. He sang loud and clear and he felt like a king. Benny had excelled himself with cinnamon *boulke,* curls of soft dough. Bobba had made cream cheese and we had wonderful sweet red plums.

The Succah has an open roof with the branches we had collected laid over the top of the Succah. We sincerely hope it won't rain, but being the season it usually does. This does not deter anyone from being in the Succah. It is a feast time with each day being of different significance.

We are told to take branches from a "goodly" tree such as date palms, myrtle and willow. These are bound together so the Jews may beat the ground and chant the age-old passage beseeching the heavens to make the earth fertile. We hold the Etrog, fruit of the citron, in our hands as we beat the branches. The Etrog is held in awe and considered precious, usually quite costly. Only the wealthy have their own Etrog. In Lithuania the Etrog was a single fruit that the synagogue was able to get, but here in Africa I learnt that families joined together, six or eight families sharing an Etrog.

As Morris had arranged for the Etrog from the shul to be brought to our Succah after the service, we awaited the messenger before we began and made sure we had suitable payment for him, as was the custom.

We were a joyous lot, making jokes and singing songs.

After our Etrog had arrived, Dorah served Kreplach soup, delicate giblet soup with tiny little squares of dough filled with tasty minced meat.

Ah Gittel, my mind wandered, I wonder if your kreplach are tender and spiced tonight. I wonder if you can imagine how happy I am and how hopeful for the future.

We began to talk about plans for our forthcoming Simcha, our wedding day.

17
THE CHUPPAH

The summer days seemed to go by so quickly.

I had asked Tuvia if she would like me to assist her in making her wedding dress but she'd looked horrified. "Of course not, I want it to be a total surprise", she laughed.

This morning I had made myself a cup of strong coffee and was relaxedly sitting down at my machine when agitated knocking on the door brought Tuvia running into my house. Hands waving, she was so short of breath she could not get the words out.

"What's wrong, Tuvi" I asked.

"Doniyel, Doniyel come quickly, The shul is on fire "she gasped.

"Oy vey, Klog iz mir."

We grabbed my keys and hat and ran down the hill. Thoughts of modesty were banished from our minds as I grabbed her hand to steady her on the cobbled pavement .We shot into the bakery and grabbed Solly.

"Lock up and come quickly, the Shul is burning", I shouted.

He ran to the back to check the ovens, while we pulled the front doors closed and locked the door, (not before grabbing a hot beigel).

The three of us ran on down the hill. Alongside us others had heard the news and everyone was making haste to the bottom of the hill.

As we reached the corner we turned into Edwards Avenue and there we were witness to a most horrendous sight. Electric flames of red and yellow leapt upwards, licking heavy smoky cloud. The synagogue wall was already blackened by the fire, the small fire engine which was available could not cope. If the roof fell in, all our religious possessions would be lost.

We formed a line—men, women and boys—some beat the flames with branches, others passed buckets of water. The congregants all prayed fervently, hoping against hope that that the precious Sefer Torahs would not be burnt. The smoke burnt our throats and the acrid smell fouled the formerly clean sea air

Hours later we sat on the pavement, dirty, sweating and tired, but grateful to know our Torah had been saved. The building was a skeleton.

What now! The elders of the synagogue held an impromptu meeting around the site. Worried looks and much wringing of hands as the Rabbi was brought to see the charred mess his precious house of prayer had been reduced to.

He reminded everyone that it was Friday and soon the Shabbos star would be out and it was forbidden to carry anything on Shabbos.

A quick and clever decision was made to move anything we could, prayer books, the Torahs, the Menorah and anything of value up the hill to the community centre in Raleigh Street. At least there they could be safe and then, after Shabbos was over, we could assess the damage.

The community really pulled together .We formed a line all the way up the hill. Old and young, mother and child, and we handed the precious books from one to the other, from generation to generation all the way up the hill, followed by the Rabbi and Chazen, his assistant, who carried the two Sefer Torah. Just before the first star came out we all entered the Raleigh street hall and gave hearty thanks for the safety of all.

The hall had a high domed ceiling. It had beautiful windows high above our heads but other than that it was very basic. It seemed this would have to be our house of prayer until things were sorted out. All the books would have to be examined and new arrangements would have to be made. Money would have to be raised to rebuild the shul.

We milled around discussing all the options and just supportimg each other. The Litvaks and recent immigrants felt extremely stressed by the fire. We all spoke in Yiddish, our common denominator.

It brought back fragile images of home that we rarely thought about in these busy hardworking days. It made us want to talk to each other about our families and shtetls, and gave us a cold feeling of vulnerability.

A week later the Rabbi called on us to complete our wedding papers as he no longer had an office. The saddened Rabbi informed us that the chuppah which had been in a cupboard in one of the walls had been badly burnt in the fire.

Tuvia wept. I felt empty and blank. I had visions of all the burnt shuls and desecrated houses of prayer I had seen before and it was too hard to think about.

"We won't delay the wedding", I said "I will make a plan." I had learnt the South African saying that the Afrikaaners used in times of adversity—"A Boer maak a plan!"

After The Rabbi left us, Tuvia was inconsolable. I walked her home trying to reassure her. As I walked back along the now familiar path from her house to mine, I was sure I heard Gittel calling me. I looked around. Have I gone *meshuggah?* Perhaps I am dizzy from smoke inhalation?

No—my connection to my mother was so strong, she was alerting me to something, something she wanted me to know. I knew it in my bones and I desperately held onto the feeling until I could clarify it in my head.

I felt weak and strange. I sat on a bench to see if I could hear it again. I looked up at the blue sky. Cotton clouds were skimming by and the leaves of the trees were rustling rhythmically. I felt the stone in my pocket. A precious ruby that I was taking to the jeweler to have set into the ring I was to give Tuvia. And then—like a vision of the Megillah unfolding—it rolled out before me! The PAROCHET, my Gittel's embroidery! I could turn it into a Chuppah, a superb chuppah and donate it to my new-found community. My Tuvia and I would be married under it and -Please G-d—one day, my children and their children's children. The Levintahls of Africa!

I ran back to The Nurek's house, banging on the door in my vigor to tell Tuvia not to worry. She was not at home so I ran all the way to the Rabbi's house and told him I'd be making the chuppah. I was so excited I didn't even wait for his answer. I wanted to get home and look at my secret rolled-up velvet parcel.

I shut the doors and pulled out my travel roll from the top of the closet. I laid it on the kitchen table. It was perfect, the size was almost suitable. I could make it more square without disturbing the patterns that Gittel had stitched and without losing any of the lions or the crown. The gold embroidery of the crown still held most of the pearls. I decided I would leave them there. I would surround the velvet with ruby satin panels to hold it up taut and high on the chuppah poles and this would make it the correct size.

I began to count the 613 stitches that Gittel had so lovingly worked but before I got past 50, I was sound asleep on the table.

I dreamt of Shlomo ben Zalkind, his twinkly eyes, his voice and his words to me. Of how he too, had kept the community calm in the face of trauma and turned them to prayer. I awoke hours later and I felt happier and found renewed strength. I would not have the privilege of him standing under the chuppah with me but their presence would be boldly evident to me and their spirits would be holding my hand as I walked down the aisle to my new life.

I fingered the velvet, running my hand over its smoothness. I separated the velvet from the grey of the blanket and I rolled the grey felt up and put it away carefully. Then, from under the floor where I had hidden them, I took out the box containing the stones that were left.

With careful consideration, I could sew one diamond back into the crown of the Chuppah, so it would be hidden away under the stitches and if ever one of my descendents needed Tzedakah – charity—as I had, I believed G-d would reveal it to them.

I shivered at my little secret and resolved, like Gittel, not to make the diamond a burden of knowledge, and to tell no-one.

18
NEW NAME, NEW CHANCE

The next few weeks were such a happy time of hope and possibilities. Tuvia and I got to know each other a little better, and the preparations began to fall into place.

I realized I had never been to a wedding in Drom Africa and it would be very different to a wedding in the streets of the shtetl.

I tried everything I knew to make contact with Shlomo and Gittel. I sent letters to Riga via the Rabbi I had stayed with. I even spent a fortune on trying to send a telegram but, alas, I heard nothing. I dreamed of having Gittel under the chuppah with me and was saddened that I could not give them the *nachos,* the pleasure I know it would have been for them to meet Tuvia and see me come to this important moment in my life. They could not even begin to imagine the circumstances.

The following Shabbos I went to the Nurek's for lunch, and I was very impressed to learn that Morris had bought me a seat in Shul as a wedding gift so that I could sit next to him. This was indeed a *shtik nachus,* a big deal, to have your own seat with a little brass plate showing your name. I felt I had arrived in the community and found mishpocha, a family!

As the time came nearer, we had to keep our appointment with the Rabbi and I showed him my new identity papers which I had been given on disembarking. He examined my papers and my ticket for a long time and I began to get nervous.

"Doniyel", he said quietly,"we live here and we obey the laws. As you are now a South African immigrant it might be a good idea to anglicize your name". He saw me frown.

"It's a *nechtiger tog*! A fait accompli. The immigration officer has written your name in English and so you must be married in your English name". "What is this English name?" I asked. "Daniel Levinthal", he replied.

I looked at Tuvia. "Will you be Mrs Daniel Levinthal?"

"Yes Mr Levinthal", she replied. I liked it. I felt I had almost become Daniel Levinthal Esq.

19
THE WEDDING

I stood under the Chuppah without a trace of nervousness. I knew this was what I really wanted to do. Solly and I had been to the mikveh the night before and he had told me how much he envied me in finding the right girl. I felt sure in time he would do so too, but for now he had Bobbe and I had no one.

I glanced up at the Chuppah. The Rabbi and synagogue committee had gasped with pleasure when I had first set it up in the shul.

A rainbow of light bounced off the sheen of the pearls and the velvet glowed with a rose coloured warmth.

I felt a curtain drawn over my pain at my parents not being there, but took comfort in the fact that they would be happy for me and I felt the Chuppah, a symbol of my home, was an omen of protection sent from them.

The shul was noisily filling up. Everyone was dressed in their Yomtov finery and the ladies' hats were feathered with a flourish.

Many Jewish farmers had settled in the Outshoorn district, near Algoa Bay and were doing well from feathers as a fashion trimming, a *must* on your wedding hat.

In the ensuing three weeks after the fire an enormous effort had taken place to get the shul ready for our wedding.

Undamaged pews had been brought up the hill. A large square wooden Bimah, the pulpit, had been built in the style I remembered from Zagare. The brass plaques with named seats had been replaced and I was very proud of my new brass named seat right next to Morris in the front row.

Guests were wandering up to me to shake my hand and wish me luck but in so doing they could have a good "squiz" under the Chuppah and each one examined it with genuine admiration.

The music began. Mr and Mrs Rosenberg, who had hosted me on

my arrival in Port Elizabeth stood up for me as my "unterferers" to give me away.

Solly, my best man, caught my eye and then I sensed that Tuvia and her parents were approaching. I could not turn and look at her but had to wait until she came to my side, and then I glanced at her and my heart swelled. My eyes watered. She looked at me from under her veil. She slowly circled me seven times, making me the centre of her world—our world together in Africa. I tried to concentrate on listening to the Rabbi and Chazen singing the Seven Blessings for our marriage.

I repeated the age-old words of the wedding promise *"Me kodeshit li*—Behold I am consecrated to you according to the law of Moses and Israel".

He read out our Ketubah, our marriage certificate, slowly and deliberately, first in Aramaic and then in English. I took the words in and I prayed I would be strong enough to uphold their meaning.

I had asked him not to say too much about the parochet turned Chuppah but simply to say that my mother Gittel had blessed me with the means to make a superb Chuppah.

Then, with great joy, I broke the glass. This custom symbolizes that we remember the destruction of the second temple.

I embraced Tuvia briefly and then we turned towards the community where we were smothered in good wishes from crowd of happy people.

The community needed some levity and strong deep voices began to sing joyously. Men joined shoulders and started to dance around me and the violinists pranced in front of us as we walked towards our new home together.

Dorah looked magnificent in maroon with her chestnut fox draped over her shoulders. The feather on her large-brimmed hat was longer than anyone else's feather and that pleased her. She preened proudly next to us, waving regally as if this was her day. Perhaps it was! With such a Chosen, a tailor from Zagare!

My Tuvia floated on my arm like a bride in a fairytale. Her soft white satin frock was draped and folded over her ample bosom which gathered at her slender waist into a Raschel lace train, which fell to the ground in yards of gently whirling floral pattern. Over her head she wore the same lace in a second fluted train and held around her brown curls with little pink buds.

Her sisters were resplendent in similar lace dresses with full gathered skirts and satin waistbands. Each had a large picture hat held to their heads with rose coloured flowers to match the Chuppah. Mendel or, as we called him, Mickey, had on a new suit which he was proudly showing off to his friends.

I had dropped Tuvia one unobtrusive little hint about the colour of the chuppah and she had run with it.

We entered our home to the sound of "Mazeltov u Simantov" being sung all around us. Laid out on the table was our pride and joy—the new Tea Set. Friends had filled the house with sweet smelling blooms everywhere. Solly, Bobbe and Dorah had made chopped herring, beigels biscuits, cheesecake and cherry cake. Everything we could feast on in one sitting.

Resplendent in the middle of the table was the Brass Samovar.

After the blessings were made for bread and wine, Dorah stood beside her samovar and loudly proclaimed that with such a smart tea set she had decided to give us the Samovar as a wedding gift as, in future, she only wanted to be served tea in a Queen Mary tea cup.

I could say "our cup had runneth over". Tuvia and I toasted each other with wine and tea and happiness.

Life is a journey,
From Childhood to maturity,
and youth to age :
From innocence to awareness and ignorance to knowing
From loneliness to love
from joy to gratitude
Birth is a beginning.

Tuvia Levinthal with Jacob and Zlatta 1919

PART TWO
Walking in the Wilderness
with Wilfred

PART TWO
Contents

20.
FINDING MY IDENTITY

I thought I heard my name being called. "Hilary—wait". I grasped my boarding pass and passport nervously. I turned round, scanning the faces. Who would know me by name?

My eyes widened as I spotted the group of my wonderful dear friends that I had made while I was in Vilnius. They surged forward excitedly with a package in their hands.

"Open it, open it" they begged.

Inside the bag was a bottle of Zagare Cherry Liquer. They knew I had searched the country for it and had not been able to find any.

"Where did you get it?" I asked thrilled to be able to take a sample back.

"We had to kill for it" laughed Violesa.

"And we needed one more hug", said Rachel.

At that moment I heard the last call for my flight. We drew each other close in a circle of multi-hugs and then I ran down the tunnel to my flight.

To my delight, I'd been upgraded on the aircraft , courtesy of the Minister of Culture in Lithuania. Here in Eastern Europe it was definitely *who* you knew. I settled back in my seat, thankful for a few long hours to sort out my emotions and file the thoughts in my head more cognitively.

It was the 21st century. I was a textile artist living in London and I'd been invited to produce a mural for the newly-acquired Jewish Museum in Vilnius.

The beautiful building was originally a Yiddish theatre and later became the communist headquarters. Now the Lithuanian government had handed it back to the Jewish community and they were attempting to make it into a memorial as a cultural centre.

After my father passed away, I wanted time to myself. I needed to mourn, to cry and to spend time with my thoughts and memories. I couldn't do this in my rushed daily life, or with the people around me as no one else really understands your own complex parental relationship.

The invitation to come to Vilnius was a great opportunity to do this as well as fulfill my life-long dream to return to my roots and find some answers to the questions I had lived with most of my life.

After three years of intense genealogical research, I was ready for the adventure.

Where had it all began?

21
A LITVAK TAILOR

In the year I turned eight, my Dad came home with an old Singer treadle machine. It was attached to a wooden table and you pedaled it with your foot.

"This will have to stand in your room as Grandpa has no place for it at the moment", my Dad said.

At eight I had no real jurisdiction as to what went into my bedroom so I accepted it with a beckoning interest. Most of my weekends as a child were spent at my grandparents' house whilst my parents, who were golf and bowling champions, played in competitions around the country.

We would sit on the floor of the tailoring room with a piece of tailor's chalk and a remnant of suiting. From this we cut out clothes for our dolls. My doll was called Pinky, as she had a pink pony tail, and Jinny's doll was called Blooz. She had a blue pony tail.

When the machine became resident in my bedroom I vowed to watch Grandpa carefully and unbeknown to anyone, I taught myself to thread the machine. I practised and practised until one day I managed to get the machine to work—I treadled away in great excitement.

Dad rushed in to see what the sound was and to his astonishment he found me sitting at the machine trying to sew.

When Grandpa heard the amusing tale, he began to teach me to use the machine, and so it became mine—to be treasured all my life, *shlept* from country to country and maintaining its pride of place in my bedroom.

My favorite time of the week was on Shabbat. As little girls we were dropped off to spend the weekend with Grandpa and Granny. On Fridays we would spend the day in the kitchen watching Gran roll the paper-thin dough made with soda water for *Kreplach* soup, my Dad's favorite. Gramps always allowed us a glass of fizzy soda to drink and we felt very sophisticated. The little kreplach parcels were filled with savory meat and then the left-over dough was sliced up to make kugel and baked in the Aga Stove. Gran could make all kinds of kugel, but our favorite was apple kugel, filled with cinnamon and raisins.

We'd help her set the table and polish the silver, and bake wonderful soft kitke, the plaited bread we ate on Shabbat.The smell of this bread remained in your consciousness all week.

On Saturdays, Gran didn't cook, so she made sure that on Fridays there was enough chicken soup and food for all the meals over Shabbat. She and Grandpa always donned their best outfits. He put on his suit, tie and waistcoat and she would put on one of her elegant stylish dresses with a crochet lace collar that she had made herself.

Routinely on a Friday morning she would have caught the bus to Rink Street to have her hair done in little waves. To preserve it all week in the "Windy City" as Port Elizabeth was known to be, she would wear a colorless hairnet.

Jinny and I always thought this was funny and very old-fashioned, but we loved the silver and cut glass dish on her dresser in which she kept the hairnets. Often, we'd creep into her room and try them on over our own unruly locks.

Their best friends from *de heim,* their old home in Lithuania, would come for tea every Saturday afternoon. Mr and Mrs Trompaitzky would arrive and they would all take tea in the dining room served from the brass Samovar

On rare occasions, or Jewish holidays Mom and Dad joined us, but mostly they played golf. So we dressed ourselves in our Shabbat dresses, which Grandma had made for us, and sat at the tea table "like ladies".

Gramps always insisted we could have tea out of the exquisite teacups, which we loved. They were covered in little yellow and lilac pansies and had cake plates to match. Gran, on the other hand, was much more nervous and would rather we had used the plastic cups, but he maintained his confidence in us and we were extra careful.

She always served an array of homemade biscuits, Grandpa had a passion for her ginger biscuits. Dad loved them too so we always took a small parcel home for him.

Port Elizabeth was a large strong community and the womenfolk were all very active Zionists and participated enthusiastically in various committees. At Pesach time, it was customary to bake your best biscuits and deliver them with good wishes to your close friends. Sometimes, if we received biscuits we didn't like, we gave them on to other friends, careful never to give them back to the family who had baked them! This was a very Port Elizabeth thing!

Gran was well-known for her stuffed Teiglach. I'm sure nobody gave those away! This was a hard chewy biscuit stuffed with juicy raisins which were soaked in ginger syrup for a while before Pesach. She made the syrup in a huge tub and then placed the biscuits in the tub to marinate. This tin tub was kept under the bed in their spare bedroom where we occasionally slept. Jen and I often hid under the bed and quietly dipped our fingers repeatedly into the syrup until our little tummies began to turn.

Such was the introduction to Litvak tastes in my early days.

The house was in the dip of a main thoroughfare called Ramsay Avenue. The bus stopped right at our gate. As little girls we sat on the red polished "stoep" stairway and watched people alight from the bus. As bigger girls we watched the "Grey Boys." These were boys from the Grey College at the top of Ramsay Avenue who would walk past after school

Our teenage friends envied our position. Mom always tried to call us in, but we found excuses to stay out there, and watch the talent.

The Garden was magical, with a palm tree growing right in the middle of the garden, surrounded by paving stones which became our bike-riding circuit. A Loquat tree laden with fruit all year round was the bank and we would stuff loquats into our purses with rather squishy bank balances! We invented many games around this tree.

At the back in the yard Grandpa built us a wooden swing and loved pushing us high into the sky when we were young.

He had an underground cellar which was dark and scary and we only went in there with him, as he had to hold the lamp. In here he kept all the articles he traded on auctions. Whatever you needed, he had one in there!

Our best afternoon activity was spent sitting out in the old Ford car in the garage with Gramps. It was kept in spanking condition. He polished it often and worked on the engine for hours on end. Our job was to polish the seats with dubbin.

He had never learnt to drive but he kept it "for love" he told us.

He was very proud of his car. He would tell us about the time Dad had borrowed the car without asking and the car had run down the hill and Grandpa had had to help him get it back. When we asked Dad about it he looked sheepish and laughed.

A few years later, whiling away a winter afternoon at Grandma's, I found an old photograph. It was a creased yellowing image of two people who looked surreal and otherworldly to me.

The man had a kindly face (I was too young to link the likeness to my grandfather at the time). His face was almost covered by long white whiskers and wonderful thick graying hair. On his head he wore a strange high priest sort of cap, akin to nothing I had ever seen before, and I noted that he had a good aristocratic nose!

She looked removed and fierce, with long hair drawn severely back. She was beautiful in a classical and old-fashioned way but her-half smile looked waxed to her face and hinted at hard times. Her elegant dress, with lace collar and jeweled brooch, must have been the fashion statement of the times. You could tell she was well-dressed. On her chest she wore a heavy gold fob watch.

They were from a world I had no knowledge of, but I felt drawn to them with an uncanny curiosity.

I waited anxiously for my mother to collect me that afternoon. When she arrived I dragged her into the bedroom with excited anticipation and enquired "Who are they?"

"Who cares?" she shrugged and hurried me into the car, having just lost the woman's golf championship.

My Gran loved magazines and collected every article about the royal family. She read them over and over again. She adored looking at Queen Elizabeth I and her dresses, discussing them in great detail. As a little girl I felt reluctant to ask her about the people in the photo fearing they were someone long gone and that it might upset her to remember.

IF only I had asked!

Many years later, when Grandpa passed away, we packed up the house for Gran. Everything lay in disarray. No one seemed to care what went where! I took the photo out of the drawer very gingerly, wrapped it in one of Grandpa's handkerchiefs and placed it carefully at the bottom of my "secrets" drawer at home.

My special treasures in life became my sewing machine and my photograph. When I got into bed at night I dreamt about those two old people, never connecting or understanding who they were, but always believing they were special to my family and I.

In 1997 Auntie Rose that is, my granny's youngest sister, turned 92. At her birthday tea, I finally had the courage to show her the old photograph and inquire if she knew anything about the couple.

"These are your grandfather's parents" she said "They lived in Russia and I do not know their names as I never really knew them."

After all these years of imagining different stories about them, I finally had a name—an identity! It was almost a shock to align them to a real life.

I flew immediately to Port Elizabeth, in South Africa, now fired by my own quest to find our roots and to find out where we came from. I trusted no-one to do this important chore for me.

I walked along the heavy old back row stones in the cemetery. I pondered over how I had never been brought to see these graves which were of such importance in my life. I saw names I had not thought of since I was a child. Unconscious memories came flooding back, the warm smell of Trompaitzkys bakery, and the doughnuts with smooth white icing my mother always treated us to. The acrid smell of Uncle Albert's cigar, and the Canasta toffees we always sought at Auntie Milly.

I stood in front of my grandfather's grave and there, for the first time, I saw the names of my ancestors

Daniel

beloved son of Shlomo ben Zalkind and Gittel Levinthal.

22
PRINCE CHARMING

My grandmother lived near a large rambling park with winding paved pathways. Here we could pretend we were explorers, discovering the world on our bicycles.

My sister and I ensured we made this park our destination as Gran was a superb cook and she kept her pantry filled with a multitude of tins, each one filled with a different biscuit, ginger, shortbread, nutty toffee and coffee creams. I can still taste the caramel on my tongue.

Later on in my life as I tried to cope with my own children eating the full week's shopping on the very day I purchased it. I used to wonder how Granny Tuvia had always kept the tins full. I have very vivid memories of the afternoons where my grandmother allowed me to help her roll out the paper-thin dough, making a wonderful light meat pie called *Perogen*.

Gramps would sit patiently at the kitchen table with his serviette tucked into his neck collar relishing the moment when the warm pies would come out of the oven and were ready to dip into the hot chicken soup which had been bubbling away since early morning.

The only drawback about riding to Gran's house was that it was too far to ride back after dark, so my mother usually came to collect us. We loaded the bikes into the car and piled into the back seat, ignoring her as if she were merely a taxi and continued our childish conversation.

On a day I shall always remember with absolute clarity, we drove down the main drag back to our house in the neighboring suburb. We passed a tall handsome lad walking home from rugby practice. Mom said "That's the best looking boy in town" and winked knowingly at me. I squirmed and scowled, as any thirteen-year-old would—thinking "I can just imagine!"

Seven years later, I was half-heartedly curling my hair for my New Year's Eve date, a big event in our small town, when the very boy in question called. He invited me to go dancing with him that evening.

Imagine the cheek of calling me at 7.30 p.m. on New Year's Eve!

He maintained he'd arrived from Sweden that day.

One might have mistakenly thought he'd called my mother to ask her out! She became quite out of control, even forgetting that her parental guidance *should* have been to keep my word to the poor soul who'd made a polite effort to ask me out weeks ago. She was excited and insistent.

"Hilary, It's a special evening—Warren won't mind—go out with someone special. It's such a lovely evening to go out with young Wilfred, he has such blue eyes" ....*oy,* it went on until I couldn't take any more. Under pressure I cancelled my arrangement with Warren and set about curling my hair with more vigor.

I hauled out the special number I'd been keeping for a wild and wonderful occasion. I wondered why I had this feeling of profound excitement at someone so unknown to me.

Dressed in my purple frilled mini culotte, (I'm serious—I still have it today) with long blonde hair left swinging loose and my 60's baby pink lipstick shimmering, I danced the night away.

He certainly was handsome. Tall and dark with brilliant blue eyes, he had a row of pearly teeth and a soft chuckle. We ate *treyf* prawns, drank wine, while we discovered the simple facts that make a new person in your life so exciting. He was sophisticated and I felt distinctly grown-up!

At midnight we pulled the celebratory cracker and, behold, mine produced a little red-stoned ring which fell onto the table!

I blushed in embarrassment, trying to look away, but he picked it up and said softly "Hold out your finger". He placed the ring on my finger. He kissed me softly and from the flutter in my heart I wondered if this might incredibly be IT!

Wilfred and I spent a magic week together. The next afternoon he took me for a drive round the coastal road.

I wasn't initially sure where we were headed until we turned into the little seaside airport. "What are we doing here "I asked nervously.

"Don't worry, we're not eloping", he teased, "I m taking you for a flip in Echo Romeo Charlie." His Cessna Skylane had a name and by now I realized it was too late to shrink under the seat and decline the invitation without losing face. He obviously thought he was treating me to an amazing experience.

Until then, I had been sporting the face of casual sophistication, but a few flips and swings later my bravado turned green. I only just managed to behave with dignity.

I returned home yelling that my mother should go out with him herself in future. He was a wild adventurer and definitely not for me!

Despite myself, the following night I found myself agreeing to go for a walk along the beach.

The sand warmed our bare feet in the African moonlight. Under the promenade we lay on the sand talking, watching the tide change its mind again and again.

We kissed with tentative exploring midnight excitement. As the passion escalated I slipped my hand into his shirt to caress his back, only to feel this astonishing thick carpet of warm curly hair!

"Oh My G-d "I shrieked, " are you a man or an ape?"

I had completely ruined the romantic moment, but we had a good laugh!

By the end of the week I was smitten. My contemporaries were watching us on the beach as we sat together, oblivious of the familiar beach crowd around us.

They wondered how this had happened so quickly. All too soon the week was over and he was returning to White River, the little Transvaal town where he lived and owned a timber business. I was headed back to my position as head designer of Loving Underwear in the city of Johannesburg. I wasn't sure I would hear from him again.

Weeks later he called. I grew to survive trips in Echo Romeo Charlie. I even helped to polish and buff him occasionally.

I visited Wilf in White River, where he kept the Cessna on a short and nasty airstrip at his timber plant. The landing on this strip was so treacherous that you had to come round the mountain, dip immediately to miss the power lines and then land quickly or you would over-run the end of the runway. I had such a fear of the landing I took lessons on landing the plane so I would know what to do in an emergency. Knowing the procedure stilled my fear most of the time.

Throughout these two years of courtship I wore my red plastic ring.

We danced—we dined—we grew close and we became friends. Wilfred definitely WAS an adventurer. By then he was a 35 year old bachelor who was accustomed to his freedom, with no strings attached.

He flew around the country in his little plane. Despite his fear of heights, he was his happiest among the clouds.

Eventually, with much parental pressure on both sides, we decided to marry.

He certainly wasn't a romantic of the universal kind. On a flight home to our seaside town, a small transparent package fell out of his pocket. I leaned forward to pick it up.

"What's this? I asked."

"Well", he retorted, "I guess everyone is going to ask where your engagement ring is so I thought I'd better get you one!"

I was so incensed at the way he had done this that I never ever wore the diamond ring preferring my plastic one. Many years later that diamond was to serve its purpose.

23

UNDER THE WEDDING CANOPY

Wilf and I arrived in Port Elizabeth two days before the wedding. This was the fulfillment of my mother's dream and I felt almost removed from the whole process. Perhaps her own wedding had been organized by her in-laws in war-time and this was her opportunity to experience all she had really dreamt about as a girl.

I arrived at our home to find it set out like an exhibition.

The gifts were laid out in categories AND she had made me a little book with all the gifts listed in alphabetical order, with the name and address of the sender. To add insult to injury, as I thought in my immaturity at the time, she had written down what I should say about the gift in my thank-you letter!

As I sit on the flight home today, I think about this and I reel with horror. "Oh My G-d! I think I do this to my children today. It must be a genetic defect!"

She was so excited at all the wonderful silverware I had received from Uncle Albert and his family All she got from me was a sulky moan about who was going to polish it!

Thank goodness for my sister, who made all the right noises for guests and kept me on track.

As a successful dress designer, I was currently designing lace for a Swiss Embroidery company.

My generous wedding gift from the company was a magnificent woven piece of oyster silk to use as my wedding gown. This I had made up into the wedding dress myself. It was a high-collared bodice made in pink satin covered with the oyster silk.The embossed raschel lace on the edge of the sleeves was complemented by the same heavy embossed border of lace at the bottom of the narrow skirt. My figure was quite good and it was an unusual design.

Mom had ordered wonderful rounded balls of flowers for us to carry.

They were the height of fashion. She had certainly done her home-work and she had saved up so hard for smoked salmon, the best wines and the best venue in Port Elizabeth.

For her, it was the wedding of the year in this little town and many friends and relatives traveled from all over Southern Africa.

Most of my own friends were away at University and as Wilfred was ten years older than I was, his friends and their wives were not my contemporaries. Therefore I knew only a handful of people at my wedding, which not uncommon in those days.

I can remember no religious significance to the wedding at all, only the tension of hairdos and manicures and getting my eyelashes fixed on properly.

Granny Tuvia was resplendent in matching hat and coat which Mom had had made for her.

I missed Grandpa and wished he could have been there. He would have given me a sugar lump and said *"my sheinele."*

Jinny looked gorgeous dressed in pink, her beautiful black hair swept up in a French coil.

Dad wore his black Homberg. He took my arm and we entered the Synagogue.

I had always had the view of our Shul from upstairs as women sat separately in the upper gallery. Now for the first time, being on the lower floor, I remember thinking how far away the roof seemed as we walked towards the Chuppah. I had an ethereal feeling as if I was part of the Chagall "flying bride" painting

My mother was beaming. She looked wonderful, young and tanned. She'd had a matching dress and coat made in silver blue and it complimented her looks.

The fairytale of her daughter marrying the man of *her* dreams had come true.

I reached my handsome husband waiting under the Chuppah. Dad kissed me and let go of my arm. I glanced at Wilfred. Complete with top hat, he gave a nervous giggle as I reached his side.

As the service proceeded I felt him leaning on me more and more. It was not really acceptable for him to look so physically intimate with me in the synagogue, but at that time I was not very well versed about Jewish law, so I didn't know this. Our generation had never learnt much about Judaism and the laws of Niddah, or purity. We were only taught to read Hebrew. I realized he was leaning on me because his brother had given him one too many whiskies and it had gone to his head.

I held on to him hoping he would not fall over. To my left I noticed his brother was leaning a little too hard on the pole of our chuppah and it was making the canopy sway at a vicarious angle. Every few moments he jerked upright, and the canopy jumped back up leaving it a little more askew!

I remember nothing much else about the service except looking above us, watching the chuppah in anxious trepidation. I thought about this Chuppah, a special Jewish symbol. It was meant to invite me into his space. No one else seemed to focus on it. I made a wish for our home to be as this chuppah—open on all sides to welcome people into a happy home, but hoping, perhaps, for a little more stability than was being provided by the wobbly chuppah above.

24
THE HONEYMOON

The honeymoon was to be a surprise. I was told to bring beach clothes and the weather would be warm. That was all the information I had to go on.

While the wedding party was waiting at the airport to wave us off, we had popped down to the beach alone for a final swim in our home town.

We parked the car right down on the sand and as we emerged from the waves, full of the joys of a honeymoon, we saw that the tide had come in and the front of our car was wedged into the sand.

We chivvied all on the beach to help us pull it free and arrived at the airport looking disheveled, and wet, only to hear them calling us over the loud hailer.

"This is a final call for Mr and Mrs. Shulman to board now."

My mother was fuming. Everyone else looked a bit peaky as we blew kisses and ran aboard.

We flew to Swaziland where Wilfred had parked Echo Romeo Charlie.

From there we flew our twin-engine Skylane down the coast to Mozambique.

I had to be the navigator and kept my stomach stable by watching in absolute fascination, how the exact curve on the map matched the curve of the coast below. I imagined that if I leaned down I would be able to touch the tree tops.

I was tense and frightened. My new husband could not understand why I didn't respond to his jokes with great mirth.

We landed at Inhambane, deep in the Mozambique bush, where we had been advised to park the Cessna in a local shed and then to take the ferry across the bay.

They had omitted to say there was only one ferry!

Five cold hours later we boarded the unsteady boat. I was now past fear, I had to keep a tight control on my imagination. I had never been on a boat and for some unintelligible reason, never equated the rise and fall of waves, with the motion of the boat. As I looked across at the opposite side of the lake, I realized with dread, that the up and down motion would continue until we touched the land across the water.

When we reached the quay, I needed some "cooling off" time so Wilfred went in search of transport. I stood guard over the luggage alone, feeling abandoned in this wild strange place.

He was gone for a few hours and I began to doubt he was ever coming back. I would have to return home and admit I could not keep a husband for a few hours, let alone a lifetime!!

I noticed people around me hesitantly moving closer. I watched and pondered as to why they were so reticent until I noticed their limbs and hands. They were lepers from a nearby colony hobbling closer to look at me and touch my cases. I suppose they longed for contact.

At that point I may have contemplated a swim back across the lake but Wilfred came riding triumphantly into view on the back of a large trundling truck, accompanied by his travel companions, none of whom spoke a word of English.

Encouraged by their wide white-toothed smiles, I climbed gingerly onto the back of the truck, sat on a box and wondered if married life was always going to be as bumpy and hard to cope with as the beginning of the road to Pomene in Mozambique.

We rode and we rode. The truck worked its way slowly and deliberately, winding along the bumpy gravel path into the deep and dense interior of the Mozambique bush. We passed no recognizable civilization and certainly no friendly service station restrooms!!

I watched them chomping raw potatoes as if they were apples and returned their toothy smiles. Was I going to be expected to eat them too?

I wondered fearfully if Wilfred had considered what sort of food we would be eating on our honeymoon? I shuddered to think of what lay ahead until, just before dusk, we rounded a corner, and before us lay a magazine view of the Bay of Pomene, our idealic honeymoon spot.

Quiet silent waters, cerulean blue sky merged with the estuary leading into the sea. Teeny tiny shells rounded by eons of waves gave the beach a pearl pink glow, and there, perched precariously on the side of the cliff was our romantic rendezvous place, a wooden hotel with 20 rooms.

The hotel was owned by Wilfred's co-partner in the Cessna, and Cooper had invited us to be his guests. It was a guest house frequented mostly by big game hunters. It boasted that all rooms had a sea view. A simple patio ran the length of the building. Inviting looking lounging chairs were dotted along the terrace, waiting for a dreamer to laze about and gaze at the sea.

It was an inaccessible remote location, deep in the heart of Mozambique and the fresh food stores were a problem. We learnt we were completely dependent on the catch of the day. Despite the simplicity of ingredients it was all served by a maitre'd with aplomb and ceremony. We had rock cod with eggs for breakfast, marlin steak for lunch and any amount of shellfish, rock cod and rock cod and rock cod—grilled, sautéed and stewed for dinner. All freshly caught and a new taste for both of us.

The second new experience was fishing. I opted to mostly walk on the beach searching for shells of infinite beauty. I found a red starfish which I kept for thirty years, held as my honeymoon treasure.

At night we sat on the stoep, sipping our cocktails. Wilfred would listen to the big game fisherman regaling us with tales of their fishy battle of the day, and their mighty struggle with the marlin who swam in the Pomene Sea. His fascination made him long to have a go at landing one but, very sweetly, he felt obligated not to leave me alone on our honeymoon. We had been cozily romantic for days now and I assured him I was happy for him to go and seek his dream, and that was the last time I saw him during the day! He was determined to catch a marlin despite his fear of the big trawler and his seasickness out on the high sea.

He became one of the seafarers at night, checking tides and swells and preparing himself for the quest and hopes of the following day.

And catch he did!

It took him five days and many grueling hours, but he pulled one in.

He was so chuffed with it. We feasted on the steaks, and the head of the fish made a piquant bouillabaisse. To my ultimate horror, he insisted on taking what was left of the huge fish carcass home with us in the Skylane. Not only did I have to survive the dreaded journey home, I had to breathe in his smelly fish to boot!

25

OUR PERFECT "GARDEN AND HOME" LIFE

White River was a small colonial community in the Eastern Transvaal of South Africa. ·

You had to live there for generations before you were accepted as a White Riverite! When I first arrived I did not know a soul, or even begin to comprehend this phenomenon. Where I came from, your status in town did not really matter, your participation was what counted.

Many years later my elder daughter took a journey back in time.

Immediately she walked into the local store, Mr Baron came forward with great warmth. "You can only be a member of the Shulman family " he declared with glee. I guess she had the tell-tale heavy eyebrows and Wilfred's smile.

"Yes," said Tirza shyly, "I am Wilfred's daughter."

They were promptly invited for sundowners. All our old local friends dropped in as word spread around town that they were visiting the district.

You only had to go as far as the only supermarket in the village to hear the day's gossip.

They sipped their drinks on the lawn watching the very same mountain view that I had watched from my White River bedroom. The Van der Merwes, our old neighbors, regaled her with all the well-remembered stories of our time in White River.

Their favorite began with the story of my first day in town.

I had walked slowly along the main road exploring my new *"medina"*. Our apartment led me past the Nederduitse Kerk, (at the time this was the national Afrikaans church). I walked down the main road, as Mr. Baron recalled to Tirza, wearing (I blush to think about it) knee-length boots and a mini skirt under a maxi-coat. He told her he had always remembered this because he was in touch with fashion trends and he thought this was a "smashing display", but, he said, the locals were *gobsmacked.* The traffic slowed as they stared and it was reported that the preacher from the Church complained to Wilfred about my being a distraction during on Sunday service. Wilfred and I laughed. It seemed to be the pot calling the kettle black. He himself was a gorgeous adonis, blue eyes thick blonde hair and very fit and muscular. It was his habit to call Wilf up at 10.30 at night and the two of them would go and have a game of squash and a few spots.

They also told her how Wilfred had been the life and soul of local parties including his well-remembered stripping routine. They told Tirza about his prowess on the hockey field, generosity and *tzadacka,* silent kindness to people in the town who were needy.

Zizi as we called Tirza loved hearing this because charity was something so close to her own heart and something she could hold onto about her father.

Monday night in White River, by unwritten law, was the "boys' night out". This meant they had to don a penguin suit and report with absolute punctuality to George's farm for a formal dinner. This was served by the butler whose family had been their butlers for generations before.

George's family were founding members of the community in White River and much admired. Their farms spread across a large area of the Lowveld

A five-course meal was prepared with freshly caught impala as the main course. This elegant procedure had been ongoing for 40 years and women had never been invited, nor would they ever be. George had remained a batchelor and George's mother Mabel was the character of the village. She was a neat little woman with a loud rasping voice—very commanding. If she entered the grocery store and there was a queue ahead of her, everyone automatically stood aside. That was the accepted hierachial pattern of this colonial village called White River.

Tirza remembered how I had told her about that the first day I had tried to put my groceries on Wilfred's account at Laudan's, the Indian wholesaler. The teller looked me up and down and said "Good Gracious! Mr Shulman only ever buys beer and peanuts on account, so WHO might you be?"

So, you get the picture of what life in White River was all about.

Living in Britain now, thirty years later, I realize exactly what colonialism is or was, but at that time it was an enigma to me.

Wilfred flew around the country meeting farmers and timber

growers in remote parts of the country. I was left to convince Floreena, his long time maid, that I intended to stay, come what may.

Each time I moved Wilfred's clothes along the shelves in the cupboard to make myself a little space, she moved them back again. She became more and more devious until one day I was forced to make a stand – "Her or me!"

Fortuitously he chose me—despite the fact that I was lonely and miserable and found social life in this little town very hard.

I did not know how much isolation I would have to face in my life ahead but gratefully we didn't have crystal balls yet.

Today I am still in two minds as to whether we should know the future and make educated choices, or take what comes and try to survive it.

A few months later we found a property which we fell in love with.

Luck was with us as Mrs Cohen, the owner, was the only other Jewish family in town and she wanted us to have the house. We didn't have a deposit to put down so we paid her off over a period of time. Very soon we managed to put up our name plate on along the Plaston Road, and I became a farmer.

We had 200 citrus trees, all the varieties of avocado, banana trees and a single grape vine. Our pride was a very proliferous litchie tree that only produced litchies when we were away on our annual leave each year.

A trusty old windmill wound its way back and forth with a familiar whine round and round as if there was no hurry and every day was much the same as the day before. I loved the regularity of the sound.

It was a strangely hypnotic thing that the babies loved to watch from their prams. Often, when I was traumatized, I would go outside and just stand and gaze at the windmill, communing with the knowledge that life goes on, round and round.

I became involved with growing a gorgeous garden. Samson was my trusty gardener. He could do anything, fix anything, and together we planted and hoed the land.

He was a gentle silent man, just smiling and doing, from Monday to Thursday. On Fridays he was paid, and despite all the schemes I devised to prevent this, he became completely blotto, aggressive and unreasonable through Friday to Monday. Then, as regular as clockwork, my silent

Sampson returned to work on the land, quietly playing with the children and pushing them patiently along on their bikes.

We learnt to live with it, myself and his two wives and 11 children who all lived on the farm.

He assisted me in winning the Garden Club prize for the loveliest "out of season" garden. Little did they know it was a *"flook,"* a lucky strike. I simply didn't know when the correct time to plant out the azaleas actually was and, because I had planted then out of season, they flowered out of season.

I seemed to do this with several aspects of my life.

Gardening in White River was an absolute pleasure. Every stick grew. The view from my bedroom looked over the Legogote Mountain.

I always had breakfast in bed, served by our trusty cook who believed in large meals. I enjoyed the view, sipping my home grown orange juice each morning so that I would be able to judge when the oranges were sweet enough, and ripe for the picking. The river ran across the bottom of our property We had visiting monkeys and the odd deer known as springbok, pranced across the lawn. We also had black mambas and boom slang, a deadly snake whose venom attacked the nervous system.

The pride of my garden was an extensive twenty year old bougainvillea tree. This grew over a broad arch and bloomed with sumptuous purple pink flowers twelve months of the year.

Samson first spotted the mean, green Boomslang. It is an Afrikaans word meaning tree snake He ran to get the children inside. We cut down part of the tree where the snake had been seen, waiting a day or two for it to appear again. All the local workers popped in to the farm from time to time to catch up on the latest development. We had to provide Buchu beer while we listened to the traditional advice of the fearful locals.

Samson's position in the community became elevated. He felt powerful, recognized as the director of this dangerous mission.

Wilfred spotted the Boomslang again early one evening and we cut back an even larger area of the tree.

The children were getting restless indoors day after day, the animals were nervous, and seemed to sense impending danger.

We couldn't take the chance that the green snake might slither out unnoticed at any moment. We ended up cutting back more and more of the growth searching for the hiding hole, until twenty years of strong beautiful plaited and twisted vine was sacrificed for a Boomslang that slid away in secrecy to some other mysterious place in the sun.

This snake story brings to mind the time Wilfred returned to "infantile male mode".

It was our habit to walk along the orange orchards at sunset, looking at what had been harvested during the day. Between the orchards was a long footpath and as I walked in front of him he tickled my leg with a branch that I immediately took to be a snake.

I jumped five foot into the air and being almost seven months pregnant with Amy, this was no mean feat.

I retired to bed to recover and held onto my grudge for a while—unusual for me.

To our left was my neighbor Diane. When we moved into our home, her husband had been bedridden with emphysema. I would go through the gate between farms and sit on his bed and read to him. He died four months after we moved in and thereafter I would then pop across and sit on Diane's bed and have coffee with her, but I always called before I went over. This was the expected behavior in this formal anglicized society.

On Sunday nights we went to Chalk Farm for a home movie. There were no cinemas in the Lowveld in the early 70s and we had to make our own social life. Occasionally, on a Sunday morning, Wilfred and I would fly to the Mozambique border in Echo Romeo Charlie. We would circle the border guards at Komartiepoort as a sign that we would be back soon. We would breakfast in Moamba, a village near the border. Feasting on gorgeous *Treif food (unkosher)* we would not eat at home, freshly-caught prawns and Portuguese bread, we would return with a strong pong of garlic, feeling fully satisfied with life. Friendships were forged with parents of other children who came to play. I was to cherish those friendships throughout my life, despite my friend Huffy declaring I was the worst driver I town.

I hold wonderful happy memories of my garden. I have learnt that I cannot live without being able to touch the earth. While Wilfred dealt in timber, I grew strawberries and each Friday I delivered freshly packed strawberries to the local hotels to serve at dinner. I was not allowed to trade my oranges on the open market as Wilfred's major clients were the Citrus Board. He was afraid I would embarrass him with the quality of my oranges because I wouldn't spray poisons, so every six weeks we harvested the crop and carted them off to the orphanage. I was resentful about this, and moaned and groaned at great length about unfair trade practice, knowing full well he was completely correct.

At this time we had French partners in the timber business. They flew out monthly for a board meeting and I would entertain them very lavishly, as we were able to do then.

The office lunch was driven down to the factory. I would lay out the best silver and crystal glasses. The home grown Avocado Ritz with Portuguese wines and freshly caught trout was served by waiters in white. The weather was always warm and the umbrellas would go up promptly at noon, looking more like an elegant safari camp than a Franco-African board meeting

My Father-in-law was the CEO of the company. JP would fly up to White River for the board meeting and over the years that followed,this became the rare occasion when he would see his grandchildren and seemingly enjoy them.

Six months after we moved into our home, we were blessed by Tirza's birth. She was named after my wonderful grandmother Tuvia and her great grandmother on the other side, Theresa Shloss from Berlin.

I had had a huge altercation with JP, my father-in-law, when he had ordered Wilfred to fly to a meeting in the Cape just before my due date. It would have meant I would have had to drive myself 60 kilometres to the hospital for the birth. Unfortunately, the father—son relationship was only one of managing director and very little of personal familial exchange ever took place.

Tirza's birth was a touch-and-go trauma. My gynaecologist, James, was also my closest friend in town. I think we both felt like misfits in this little community and we developed a very special friendship, particularly after I painted him a large fertility mural in his rooms. He was the only gynaecologist from Mozambique to Zambia, and he began to have amazing success with fertility. I said it was my magic, he said it was his talent!

Tirza was delivered in the lift, ripping her out of my tummy in extreme haste following a caesarian as an emergency after he realized that I had had a placenta abruptio, and she might have been deprived of oxygen for a while. James had felt there was no time to waste in getting her out. When someone is a close friend to you, the thought of failure must be more than daunting. It was days before they allowed me to see her and I was not well enough to walk to the intensive care unit.

Tirza maintains that this is the root to her fear of lifts today!

A tiny premature incubator baby, she was a fighter then, and remains a fighter now.

Seventeen months later, gentle, quiet Alissa was born. Her name meant noble truth in Hebrew and she grew to be a noble and of great truth. We had to go back and forth to hospital a few times but finally she could delay no longer and Alissa was born with the cord round her neck, lying back to front and breech. We called her Lissi for short. It was the first epidural caesarian section performed at Nelpruit hospital. This experience created an enormous bond in my friendship with James. It was an experience I remember with joy. Alissa was a healthy eight pound ten ounces, and I was lucky enough to have so much milk I fed a baby in the ward whose Mom had fled from the bush war in Mozambique. She was too traumatized to feed her baby, and I could manage both.

Zizi and Lissi grew round and bonny. They ate mulberries and grew silk worms and played with the *piccanin,* all the other black children on the farm. Life in the bushveld was simple and quiet. We had no television and no movie houses.

I began to paint again and when I was really concentrating I'd put the two carry cots on the kitchen floor and they would lie there quietly and watch me at work. At the end of the day, my special friend Cherry and I would ride round the Plaston Road to "crit" each other's paintings. During this period we formed a painting group of like-minded artists with members who were as diverse as an ex-nun and the postman. At my home we had monthly sessions which were conducted with great intensity, and a good measure of talent. Life was a bowl of cherries.

26
A GIFT FROM G-D

In the fading light of a lowveld evening I drove home slowly, through the open country-side up the·hill from Nelspruit. I was pleased I had time to myself to adjust to this astonishing revelation. I tried to comprehend what I had just been told. Lissi was 6 months old, I was still breastfeeding her and I had gone for a check-up because I just wasn't getting my waistline back!

"Well", mused my gynaecologist James," the reason is that you have a very active rugby ball growing in there."

I spent five hours in his consulting rooms in total disbelief. The fertility mural had turned its magic on the maker.

Slowly I awoke to the amazement and wonder of this idea. This was definitely going to be my son—my David or Jonathan. I was absolutely sure from the kicking that I now realized wasn't just a cramp, that the impending addition to my family was a male. It was not common practice to do a scan in those days, and we never knew the sex of the baby beforehand.

Wilfred was just as amazed at the news , and my mother-in-law was totally speechless. She had only just congratulated me on the last addition to our family.

Around this time, I had noticed Wilfred becoming very reticent and very withdrawn. I wondered if he was no longer interested in me, or whether the business tension he was feeling with his father was getting to him. So often I looked back over this period, and I realize in hindsight that I could never have imagined the problem, as I had no conscious knowledge of anything like it.

Late one evening the telephone rang. It was JP. I heard Wilfred exclaim "Oh no! How could you, how could you have done this without discussing it with me?"

He NEVER EVER confronted JP so I assumed this must be really serious. He put down the phone, turned to me with such pain on his face I couldn't imagine what the reason could possibly be, and he sank brokenly down onto his bed.

It is a very poignant sight to see a grown man sobbing heartbrokenly. Over and over he exclaimed "How could he, how could he? "

It is one of the grudges I will always hold against JP. I could not comprehend the absolute thoughtlessness of it all! The pain it caused.

JP had sold all the shares in the business to the large Belgian consortium without even discussing the prospects with Wilfred. Wilfred had devoted his entire working career to this business and always accepted this miniscule salary because he expected to become the CEO and never remotely entertained the idea that this would not be his inherited, but additionally, his well-earned right.

Most of the larger development in the group of companies had come from Wilfred's genius in building up the industrial side of the timber business, and this had contributed to the large growth spurt of the company.

Wilfred had been a man who rose at the crack of dawn filled with enthusiasm for the day ahead. He always got to the factory by 6.30 in the morning. The workers expected to see him and followed his example. He was a much loved managing director and being a large industry in a small town we employed a large proportion of the people in the town.

We had a very easy social structure because everyone was well-acquainted and met at the golf club over weekends. There was no standing on ceremony and Wilfred didn't go with the idea of formality. His staff were his loyal friends, and he was considerate and involved with them.

We often gave wonderful family "braaivleis," a South African barbecue with whole lamb on the spit and what we call boerewors, a fat sausage filled with a mixture of beef and lamb and special herbs which grows crisp on the outside and soft and juicy on the inside. The cook would set the fire up during the afternoon allowing the coals to simmer slowly. Beside it he would stand with a smaller fire in a big black iron pot and make the putu. This we always ate with the braai. This was made from maize meal and the standard daily diet of our African workers, but we ate it as a special delicacy with our braaied wors.

The many children and grandchildren whose parents worked at the factory ran around the fire laughing and jumping with the freedom happy kids have.

At Xmas we held a very festive Christmas party in our home for all the workers. I sent out a "wish list" to parents for their children and my hard work was amply rewarded by the parent's excitement when the children found their wish fulfilled under the tree.

I remember one year when the Pienaar family had such a good time they loaded all the children up to go home, only to leave one running down the driveway after the van shouting "Pappie pappie." I recall another less enjoyable year where the youngish managers got totally trashed and at 3 a.m., I called our older factory manager John to come and take them all home before they fell into the pool and drowned.

On Sundays all the local factories got together with their gumboot dancing teams We had the largest factory in the area,for this reason the competitive venue was usually on our grounds.

The timber factory team made Tirza their mascot because, although she was tiny, she loved to dress up.

On our arrival, they escorted her with great ceremony to the throne they had made for her, a high seat proclaiming to the other teams that she was the *"Makoola baas 's daughter*, which, in Tswana means the "big boss!" She loved this and handled it in a most regal manner, stepping up to her throne and sitting down carefully as if she were born to be queen.

So this was the background to our wonderful life where the two little girls ate lunch sitting in the green pea patch, until the fateful day when I saw Wilfred trying to lift a cup of coffee and his hand shook so badly he did not have the strength to bring it to his lips.

I was extremely perturbed. I sat down to think it all over, and realized that for weeks he had been lying in bed late. Each time I would come into the room to say "are you not working today," he'd mumble "I'll go later." I had thought he was so angry about the sale of the business he couldn't bring himself to go to work but on this day I thought perhaps he was overtired and needed a medical check up. He was due for his annual pilot's license overhaul, so I called a physician friend of mine in Johannesburg and made the appointment.

Wilfred flew himself to Johannesburg in Echo Romeo Charlie. He couldn't find the Rand Airport and flew around for an extra two hours looking for the runway. Afterwards I learnt with horror that he had less than 20% vision and had landed on the wrong runway!

The doctor with whom he had an appointment was flying to London that evening, and had waited for him at the medical rooms.

At three o clock that afternoon I was waiting to hear from Wilfred when the telephone rang. I picked it up and heard a voice introducing himself as Dr Rosen.

"Your husband has been referred to me today. I'm sorry to tell you he has a brain tumor and it appears to be malignant. There is little I can do for him. It was 1973.

My mind could not make sense of these words. All I could think of was my son, my son. "But it can't be", I screamed "I m pregnant!"

"Well," he said in distant removed coldness,"if you can't cope—don't come to Johannesburg. I will operate tomorrow," and he replaced the receiver.

I must have sat on my bed staring at the phone for a long time. By some miracle my neighbor Diane came through my kitchen door, an unheard of event, as I explained earlier. We never visited each other without the courtesy of calling first.

She said she was sitting on her stoep, looking down towards Legogote, when she felt this urgent need to walk over and connect with me.

Was it a predetermined moment in time that changed a habit of years? We'll never know.

She took one look at my face and listened to my halting words trying to make sense of what I had heard him say.

"He has a brain tumor, I kept repeating, "He says there is nothing he can do"

None of this could be real, I thought. I must have eaten too much chocolate, or I must have misheard him. This could not be happening.

She assumed I would have to go up to Johannesburg urgently.

Diane sprung into action. Friends were called—the house seemed to be filled with people but I could not focus. They yanked out our suitcases and went through my grossly untidy cupboards, packing clothes and searching for identity documents. They dressed and fed the girls, making us ready to travel on the overnight train to the city that evening. I moved as in automatic pilot.

I went where I was told and soon we were click—clacking across the tracks in the dark of night on the cold and foreboding journey.

My aching heart thought about how he would feel when Dr Rosen told him the awful news. Over and over in my mind I ached that it would have been received without me there to hold him and reassure him, to love him and give him strength. I willed him to be strong all through the long uncomfortable night.

In the morning, as the sun rose, we reached the gold mining masts of Johannesburg.

I seemed to be so lucky with friends, with associates, with everything except my husband's health.

Dr Moore, our pediatrician, was on the station platform. He took the girls from me saying "Hilary, do not worry, they will stay with me until the operation is over and you can concentrate on being with Wilfred." I felt completely confident that he would look after them

Ahead of me I faced a new challenge and at this point I knew there would be no option or choice. I had panic attacks driving in traffic. In White River there was no noticeable traffic and I only drove on country roads but now I had to get into a car and drive into the hub of Johannesburg where the clinic was situated and Wilfred was waiting for me.

I talked very quietly to my inner self as I got into the car, eased into the traffic, took a deep breath and I just DID it. I felt like Stirling Moss! I astonished myself.

I dreaded seeing how he had responded to the idea of a brain operation. I ached with trepidation at the thoughts that might be going through his mind. I felt such fear for him and for me.

I arrived at the clinic to find a very agitated Wilfred pacing up and down and totally pissed-off at having to spend the weekend in a hospital when he had a rugby match to play. Dr Rosen had told him that he had "a cyst"- that it would be removed and life would carry on as before!

I was nauseated and aghast. In the early seventies "malignancy" was still an unspoken word and doctors rarely discussed the details with their patients.

Wilfred threatened to get into his plane and fly home. He had no patience for any of this nonsense.

I was devastated at the management of this scenario in our lives. How could he allow him to go into the operating theatre with no knowledge of what might lie ahead? How could he deny him the opportunity to discuss as man and wife what our plans and future plans should be or to be able to exchange feelings (I wasn't to know for the last time ever)— but, Dr Rosen must have known.

Being totally inexperienced at any of this, I accepted his decision. After all, he was the neurosurgeon! I didn't have the remotest idea that following the operation, Wilfred would never again be able to make a logical decision, or share any of the responsibility for our family, let alone our unborn son.

I was going to be left to do it alone.

Birth is a beginning
And Death a destination.
And life is a journey:
From Childhood to maturity
And youth to age.
From innocence to awareness,
And from ignorance to knowing:
From foolishness to discretion
And then, perhaps to wisdom.
From weakness to strength
Or strength to weakness
From sickness to health
And back
We pray to health again;

The Angel of Death.

During the 60s and 70s, more cancer was being diagnosed. Medical staff carried as much fear and reticence in dealing with patients and their families as did the sufferers.

Dr Cecily Saunders was the first nurse who acknowledged the need to discuss people's fears and feelings about dying.

In the late 70s, Dr Elizabeth Kubler Ross began a programme of counseling patients and their families for help with their thoughts and fears. This only for people who requested help, as often doctors were too busy to handle the issue.

It was the beginning of the hospice movement, where patients were afforded the right to their feelings as a human being, and not just as another diagnostic number.

Death has always been a distasteful and fearful event to man. We cannot concretely conceive of it and over the decades it is usually portrayed in our cultures as evil and painful, as an accident or a fearful event about to bewitch us. It has been used as a threat, and in religion as retribution. By law, it is not an option we are allowed to choose.

Part of grieving is expressing anger, whether we do it consciously or not.

My anger grew over the years and was directed at many sources. Only decades later did I understand my anger was all the vehicle of my grief at what happened to Wilfred and to my family life.

And then came the Star Wars.

I held his hand down the long concrete corridor. At the double doors I kissed him goodbye. The man I knew rode on to a new and uncharted destination.

The operation to lessen the pressure on his brain took eight hours. My sister-in-law had offered to sit with me but I needed to be alone with my thoughts, so she went off to collect Wilfred's parents who were summoned urgently to Johannesburg.

It is well documented that just before a near death experience, you review your life before you, like a slow documentary. Those hours seemed like minutes, the cold stone floor acted as my only connection to reality. I sat as if I was a Buddha, unmoving, unthinking.

The theatre door opened and Dr Rosen came out. He was a little man with a moustache and a non-smiling face. He took my hand gently and said, "What I have to tell you now is more difficult than the operation I have just performed." Your husband's tumor is malignant and there is nothing more we can do for him. I have worked in the motor area of his brain and he might well be paralyzed. His life expectancy at this point could be three months as the pressure will build up again"

Then he patted my shoulder and walked away grimly.

I dragged my feet, choosing the long route back to the hotel. How would I tell his parents? His mother was a frail and gentle lady.

I met them all waiting in their suite at the hotel. I repeated Dr Rosen's words as I had heard them. I explained as carefully and truthfully as I knew how. There was a stunned silence and then his mother said brightly "Let's have tea."

I needed to shriek, to wail—to be comforted. I needed my Mom to hold me and rock me. I needed my Dad to get me a glass of water and make the nightmare go away.

All I got was tea!

No one mentioned his name and no one asked a single question.

The subject was too hard for them to confront. I didn't understand their inability to do so and they did not understand my need to unload my ultimate heartache.

I believe this was the point where the parting of the ways between his family and I began. Wilf's family and I dealt with the issues of life in very different ways. We could not possibly have shared the problem, because we did not recognize each other's very diverse coping skills.

Today I have come to understand the pattern of my life and how I have coped with its hardships.

The only way I knew, was to face the problem full on and look for a solution. I had been brought up with an attitude that taught to ask for help was unsavory. I was taught not to borrow other people's clothes or money—heaven forbid!

I made a plan. I would be realistic, decide which of A, B, C, was the best way forward and then step to it and take action. I had never cried on anyone's shoulder.

On the opposite side of the color wheel, if you can imagine orange to blue, were Wilfred's family, introvert people who believed it distasteful to show emotion or feelings. In the early years of our courtship I thought I would be able to teach him to express himself, but I soon gathered from his background of European gentility, that his only experience of relating to someone was where no one ever touched, or reached out.

Years later, when trying to understand his family's repressed attitude, I recalled a conversation with him where I shouted "Why the hell did you marry me in the first place?" He had looked at me quietly and said "Probably because you were different from them"

Being "different" brought me so much shit all my life. I perpetually resented it. How many therapists were to listen to me swearing that I truly wanted to be conventional and ordinary, just an everyday mortal in the sea of beings

When I was five years old, I am told, I had my friends to lunch and I colored the mashed potato green. I reportedly told them it was to make it "more interesting" and I never lived it down in Port Elizabeth! Sharon, my oldest childhood friend remembered it forever.

I guess I set the pattern then, and the green mash turned to purple and chartreuse as my horizons and solutions to life became more complex.

After tea, I returned to the hospital. Wilfred was regaining consciousness, and at the time there was a serious shortage of nursing staff so I agreed to sit with him until it was time to return to the hotel and bath Tirza, who was nearly two, and little suck-a-thumb Alissa who was just nine months.

Paralysed he certainly was not! The first leggy nurse who waltzed by the bed caught his eye. He tried to get out of bed and seemed quite mobile, despite all the tubes he was attached to.

So far so good!

He didn't really relate to anyone in particular around him, but I had been told he might be confused for a few days and not recognize me.

At night I returned to the hotel where Tirza and Alissa were holed up on the eighth floor with a Canadian day nurse looking after them. In the dark of the night I would take quiet time to talk to my son in my tummy. To tell him how much I looked forward to his coming out into the world, how we would do our best together come what may, and how he would have to stop kicking me during the day to allow me to do my job.

The next few weeks were a blur of rushing to the hospital, sitting there during the day, watching Wilfred cope with the physical momentum caused by the alteration in his brain pattern. His right side was very weak and he dragged his arm and leg,

His speech was not that coherent and he really didn't know what time of day it was. I don't think he knew who I was but, being a wife, one can be more authoritative than a nurse, so he seemed to follow my suggestions. The circumstances of his altered state became the centre of my focus. Each hour brought new behavioral aberrations, each time unexpected.

By the third week, Dr Rosen agreed to allow him out for the day to ascertain just how he would cope in the everyday world.

He did not give me any information on what he could or could not do, or any advice on how to manage him. He just threw me into this new thing blind, but I felt I had the confidence to manage.

We decided to go to the Zoo Lake. The two little girls were pleased to see him and didn't seem to notice too much difference. We ambled carefully along the lake until we came to the boats and then to my absolute horror, Wilfred insisted he wanted to go on a boat!

Thirty years later I still can't believe my stupidity, but he was so insistent and became very agitated. It was that agitation that I feared might harm him. Rather than upset him in this fragile state we all climbed into the boat—a brain damaged man with a bandaged head, two little girls and a very wobbly pregnant mother in a little boat on the lake….. He rowed out to the middle laboriously pulling the oars while the girls pretended to row, while singing "row, row, row your boat "as loudly as they could to cheer him up.

Half-way there, he seemed to lose his strength. He sat back looking tired and listless. He had completely lost interest in the project.

I certainly could not row, so we began to float round the lake. People passed us and waved. Eventually I had to shout "Help—help," gesticulating to the boat people who came out to fetch us.

My nerves were shattered, I couldn't wait to get him back to the hospital.

On our arrival Dr Rosen was walking down the corridor. He smiled benignly at the children and asked us if we'd had a pleasant day. Wilfred explained we'd been rowing on Zoo Lake. His face went white and then slowly puce. "YOU WHAT?" he roared," I spent eight hours repairing his brain, and you took him out to do the ONE thing that puts pressure on his head." I thought he was going to strangle me. No one told me what he could or could not do. In retrospect, I know it sounds like common-sense thing, but nothing at that point made any sense.

So Rosen kept him under observation for a few days and he was none the worse for his experience.

I never went rowing on Zoo Lake again.

27
HIS ALTERED STATE

When the time came to leave the hospital and take him home, I asked Dr Rosen to speak with his father personally. I really feared going back out to the country where medical facilities were very rudimentary.

I made an appointment to take JP to his rooms, Wilf's father listened intently.

"Your son will never again be able to manage the business, drive or make reliable logical decisions, and it would be wise if Wilfred and Hilary and family stayed on close to medical facilities permanently."

JP asked no questions and raised no queries.

They shook hands and as we walked back to the hotel my father-in-law said "Oh well, he can rest here for a few weeks and then resume his normal life again in White River."

Had he heard, or had he blocked it all out?

The situation remained unchanged.

We returned to White River and JP never changed his mind.

I was extremely nervous about taking him home on my own, after my last experience, and made a long list of all the questions I had to ask Matron and the staff. Apart from the responsibility of organizing his cortisone tablets and dressing his head wound daily, which was quite complicated for me as a lay person, I wondered how to handle life as a new young wife.

I decided to brave the question and ask Doc Rosen himself.

I met him walking down the corridor and very uncomfortably, I enquired about what I should do if Wilfred approached me sexually, thinking this would surely raise the head pressure!!

This short man looked me slowly up and down, paused, and then with infinite iciness he said, "IF the question ever arises, come back to me?"

I felt so embarrassed. I slunk away, hating him for his unkindness, feeling sad for a man who worked in a field where most cases are terminal, and he probably had to be harsh to everyone, shutting out his own feelings most of the time. I was finally beginning to experience a feeling of crushing fear at what my life was going to become!

We took up residence in a kind relative's house near the golf course in Houghton. My due date for the coming baby was approaching fast and I was extremely broad and badly stressed. In later years I was astounded to find a photograph album of this period, showing that my bulging shape had not stopped me wearing a halter neck maternity suit! I won't attempt to describe how I looked in the photograph. Albums record this anathema …… .

In addition to not being in my own home I had a grown-up baby who became increasingly aggressive and unreasonable. He had to be very carefully managed and could not be left alone for a second.

One day I quickly nipped out of the room to change Alissa's nappy. When I returned to the room I found he had disappeared.

I prevailed upon the gardener to keep an eye on the children and leapt into my car. I drove slowly along the road searching the nearby holes of the golf club, hoping he hadn't ventured onto the course. A golf ball could end the saga right then! As I reached the main road I saw him calmly limping along the busy main road, head bandaged, oblivious to the traffic and traffic lights.

I slowed down and tried to coax him into the car, but he was determined to walk alone. He ignored me. That determination remained his battle shield, his strength and his life force.

In the years to come he never *ever* let it lapse.

I followed slowly in the car, praying drivers would see he was not coping all that well. Eventually, he turned round the block and headed towards home which was luck, not intention. As he was tired I hoped he was more manageable. He got into the car meekly.

Did he have his own thoughts of rage at his non-independent status? Perhaps he was testing himself. I had no way of knowing because one couldn't communicate with him, and there was no relevant conversation where we could have shared his frustration.

During this very trying time, an angel of friendship came into my life.

The doorbell rang and there stood an elegant blonde woman about my age with a soft-spoken voice. In her kindly manner she explained she had been sent to help me via a friend as she was going through a similar experience. Maureen's husband had been under Dr Rosen's knife more than a year ago. She turned out to be a gift from G-d. We became firm friends. Sometimes I felt she was more another sister than a friend and we shared so much in our lives in the years to follow. On many dark days she was my Rock of Gibralter.

During this period, I was also blessed with the help of an English friend Tessa, who was living in Johannesburg. She had been a work colleague and we had married at the same time. She popped in often, always a kind ear and a helpful suggestion. Her daughter was the same age as TIrza and it was comforting for them to play together as if life was perfectly normal.

She coined the nick name for Tirza "as small as a tickey" a coin we used in the early 50s. It stuck. She became my Tikkele, little Tickey, and even at thirty she was still my little Tikkele! Tessa and I sat together and sipped our Earl Grey tea. We talked in whispers.

She promised to come to White River and she offered to host Alissa's approaching first birthday party.

Eventually, I ran out of excuses to remain in Johannesburg and we were forced to go back to the isolation of White River. My gynaecologist wanted me to deliver the expected baby at Nelspruit hospital and we returned to live on the farm.

28
EASTER FRIDAY

We think of bunnies and chocolate eggs and baskets of spring daisies, but I didn't have time for Belgian luxury.

I had begged James, the gynaecologist, to allow me to have an induction in order to have the baby on the Easter weekend. It was the only time I had company to help me look after Wilfred and the little girls. He refused to induce the birth. We really couldn't tell how mature the baby was because I had not known I was pregnant until nearly five months along the pregnancy.

I drove home, packed my suitcase, made a large foaming mug of hot chocolate—camomile tea would not suffice at a time like this—and lay down to talk to my boy! I was absolutely sure these were not ballet jetes, but soccer kicks that I had been feeling.

"It's now or never chum, we have to do this today", I told him. The house was ready, the girls were organized. I fell into a peaceful doze. A few hours later I was awoken with medium strong labor pains. This must be the only time HE had happily agreed to do what I told him!

I lay soothing him with my hand on my tummy as our last peaceful moments together before he came into the real world, where not everything goes according to plan!

I had to be quite sure this was happening.

I got up in a leisurely style, took the two little girls into bed with me so they could feel mommy's tummy contracting, and waited the long sore night for the train to arrive early next morning.

At 5.30 I rose, kissed the girls goodbye, leaving them with Gladys, the loving African nanny. I drove Wilfred and myself the 60 kilometres to Nelpsruit Station to await the train and arrival of Wilf's brother and sister-in-law.

As they stepped off the train I lurched forward and said " Come on, we need to go to the hospital in a hurry, the baby's coming."

They looked aghast, "But we've only just arrived" they shrilled.

"Let's go" I said.

Ten minutes away we arrived at the hospital, but it was far too late for me to walk upstairs.

Panic stations! A parking lot drama ensued. A trolley was brought to the car and I was unceremoniously plopped onto it and rushed up to the theatre, where I tried to convince the matron I didn't DO enemas!

James had been alerted to my pending birth. He came flying into the room. He yelled at me for waiting so long before checking in, but at the same time he calmed me down because I knew how much planning we had done to do this thing together. We had talked over every aspect of the operation, and I was carefully informed of every step.

The theatre was calm and quiet with all machines ready and flicking. I remember thinking how narrow the bed was. James talked softly to me, explaining step by step, what he was doing. He had arranged a mirror above my tummy, as promised. I was to watch the operation in progress.

The bed was surrounded by gowned and capped green figures. Only their eyes told me they were alive.

There was absolute silence—no one moved. I saw him take a breath and then—he slit my tummy open in one long stroke, but HE was so far down the birth canal already, that James had to cut horizontally across my tummy as well. As this was my second caesarian in a year, we could not chance a natural birth.

With precise deliberation, he took a long silver instrument that looked like a letter opener and just lightly pricked the huge pulsating womb. It peeled open to reveal my large and wonderful baby boy, waiting to make his entrance into the known world on Easter Friday. He had to be special!

I had already had Alissa by Epidural Caesarian so I knew the drill, but here we had student doctors and James' new gynaecology partner from London, all standing and watching the procedure.

James dipped his hand into my body and withdrew the baby. Holding him aloft for all to see, he said "We're going to need a Rabbi!"

He was a great actor in this role and everyone at Nelspruit hospital had heard of his wild rages in the operating theatre, as well as his prowess as a surgeon.

At that moment it became real. This was actually happening to me. In all the months since I had heard I was pregnant I had not really believed it. I had floated along coping with practicalities only, but now I was confronted with the real thing. My son.

I wept, buckets of copious tears. I needed an extra nurse to just keep blowing my nose and wiping my eyes for me. In exasperation, James growled."Are you happy or sad—stop it already."

"How will I bring him up on my own?" I sobbed.

"He looks big and strong", James declared. "He's a special gift and you'll be fine", he said gruffly, knowing full well what lay ahead.

Wilfred was much too "*pieperig*" as we say in Africa to have been inside the theatre with me, and it was not common practice in those days, but at this point, the baby was taken outside to show him off. Wilf was absolutely speechless with joy and was brave enough to hold him with the help of the nurse who had been warned not to let go of the baby while Wilfred held him.

Meantime, back inside the theatre, people were scurrying back and forth with instruments and gauges. James was slowly stitching me up and by the 44th stitch I was beginning to get the feeling back in my lower half and counting each prick.

I knew I would have to take Wilfred to London for radiotherapy treatment very soon. I asked the Londoner present all sorts of travel questions to keep myself from concentrating on the stitching. I had never traveled abroad and really had no idea of what I would be confronted with.

After ten minutes he seemed to reel and left the room hurriedly.

It was later reported that he had come out of the theatre green and told Wilfred he had never attended a major operation where the patient was talking about which tube to catch in London in the following week.

Once the baby was safely born, Wilfred and brother were so excited they wanted to celebrate. Men don't shop, eat chocolate or have bubble baths—they get pissed. That's exactly what they did!

They drank a whole bottle of Wilf's favorite Jack Daniels bourbon, with no thought to the consequences. His brain swelled up totally and fluid began to accumulate around the brain causing headaches, visual disturbances and imbalance.

29
BRIT MILAH IN THE COUNTRY

I longed for a well-earned sleep after all that action, but James and I were on a high, discussing the operation in all its infinitesimal detail from all aspects. It had created a talking point all round the hospital. It was the first time a patient was awake and watching her own operation.

This country hospital in the Lowveld of the Transvaal was agog with the event, and the comments were filtering back to us.

Eventually he left for home and I fell into an exhausted sleep.

When I awoke, my handsome blue-eyed boy was sleeping peacefully next to my bed and we awaited the arrival of his father.

However, Wilf wasn't well enough to come and visit and it was two days later when our driver Edward helped him up to the ward that I began to acknowledge we were running out of time. His tumor was behind the optic nerve and his eye and vision were evidently becoming pressurized again.

I lay there trying to contain my fear, wondering what to do, watching the peaceful face of my bonny baby boy and accepting I had no choices. I had to do whatever had to be done. There was no time to groan about my caesarian scar, my tummy, or feeling weary.

"Get up and get it done." That was my only option.

I waited anxiously for James to appear. Around 3 a.m. that morning after another lucky lady had delivered successfully he came by to check us out.

"I must leave for London soon", I cried. "I must do whatever I can to save him."

James's face darkened. "Look Hilary", he said, "this is your second operation in a year. Between you and Wilfred, who is ill, who will carry the baggage and how will you travel in this weakened state. If you do this, the consequences to your body will be long term damage. Your insides will sag and you will know all about it!" In my untraveled ignorance I imagined that London was like South Africa, where help and porters were easily accessible.

James "hrummphed" in exasperation, then shrugged his shoulders, turned to walk away from me and said simply and strongly, "If you leave this hospital, you do so without my permission and I wash my hands of your care".

I think he felt it would deter me, but I had no responsible thought for myself at that point. I could only think of Wilfred's options and how unstable his condition had looked this morning.

When the sun rose, James must have been back on his ward rounds. He popped his head round the door and scowled. "Still here?" he said sarcastically, and walked away.

I knew he was worried, but in a way that was my permission, the only one I was going to get from him!

I set the journey in motion. I arranged to interview nursing sisters to look after my baby and called long haul airlines.

When the matron came in, I explained I was checking out .She looked at me in total dumbfounded silence. "Are you taking the drip onto the plane too?" she asked, and then she too, turned her heel on me.

At this point I have to introduce you to Gill

Gill arrived at the hospital with wild red curly hair, freckles, and a curious Australian accent. She was bubbly, loving and confident.

James had interviewed her with me and afterward I had commented "Well, she's large." he retorted, correctly. "It does not matter how she looks, what matters is how efficient she is," and there I had to admit, her C.V. looked very impressive.

She was only 21, but had been the matron of a hospital in her native Australia and was now exploring Africa on a working holiday.

My gut feeling told me she could be independently trusted.

I tried to ascertain if we could get permission to hold the baby's Bris Milah (his circumcision) earlier than eight days, but religious law forbade us to do that.

As we had no Jewish community near us in White River, we had to get a traveling Rabbi and in the end I decided we would go with what we knew and invite our childhood Rabbi from the small seaside town of Port Elizabeth to fly up and do the circumcision. He was immensely proud and honored at our invitation. However, he omitted to mention he was actually retired and hadn't done a circumcision in twenty years!

He arrived amidst great excitement. I stood at the kitchen table holding my stitched-together stomach up with one hand and slicing the endless platters of cold meats with the other. I was in a complete daze, smiling and greeting people I didn't know.

This was the first Bris Milah held in the Lowveld for a hundred years.

Farmers, grocers, gentlemen, any man worth his salt, all Wilfred's clients, the Banana board, the Industrial Development board—a government body at the time—and friends from far and wide, were intent on being there.

Our neighbor, Paul Davis, was a wonderful old man who had only discovered his Jewish roots very late in life. Living in an area isolated from a Jewish community as this was, he had never been to a circumcision. We gave him the honor of being the Sandak, that is, the godfather who holds the baby, and he went to enormous trouble to search and find him an unusual antique silver Kiddush cup as a gift. This he would use to make his own Kiddush on Shabbat.

I adored Paul. He was interesting and worldly. I had spent a lot of time just running my eyes over his vast collection of antique books which filled every available room in his house. He knew the history of them all and I never tired of listening to him talk about them.

He taught me to go to book auctions and Wilfred learned to rue the day I happened to set my heart on a set of signed first edition books on the Kruger Park Game Reserve by Stevenson Hamilton. I wanted them so badly but this dratted old lady started to bid against me. I lost my sense of reason and I kept the bidding going long beyond the realistic value, only to discover, to my embarrassment and horror, that I should have let her have the books as she was Stevenson Hamilton's wife!

There were 700 people at this Bris, all crowded into and flowing out of the large front porch and over the lawn of the farm-house. No one had ever attended this ceremony before, least of all me. They weren't quite sure what to expect but they all respected "Wilfred the Jood" so highly they wanted to be there. They came laden with their special gifts, their prize pumpkin or a newly grafted rose bush. Thankfully, nobody brought me a slaughtered sheep!

I stood outside the room imagining what was going on and when I heard the baby give a shriek, I thought I was going to faint until I saw our young GP come out of the room, wide eyed and ashen.

Our old Rabbi's hand had not been too steady and Justin himself could not watch!

For years afterward the Rabbi used to call us up nervously, to find out how our new son was doing.

We named him Daniel Anton after his two great grandfathers. I had a feeling he would be as talented as Daniel Levinthal was. Sadly, I had never known Anton but Wilf had happy memories of him

Wilfred stood at the front door after the circumcision. He shook each person's hand. I remember that he was wearing his "wedding suit" because he still had the imperial mints from our wedding in his pocket. When the very last person left he looked at me for a long time, then he walked woodenly towards our bedroom, lowered himself onto the bed and lapsed into a coma.

30
LOSING MY SENSES

J ustin was our General Practitioner from our home town in Port Elizabeth. He had come to live in White River and been instrumental in saving Tirza's life. He'd come to call on us, found Tikkele extremely unwell and called the Lions charity helicopter to fly us to Johannesburg as an emergency.

I trusted his judgment. He came immediately when I called him.

He sat at Wilf's bed and then, in his presence, I called the radiotherapist in London and he told us to pump Wilfred full of cortisone to control the pressure on his brain and get him to London immediately.

The next few hours were filled with decision-making trauma.

I called Dr Rosen, who felt going to the UK was our best chance. I called the local neurosurgeon. He came over to see Wilfred lying there in a compromising state. He was unsympathetic and he asked me roughly "Do you think they have some magic in London that will bring him his healed brain cells back?"

I was so confused, so scared and so tired.

My caesarian scar was not healing and I felt woefully swollen and awkward.

My brother in law, ("the one with no hair "as our family joke went) took my hand gently and told me "Listen to your own head. If you feel this is the only chance you have and you want to try it, then go, forget everyone else's opinion."

Under these circumstances, people were beginning to constantly tell me how brave I was, but this was not true. You just do what you have to do when you have no other recourse and in this case you don't know any better and it was all completely out of my range of understanding.

Justin and I sat at Wilf's bed without moving for 36 hours. I held his hand, waiting for some response, while Justin slowly dripped the

Decadron into him. Eventually it began to reduce the swelling. He opened his eyes and recognized us.

In preparing to go to London, we would have to get Wilfred onto the aircraft without the airlines knowing how ill he was. The normal procedure would have been to have him examined by an airways medical board who probably would not have allowed him to travel.

We couldn't chance it!

I would have to control all medication until we reached the Royal Marsden Hospital in London. In the early 70s this was the only place we could be treated on the Linear Accelorator. This was a new radiotherapy machine which plotted exact cells to radiate, rather than the cobalt treatment of the time which hit the general area, annihilating all the cells in the area and causing much more brain damage.

Gill had to teach me to give an intra-muscular injection of morphine and this would be how we controlled his pain until we got there. She made me practice by injecting into an orange. You had to kind of close your eyes and stab hard with the needle.

While this was going on we had to keep watch on him at the same time so she gave me these lessons in the bedroom where he was lying.

It was only later in this process we noticed he was awake and watching us. Even in these dire circumstances, he kept his sense of humor and he indicated to us that there was no way he would be having a headache or needing my services. I hugged him, knowing he did not understand what was at stake and if he did, he gave no indication.

How I bid my young children goodbye, left my new-born son with Gill and got onto that aircraft will always remain a blank in my mind. I would prefer to keep that door closed. I know I was so concerned with Wilfred's physical needs as his left leg was not functioning normally. I was so fearful that they might prevent us from traveling that I probably didn't have time to fear for my babies. Tirza was already a mature and reasonable little lady aged just over two .She took charge of Alissa in a manner way beyond her years, often talking in my voice, to my embarrassment, but I think she was pretending I was there and it comforted her. They took on Daniel as if he was their own baby, playing with him and talking to him, holding his bottle while he drank, patting him to sleep, and helping Gill in a most admirable manner.

This was an era of several bombs on board aircrafts, and terrorism in South Africa was rife.

Restriction and security at the airport was tight. We placed the morphine capsules into the lipstick container removing the lipstick first. The syringes were laid between the fabric and the plastic lining of my padded make-up bag and Wilfred was filled with cortisone so he could limp his way up the gangplank. I hoped he would not walk towards the wrong aircraft.

Once he was confirmed on board, I proceeded through customs.

I passed the barrier, looking very flushed, trying to avoid eye contact. I was immediately pulled aside and invited to enter the cubicle to be searched by a female warden.

I suppose I must have looked stressed. I felt as if my beating temples were going to explode. She searched me slowly and methodically. She then proceeded to unpack my make-up bag in slow motion. Examining each article from all angles, she held it to her nose and smelt it. She turned it over and shook it.

But, she never OPENED the lipstick! Then she packed it back even more slowly and went off to talk to her superiors.

It *rained* under my arms. Could they arrest me and leave Wilfred on the plane? Could I explain why I had morphine capsules on me for a holiday in London? Would I go to jail forever and not see my children?

I couldn't survive much more. The breast milk began to pour through my shirt and I prepared for surrender.

At that moment she came through the South African Airways curtain and said lightheartedly, "Have a good flight, Madam". She shook my hand with a smile.

Fiery dragon claws clutched my shoulders and dragged me forward. I had come to the end of my strength.

As if I were a puppet on strings, spirits forcibly led me up that gang plank and down the aisle as we prepared to head for London. I was the last to board.

31
THE LONGEST NIGHT

I walked wearily down the aisle to where Wilfred was concentrating on the menu, completely unaware of the odds we were up against.

Unlike my journeys in Echo Romeo Charlie, I loved the take-off in the Jumbo jet, but tonight I didn't have the *keiach,* the strength, for excitement. I only hoped we would both survive the journey.

Pretty soon I gave him his tablets, per mouth he was very relieved to note, and he fell into a deep and sonorous sleep. He seemed to be breathing so shallowly and slowly at times that I had to keep poking him to see if he was still conscious.

I hugged myself tight, the realization that I was going to this unknown place so far away, so foreign to me and what had happened to me over the last twenty-four hours was beginning to kick in.

My body was suffering from such stress I felt devoid of a pulse and my head and neck were made of wood.

The cacophony of sound from 300 passengers shifting up and down was almost more than I could bear. The dinner was served and the clatter of trolleys down the rows finally quietened. The lights were dimmed. Eleven hours left to go. I was alone with my thoughts – or nearly alone!

A little girl was standing at my elbow with an enquiring look. She was dragging a silky blanket and her halo of soft blonde curls was clad in a yellow ribbon. We chatted simply. "What is your name?" I asked. "Yes"she nodded, happy to agree with me on all subjects.

I leaned over and swept her into my arms, she smiled warmly, wriggled herself comfortably into my lap, put her thumb in her mouth and shut her eyes.

The thumb in the mouth absolutely finished me off!

My Lissi was a thumb sucker. She was eleven months old, just recently weaned and I had left her alone for G-d knows how long.

I hugged the little girl hard, trying to send my hug through the universal sound waves to Alissa I wondered painfully if they were managing to carry on their normal routine and I couldn't even think about what they thought of all this. Wilfred never stirred.

Half-an-hour later a frowning hassled young mother came down the aisle.

"I'm so sorry" she said. "I was feeding my baby and didn't notice her missing, I'm so sorry to have disturbed you."

I couldn't very well go into a long explanation about how much her daughter had comforted me, so I prepared to give her back. She woke up and screamed blue murder, fighting and spitting at being moved. She was determined to travel in style and she'd located her upgrade, and she was sticking to it!

I assured her mother I would bring her back later and we cuddled up for the night again.

The journey seemed an eternity. Wilfred slept the whole night and I kept my eyes on him all the way.

We landed at Heathrow Airport.

As I write this today, a seasoned traveler of many international airports, I can still remember my staggering surprise at the overwhelming size of Heathrow airport. I finally understood why James had been so anxious and angry with me. Now all I had to do was get Wilfred safely off the plane and onto a bus. Should be simple enough!

I woke him up with difficulty. He was extremely disorientated

I threatened him with very dire consequences if he looked even slightly wobbly on his feet. At that stage he was able to walk in a slow ungainly manner and we might get away with looking like holiday makers.

We reached the immigration counter and were allowed to get our passports stamped together. I prayed Wilfred would not open his mouth

I gripped his hand very tightly. Suddenly, we were through the barrier.

The long escalators seemed to stretch ahead like elastic, confusing signs directed you this way and that, and throngs of people from so many different nations hurried into long passages or up other escalators It made my mind jangle as I struggled to find out where we could find transport.

At least I spoke English. We headed for a sign reading "Bus." I loaded our suitcases, my now sagging husband and my own bundle, the large and mobile aching stomach I still had from the birth, onto the bus.

When you grow up in a relatively young country where the buildings and town planning is mainly 19th Century, you cannot conceive of a concept such as this, the age of the city of London, until you see it with your own eyes .

My mouth was wide-open as the bus wound its way along the streets. Old red brick houses with these amazing Georgian windows, the little turrets and roof windows where I imagined witches and slaves slept. I was enchanted and turned to share it with Wilfed, but alas, he was asleep. It reminded me that we weren't here to be tourists at all.

We made our way by taxi to the hotel that I had arranged in South Kensington.

On our arrival I noticed a fascinating scene in the lobby where formal afternoon tea was being served with little cakes on dainty floral plates and iced friandes—my absolute favorite!

The concierge was cold and brisk. I realized he had looked long and hard at our South African passports. We weren't the flavor of the month at that time in the early 70s.

We were hurded into a teeny elevator big enough for two people and once again, I had to lug our suitcases, holding my post partum stomach.

We unlocked the door of this stuffy little bedroom. Wilfred stepped inside. I saw the bed and made a supreme effort to aim for it. I knew I could go absolutely no further.

I felt myself fainting in slow motion towards the bed and the next thing I knew, I woke up 24 hours later in a strange hotel in London. I lay disorientated, trying to get my bearings and my strength. A much more difficult journey was about to begin.

Life is a journey ....

32
THE LIGHT OF RADIATION

We awoke knowing this was *THE DAY*. I was pleased to note Wilfred making a conscious effort to look his able-bodied best. He allowed me to blow his hair dry and wore his most elegant sports jacket and needless to say some precious rugby club tie.

He was not conscious of the fact that he was dragging his left leg along after us, but he felt confident that he looked good and that was all that mattered.

We took a black cab to the Royal Marsden Hospital in Chelsea. This in itself was an exciting first for me. The cabbie realized we were first-timers in London and took us on the scenic drive to our destination, but I didn't mind the slight extra charge. It gave me time to prepare myself. On arrival we met Dr Julian Bloom, the man we had travelled so far to see, reputed to be the top radiotherapist in the world at that time. A handsome warm all-welcoming man, he greeted us as if we were family.

We sat down in his office and his first enquiry was to hear all about my friend Maureen and her husband who had been treated there the year before and returned home. We were pleased to report he was stable. He repeated several times how beautiful Maureen was and how much he had enjoyed meeting them. It made me feel all the more shapeless and exhausted.

Then he proceeded to examine Wilfred slowly and methodically while I waited and watched.

After an eternity, he was done. He sat us down, turned to Wilfred and very gently he told him, "I'm sorry but I will have to admit you to the Royal Marsden in Surrey."

"But why?" asked Wilfred, quite devastated. He did not realise that the reason he felt mobile and good was because he was on such a controlling dose of cortisone.

"Yes, you are doing well," he explained, "but we must reduce the cortisone now and that must be monitored in hospital. In addition, you will have to spend time in the "art department" while technicians plot your radiation. Here they would make a mould to hold your head in position so that the radiation could be pinpointed at the tumor.

"I will see you every day and we will work as fast as we can to get you home to your children," he said kindly.

Wilfred was so disappointed and for the first time I think he registered fear.

I learnt while at the Marsden that there are two kinds of cancer patients, those who want to know all the details and those who remain in denial throughout. When they are faced with evidence of their own cancer, they talk themselves out of it and that way they maintain their equilibrium. Wilfred was definitely one of the latter. By the next day he was resigned to booking into the hospital in Surrey.

And so began a journey, where the Royal Marsden became the centre of our world and our "club "so to speak.

The next day we had to hurry to Chelsea to meet the daily Marsden Hospital bus which took patients out to Surrey.

There we met our travel companions for the next few months, all of whom were being treated for brain tumours and had come to London for the most up-to-date treatment. It seemed there was no genetic predisposition. They came from every country in the world, large, small, old and young. The children who were in London for treatment, with their bald heads and wide-eyed fear, were very hard for me to watch.

It was murder getting Wilfred ready in time to catch the bus in the mornings. I had to chivvy him for hours, I missed breakfast out of choice as I couldn't stand the waiters who kept asking me where I came from. I was too nervous to say South Africa as the suggestion of "Apartheid" was the daily newspaper headline. Instead of breakfast, we made a habit of grabbing a sandwich on the way.

I remember sitting on the pavement with him and laughing at ourselves eating huge loaves of french bread which we tore with our hands. No one knew us and I loved the anonymity!

We likened it to the way we knew the Africans back home would sit on the pavement tearing the middle of the bread out and then throwing away the crusts.

We joined the bus. We were the obvious new arrivals for treatment and everyone acknowledged us with interested nods, although no-one spoke to us. The ride was long and treacherous, winding through the narrow back streets of the suburbs of London. I am not very good in traffic and I held my breath each time we careered round a corner and I thought "he'll never make it!" The bus driver was obviously well versed in negotiating these little streets and within an hour, although sometimes as much as two hours, we arrived at the big and busy Royal Marsden in Surrey.

We were escorted underground. It felt as if we were to take part in "Star Wars." We had to attach radiation monitors to our collar. There was a silent humming eeriness. We went through many sections separated by steel doors until we reached the radiation department. I held his hand. He was shivering, I felt his misgivings. I sensed fear at the unknown element which lay beyond those doors.

The underground lift opened and we were met by a pleasant young lady who showed us round the facilities. I looked at her and listened to her accent. She looked very much like our Cape Coloured people. She read quietly through our records and then she looked up directly at us, smiled and said "*VRYSTAAT!*—Welcome to London". This is a well known rugby greeting. I broke into tears, I guess Wilfred was pretty close to tears and I just had to hug her; there was something precious and familiar in this very foreign experience.

Later that day we learnt that the art department would make a plastic mould of his head to enable them to radiate him. This would map the exact point of entry and building a model would prevent his head from moving. In this way it would direct the radiation, as far as possible, only at the malignant cells.

I learnt with horror that this procedure, combined with all the other tests we needed could take up to six weeks and only then, would they *begin* the treatment.

This meant we were going to be away for months and my heart sank. My new baby was changing every day and I was not there to see him and hold him. Tirza and Alissa were at such vital stages of their development and having to play Mom to each other.

I left Wilfred in the waiting room. I walked around the block alone. For the first time I felt anger, frustration and total mental exhaustion at the road ahead. I tried to tell myself it had to work, otherwise why did we have to go through all of this and why did my children have to bear all of this, if not as a cure for their Daddy.

At this time, in the early 70s, doctors were not very forthcoming with information. Had I been informed of the side-effects I would have understood how to cope with them. As it was, I learnt each lesson from the various experiences, which I could have avoided with better warning and explanation.

These side-effects, the all-consuming hunger which high doses of cortisone give you, were difficult to manage. He ate mountains of food, every food barrow we passed he had to have something to eat. He was continually ravenously hungry.

As my shape went down by a size each week, and my post-partum body tried to return to normal, my waist slowly began to curve inwards instead of outwards. I walked around with clothes hanging untidily around my hips. In contrast, his clothes grew tighter and tighter till he started bulging at the seams, his buttons scarcely holding the cloth together. This was a strange vision for me as he'd always had such a good body. He started to look so unlike himself. His cheeks ballooned and his eyes grew vacant.

The unreasonable temperament with one moment high and energetic, and the next raging over some insignificant matter was traumatic. The emotional withdrawal, the cringing from being touched, the passive objective syndrome where he just would not do what he had to do, or what you asked him to do was very trying. Some days I just wanted to hold my baby and be in another place. I tried not to think of other young married couples going about their normal family lives, while I was holed-up indefinitely in an oncology unit with hundreds of patients in varying degrees of decrepitude.

One morning while he was in the bathroom I heard this dreadful agonised cry.

I leapt out of bed and burst into the bathroom. There stood Wilfred with half his head of magnificent curly black hair in his hand. We both wept.

We went straight out to buy a series of hats and he became compulsive about wearing his hat at all times. Perhaps it is easier for women to cope with this aspect of treatment. Each day on the bus another "cancer compadre" was faced with the decision of whether "to wig or not to wig."

So began the pattern of our day. When Wilfred was not an "in" patient, we would run lumpily along the road for the bus. I would beg him to take a seat but in his mindset he remembered a gentleman's way only. If he saw a lady standing, he would insist on giving up his seat.

As we were usually late, we would be near the back door of the bus. The bus would be crowded with other patients. Each time this single-decker lurched its way to Surrey, Wilfred would be holding on to the rail with his weak left hand. His weak hand would let go the rung, he would topple in slow motion and then, at the last second, grip the handle again. I tried to stand behind him on the bus but he was not going to be told what to do. Each day I thought he was going to fall off the bus and by the time we arrived I felt so nauseous I needed a cup of weak black tea to revive me.

This must be where my English habit of tea drinking for comfort began.

We would sit in the extensive waiting rooms with hundreds of other people whom we got to know by sight. We would nod as a concession to a greeting, and sometimes the partners would talk to each other. Most of the patients felt so lousy they dozed off in their chairs.

As I exchanged stories with many partners from other lands and cultures, I began to realise that we, the partners, were the visible sufferers.

We were away from our daily lives, carrying the responsibility of the person who was ill and trying to cope with all the uncomfortable limitations this treatment brought with it in a totally foreign place. This hardship bonded us together. Each day we would bemoan the long wait and the management troubles we had struggled with as partners of the patient on the night before. Seeing and experiencing that you weren't alone in this struggle was reassuring. The other partners became my friends and the radiographer became my cousin from home. Wilfred enjoyed the greeting of VRYSTAAT which, loosely translated, referred to the province of Free State, who supposedly had the strongest rugby team in South Africa. This was an important issue for Wilfred and one he could still relate to.

Some days we would wait more than eight hours for Dr Bloom. He left home before 7 a.m, and if you had to speak to him personally, you were asked to call him after midnight as that was the end of his day, travelling between the two hospitals, treating the hundreds of patients with brain tumours.

We sensed his arrival. Nurses who had been lounging around, took to rushing up and down with lists, the atmosphere in the waiting room changed, the expectant in the queue murmured to each other: "THE KING HAS ARRIVED" "Patients sat up, trying to look well, and then, with a rush, he swept in.

Dr Bloom appeared, marching down the corridor in long purposeful strides. He was followed by a flurry of junior doctors clutching their white coats, running to keep up with him.

We waited our turn patiently as we were all in the same boat. hen we were called, I always wished I could sit down there and then, and paint the pathos of the scene. The junior doctors lined the office wall standing straight and tense, silent and still, as if they were terrified of him, this kind, wonderful man. He questioned, he examined, and then our one minute audience that we had waited so many hours for, was over.

We always felt a bit deflated so we kept our treat for after the event.

The tea room offered a very limited fare of watercress sandwiches or a blushing bunny. This was a toasted cheese and tomato and cost 2p at the time.

Our budget was extremely limited so we had our blushing bunny each day, sharing a pot of tea which we stretched to as many cups as we could.

Then came the equally treacherous journey home. Each day I sat in the bus and looked out of the windows at the shops with such longing. I vowed one day I would come back with my children and we would wonder care-free around the shops with no limitations, just touching and trying on and exploring the exciting clothing, shoes and hats I saw from the window of the bus. Biba's store had recently opened. As an ex-designer, I was reading all the newspaper articles about Mary Quant's merchandise and I was drooling to see it all.

Many were the times when Wilfred was admitted as an in-patient. He had relapses in his progress when they had to stop treatment and allow his body to rest. He would seem to be in another world, just lying there, trance-like.

On one occasion, the man in the bed next to him was dying. I asked them to move Wilfred away fearing he would get frightened. That was when I learnt the power of his blocking out process.

When I came into the ward the next morning, the nurse had told him Jim had died during the night.

"Where's Jim" I asked Wilfred pointing to the empty bed. "oh!" he said unconcerned," they moved him to another ward," despite having been told the facts by the nurse.

When he was not too well, I would hide in the loo until the night nurse had checked him for the night and then lie on the floor next to him, knowing it would be hours before they came back. They were so busy, I was too scared to leave him alone and travel all the way back to London.

On other nights I took a mini cab back to the apartment we now had in Mayfair. I was very embarrassed at having to eat alone so I would take my book into the café near our flat and read while I ate.

One evening the owner of the café came over to me and proclaimed very loudly—"This is a restaurant, not a library". I crept out and relied on takeaways in the bedroom after that.

On another occasion, I was so completely wrapped up in our daily progress and treatment I tended to forget practical things. I would stay at the hospital until Wilfred was asleep and then catch a mini cab home. On this occasion I was dozing off in the back of the cab on the long ride home, when I realised with trepidation that I had no cash on me.

I asked the cabbie if he took travellers cheques and he said "I DO NOT." He squealed over to the sidewalk. He was totally unsympathetic to the fact I had no clue where we were, and he chucked me out into the dark and moody night.

I felt lost. Not only lost in London, lost in the scheme of things generally, lost in my ability to carry on, lost in my belief we were getting anywhere with Wilfred. The progress was not very evident. I walked along dejectedly. A kindly black cab must have seen a lone lady walking in the night. I tearfully related my silly story and he took me home without asking for a fare.

Early on in our London stay, I took Wilfred to a neurologist in Harley Street. Dr Williams was an old friend of the family. I think my motive for the visit was intended initially to deliver the prune chocolates which my mother-in-law had sent him and knew were his family's favourite. He was a gentle knowledgeable man whom I felt I could relate to.

I was still puzzled as to how to cope emotionally and Dr Rosen's "non answer" had not helped me.

"Should I try to keep the physical side of our relationship going?" I asked. "Should I continue to be loving even though there is no response? I find it so hard to judge whether he wants to be close or if he's just reticent". I wept.

With great loving patience he explained to me what Dr Rosen obviously had not had the skill to do.

The tumour had invaded the emotional area of his brain, and this, coupled with his emotional background and the scar from many rugby injuries, would annihilate any chance of him ever having an emotional relationship again. He understood my need for companionship, especially being alone in a foreign country, but he maintained that if I stopped hoping and trying and learned to accept that I was there to protect him, provide for him, but that I could never again expect him to share the thoughts of husband and wife, my acceptance would eventually make it easier for me—and for him as I would not have expectations of him.

My caesarean scar was not healing well. I felt anaemic and tired and I guess just coping with the daily responsibility was as much as I could manage then. Gill was sending weekly photos of the children and Daniel's progress and I couldn't actually cope with additional emotional trauma at the moment. So I left it as such, with a very sad realisation that my marriage had ended really before it had even had a chance to begin.

33
LOST AND FOUND IN BOND STREET

The days in London became routine. My view of London was the trail to the Royal Marsden Hospital in Surrey.

I kept my sanity by trying to be creative with my limited resource.

I made picture collages of my growing children, copying the photos and rearranging them in different forms with headings cut out of magazines. I needed to do something creative, however simple it was. I pinned them up on the walls of our apartment and wondered how long it would be before I saw them again.

Initially, I had asked Dr Bloom what he thought Wilfred's chances of recovery were. He replied that there was an enormous area of brain damage and they could only do their best?

I begged him to keep in mind the promise he had made on our arrival that if he thought Wilfred was not going to survive, he would try to get us home before he died. I believed that at least the children should see him and be able to say goodbye, young as they were, I did not want them to be left with an incomplete feeling of him disappearing, never to be seen again.

He promised me he would do this.

As the weeks turned into months my horizons shrunk. I separated myself from home and thoughts of family. I focused on getting him through each day's treatment. I lost sight of getting him home and began to just worry about whether today would be a day when he came home to our apartment in the evening or was "kept in" the hospital for observation. This happened on a fairly regular basis.

Halfway through the radiation, his teeth on the left began to crumble and fall out. The point of entry for the radiotherapy was through his jawbone, and this too began to disintegrate.

Treatment was halted for a period and he was hospitalised and put through a battery of new tests. No one answered my questions and Dr

Bloom became too busy to talk to me. It was during this time in hospital when Wilfred had become silent and inaccessible that I marveled at the innate strength of the human species.

Our behavior patterns are the ingrained conditions in our childhood enviroment and despite our intellectual capacity, in times of stress we seem to revert to our unconscious basic references. Early on this morning we lay waiting for the new registrar to appear. The door opened. In walked an awesome looking man, tall and imposing with a wonderful resonant voice, and marvellous gleaming black skin.

Wilfred was an unwitting son of the apartheid era in South Africa. As suburban whites, we had never really met an African man of this calibre. I realized the doctor was going to examine him and I was absolutely sure Wilf would roll off the bed and hide underneath it.

I held my breath. There was a moment's hesitation, and then Wilfred laughed broadly and held out his hand to shake the doctor's hand. I knew exactly what he was thinking. KYK HOE LYK HY NOU! which means "If only they could see me now in South Africa!!"

This was the beginning of another instance which illustrated Wilfred's amazing strength of character. Dr Hoburn talked to us about a new treatment they intended to try. He told Wilfred the side-effects were very severe and he should expect not to feel too good for a few weeks, but that they would monitor him closely and support him at all times.

"Are you strong enough to go through with this?" he asked Wilfred. They did a lot of jovial bantering and Wilfred assured him they "grow them strong in Africa!!"

I loved him so much. Through all this horror, his sense of humor still came to the fore, albeit it was buried in fatigue most days.

I was called to a conference. "This chemotherapy is devastating and he will either survive and get better, or it could finish him off", I was told. If the body reacted negatively, he would hemorrhage, "You will then have two minutes to get him to an emergency hospital."

I listened in incomprehensive silence.

In retrospect, I guess they did not consider I was a stranger in town – I didn't know my way around. It was a heavy responsibility to give anyone untrained in nursing or medicine.

I became totally traumatized by the anticipation of what could happen. Before we left each day, I plotted our long route via the nearest hospitals, being sure always to have cab money and the telephone number of the nearest hospital. I was terribly nervous and became abnormally stressed waking up constantly at night to check his body for signs of bleeding.

One has to bear in mind this was the early seventies. Chemotherapy was in its infancy and details were mostly scant because they simply hadn't had the opportunity to collect information yet. Still, it rankled that at no time did anyone approach me, or us and discuss whether we wanted to proceed with this line of treatment. I learned much later that they only tried it on terminally ill patients whom they thought would not survive and as a last line of hope.

Each day they brought him the capsule, Every day he had high care in the ward—nursing staff stayed close by. Wilfred showed no reaction.

Each day Dr Hoburn arrived, expecting to see a strong reaction to the drug, vomiting or some form of bleeding. Wilfred took great pleasure in informing him how good he felt and how strong this son of Africa was.

The friendly banter continued. "Are you really swallowing the pills?" the doctor teased him.

"Sure" said Wilfred "you can double the dose."

They became friends. He would sit and they would chat about their homes. He came from Ghana, and was becoming an oncology specialist in the chemotherapy field.

Eventually Wilfred was allowed home to Mayfair.

I was terrified of the responsibility.

I began to notice he couldn't button his shirt correctly, or he'd leave the tap running and not notice. He seemed to be in another world and often couldn't respond logically to conversation. I didn't know whether this was a drug reaction or deterioration of his mental capacity.

I wondered if he was depressed but I had no way of knowing how he felt. It was impossible to gauge what, if anything, he was thinking, and he didn't make any effort to verbalize any thoughts despite my constant enquiries.

This isolation from his feelings, his cognizance was the hardest part for me to bear.

I thought a day at the shops might take his mind off things, and I was so longing to just have a quick look around. He had left his hat somewhere and with his broad hairless patch he was very concerned about getting another.

I had heard one must see the pets department at Harrods with all kinds of weird and wonderful goods. So off we went to the West End. I held his hand tightly as he was extremely wobbly and very unfocused. We caught a cab to the store.

I had great difficulty keeping him close to me while my eyes devoured the magical departments, the Egyptian floor, the fashionable silks and satins, the gold and silver coated almonds, the elderberry flower drinks. I hoped my mouth was not open all the time as we looked at the goods, remembering that apartheid South Africa was embargoed by most suppliers at this time and the goods in our stores were limited.

We purchased an East Enders cap for him. I went to the till to pay for it, entreating him to stand still for a moment. I let go of his hand, reached into my purse, and paid the bill.

By the time I took my till slip and looked up, he was gone. He'd literally disappeared into thin air.

I screamed, "Oh my G-d." The assistants looked alarmed, people turned and stared and I became really frightened. I garbled my story out as quickly as I could. Store detectives were summoned. I tried to give a description of him wearing his East Enders cap, only to realize with despair that this was the regular look around here. Most men wore caps.

The ladies who had served me agreed he looked slightly "different," so the store was put on alert and everyone was running around in circles, not knowing where he would have headed. By now ten minutes had passed, he could be anywhere, and all because I so badly wanted to shop. I felt so guilty at having tried to take him shopping, I became more and more fearful as we could not locate him in the store and eventually they decided to call the police.

Within moments the department was filled with helmeted British bobbies, so kind and reassuring. They took me into the street and spread out left and right while we left the store detectives looking out for him. I rode in the cop car with one of them. We moved up and down the surrounding streets searching the crowds for a wobbly man not sure of his name.

Well past busy Piccadilly, about four blocks down on Bond Street, he was standing at a congested pedestrian crossing not sure when to walk, looking like any other tourist.

I leapt out of the police car and ran towards him. I was terrified that if I called to him he would determinedly cross the road, so I crept up and grabbed him.

I wasn't sure whether I wanted to strangle him or clobber him, but I hauled him into the police car to his wide-eyed amazement and they delivered us home.

I fell onto my bed and wept.

I wept with relief, I wept with fatigue. I wept with the utter frustration of having no-one to communicate with. I felt like I couldn't last one more minute without my children. As I cried my longing became worse, I hugged myself as I longed to hug my babies, I whimpered myself into a deep and exhausted sleep, while Wilfred just sat in a chair and stared blankly at me.

34
HOPING TO GET HOME SAFELY

I can't believe how the months have passed. Wilfred is frail. He walks slowly and everything is a huge effort. His uncle in Britain, an O.B.E, had invited us to the Connaught Hotel for lunch. We knew it was a very expensive restaurant and we were thrilled to be invited to experience this change from our blushing bunnies, which had begun to taste like sand.

I put my arm around him as we walked towards the hotel, thinking how uncertain our future was. Did he have a future, I wondered?

I tried to cheer him up by challenging him to make this a worthwhile meal and order the most expensive thing on the menu, knowing that Uncle Arthur would not mind.

We joined the family party and tried to chat but I could see he wasn't feeling very well.

He ordered a crocodile schnitzel, looking slyly at me to see if this was expensive enough and I winked back. But, sadly, it was really just to please me. He had no appetite, the pills were finally beginning to react in his system.

We left lunch early and went home. He stayed in bed for a week, just lying there resting listlessly looking out of the window at the endlessly grey sky. I prayed that he would see the blue sky of Africa again

Bursting through my thoughts the shrill sound of the telephone brought me down to earth. I had a surprise call from Dr Bloom. He told me I should prepare to go home as he wanted to keep his promise to me. I asked him how long he thought Wilfred would live and his words remain illuminated in my head.

"Don't hope for more than a month, I'm afraid we have not been able to achieve much."

How to explain our sudden departure to Wilfred? I need not have lost any sleep over that. He knew there was a rugby match in Johannesburg on the weekend and he was determined to be there. He perked up considerably and began staring repeatedly at the children's collages, whereas he had previously shown no interest. Perhaps he too had shut off his feelings and now he knew he would see them soon. He wanted to call and tell them. I was wary, I wanted to get him home first. His sister had now had the children for nearly eight months.

How much I longed to discuss his feelings with him, to know how he felt and what his desires and fears were. This blank non-communication was so hard to live with, so stonewalled and so cuttingly deadening. I yearned for love and warmth and someone to share all the hardship with. My own fears were so mangled up with anxiety and trying to cope with practicalities of getting him safely from A to B.

We booked a flight with great excitement. Nearly seven months had passed, Daniel could already make comprehensible sounds. Gill had spent all her time talking to him and he was verbally very advanced. He was looking splendid in the latest photos. Would he relate to me or would he only want Gill with whom he was familiar? In the back of my mind I worried about this, but kept busy preparing.

We were handed three capsules in a special container to get us home. From there I was loosely informed that I could link up with South African oncologists and they would continue the chemotherapy treatment.

I packed our belongings while Wilfred lay on the bed watching me. We had been advised to take the easiest route home as he had to have cortisone injections at some halfway stop and at that time, stopping over in Madrid was the shortest hop to South Africa

As Wilfred had to rest for a day en route, I had a brain wave. I decided to reward myself with a day's shopping in Spain. I wanted at the very least some gifts for the children. Through the hospital, I arranged to have a nurse come in for the day to stay with Wilfred while I roamed the stores. I fantasized at the thought. Of touching things exotic in shoe stores and buying lovely European underwear, not available once we got home.

Once more I carried the suitcases. I was stronger, slimmer, but still very nauseous.

I subsequently found out that this was from months of living in a radiation hospital in the early 1970s when protection from radioactive isotopes was not as good as it is now.

We arrived in Madrid around six o'clock in the evening. I was enchanted with this Spanish city, its sights and its unfamiliar sounds. I enjoyed the drive to the hotel. Wilfred was very tired. I settled him in the room first and then came down to register. After signing my name, I politely asked the concierge what time the shops would open in the morning. I intended to be first through the door.

He smiled at me apologetically and said "Madam, regrettably, tomorrow is a public holiday".

In retrospect, I was so ashamed of my reaction, but months of frustration exploded in a giant waterfall through my disappointed body and mind. I ran up to the room. I ranted and raved and cried and spat. I was so angry with myself and the world in general. I cancelled the nurse and we both stayed in bed for the day. It should not have been a big deal, but it was!

I must have slept very late because when I awoke the room was empty. Not again! I didn't have the strength to move but a few moments later the door opened and Wilfred came scurrying in carrying a parcel.

My display of hysteria had upset him. He had wanted to do something to ease my disappointment and had remembered seeing a little jewelry shop in the lobby.

He handed me a gorgeous necklace. It had alternate black and white Majorca pearls separated with gold bars. Very elegant, very fashionable, and, in addition, he'd also purchased a brooch for his mother. I was so touched. Was my old Wilfred still in there somewhere? Would there be some hope of loving communication in the future? I never stopped hoping.

35

THE JOURNEY HOME IN THE FAST LANE

The Spanish doctor injected Wilfred with cortisone as arranged, and pronounced him well enough to travel.

The reality of going home was within sight.

I knew we had to be at Barajas Airport to catch our flight at 6 pm. We made our way in plenty of time and walked towards the check-in. As I proffered our tickets forward to the flight check in I was mortified to find we had just MISSED the flight.

No-one had thought to tell this twenty-three year old first-time traveller that there was a two hour time change between countries in Europe and I had absolutely no idea!

I could not believe my ears. What on earth would we do now?

"Can you get us another flight?" I asked the counter hand."

"There isn't another flight to South Africa till next Tuesday."

Four days away! I knew Wilf needed treatment before then. I began to feel panicky. I watched him for any sign of fatigue.

The airline called around to other airlines. Eventually we were advised to catch the plane leaving shortly for Paris and there we could pick up a connection to Johannesburg.

I dragged Wilfred down the runway to the aircraft. We took our seats as they closed the doors and the aircraft taxied out. He was looking pale and wan and I was nervous and tense. An hour later we disembarked in Paris to be confronted with the most goddam awful sight ahead.

The airport workers were on a "go slow". The queues at passport control were spilling out onto the tarmac. Hundreds and hundreds of people were waiting.

Everyone was throwing their hands up complaining and *"mon dieu-ying"* The chaos sounded like a morning market and no-one spoke English.

I tried to get preferential treatment because Wilfred needed to sit down, but no one would take the slightest notice of me. I was watching

Wilfred looking very jaded and dragging his leg badly. I placed him under a tree, propped up by the suitcases, and took my place in the long queue.

If we didn't get through passport control, we couldn't go through to the departure lounge and we would miss the next connection to South Africa again. I thought of anything I could do to attract attention without getting arrested.

I begged the guards standing around but they didn't understand me and in the end I had to take my place in the queue and wait. I was weak with stress and very worried that Wilf's platelet count would drop too low.

After almost two hours of standing, we came to the front of the queue. We had missed the connecting flight directly to Johannesburg and our only choice was to fly on to London to catch the South African Airways evening flight.

Could this be happening? We had flown half way around Europe as the supposed SHORT cut to get home and we were still going in the wrong direction.

We boarded the flight to London with heavy hearts and no energy left at all.Wilfred just followed me up the gangplank completely unaware of why we were making so many short flights before the long haul.

An hour later we were again confronted with long queues but this time they spoke English, and I could no longer behave with dignity. I demanded they call the supervisor and told them our very stupid sounding story.

We were taken straight to the head of the check in queue only to be confronted with the fact that the flight was full except for two seats in first class.

I wondered what to do. I didn't have a credit card in those days, so I resolved to cash in all the air tickets I had on me with which I intended to collect Gill and the three children from the coast. I tore out all my remaining travellers cheques that I had so carefully saved. We were assisted up the gangway and helpfully seated in first class. The steward could see Wilfred was in no condition to sit up all night so they made up a bed on the upper floor for him and he slept peacefully all night.

I sat in my seat, tears falling down my face while the kindly gentleman next to me held my hand and tried to placate me. We didn't exchange names, but I knew his face. He was the chairman of a very large consortium and many years later, with no connection inferred, I was the recipient of a grant from him to travel to a conference in Canada. He never tied the face together and I never reminded him what a weepy traveller I was.

We arrived at Johannesburg Airport. I was a little worse for wear but Wilfred was refreshed and excited. His brother fetched him for the rugby, His family were a little taken aback at the change they saw in him but there wasn't time to dwell on it.

He managed half the rugby game and then requested to be delivered home, but that satisfied him and gave him a feeling of coming home to familiar territory and things that were important to him.

I called the children at the coast. Each sweet voice could not really understand that we were soon to be reunited, but they understood that they were to be coming to the airport soon.

Early the next morning we set off for Port Elizabeth.

There, standing at the door of the airport building, was an indescribable sight for me. I couldn't walk, I was afraid I might faint. They held each others' hands, my sweet little daughters. They came forward holding the freshest bunch of flowers I had ever seen.

They were so grown up, so in control, so bursting with unknown expectations.

So Incredibly Beautiful.

I gathered them up in my arms and I squeezed as hard as I could. We had both arrived home safely to hold them once again.

Then I stepped forward to do the hardest thing I have ever done in my life

My son, sat proud and upright in his leaning chair. I bent down, and I said "Hello Daniel". He examined me carefully from top to toe, he considered exactly who I was and as I spoke he seemed to recognise my voice from the telephone and he slowly broke into a broad smile and put out his arms to me.

If I ever felt burning wondrous love, I felt it then, the miracle of a mother and child.

I picked him up and held him close, rocking him to my body as my milk flowed freely down my shirt—seven months and a half months later.

36

MANAGING CCNU

Birth is a beginning
And Death a destination.
And life is a journey:
From childhood to maturity
And youth to age
From innocence to awareness
And ignorance to knowing:
From foolishness to discretion
And then, perhaps, to wisdom:
From weakness to strength-
Or strength to weakness
And often back again:
From health to sickness and back
we pray, to health again.

I t seemed a long and winding road. It was all uphill and no bridges. We returned to White River in a blur of coping with Wilfred's current fragility. Gill accompanied us. This gave me time to readjust to having children around. I had to cope with changing nappies, making bottles and alerting my numbed senses to little voices needing attention. I had grown used to focusing all my energies on Wilfred's needs. Thank goodness Gill was around to help the transition.

She had been with Daniel since he was born. He'd slept in her bed, learnt to walk and nearly talk and been the centre of her focus for so long that she too had to adjust to eventually going back to Australia and leaving him with me.

Samson and his family were delighted to see the "Makoela boss" return home but very upset to see him stooped, minus his wonderful head of curly hair, and barely able to walk. They greeted us with ululating songs and welcoming dances. Neighbouring workers drifted in as the news of our return spread.

The men came forward to shake his hand shyly, but eventually he had to excuse himself as too weary to cope.

The children were delighted to be back in their familiar surroundings with Gingie the cat and Brady the Labrador. All the farm children leaped around, touching them and dashing too and fro.

Nunoo and Lalla, Samson's little girls, took Tirza and Alissa by the hand and pulled them off to play.

Pompie the youngest was just walking when we left. Now he was strong and confident. He came up to Daniel with a little injured bird in his hand. I watched in wonder as Dan looked at his proffered hand, unsure of Pompie's intention. Dan carefully stuck out his finger and tried to stroke the bird who immediately fluttered his wings. Frightened, Daniel burst into tears and Pompie ran away laughing.

The chemotherapy had to be administered every six weeks. We had enough capsules to last us for two months. I was to obtain them from the John Hopkins Hospital in Maryland USA. My final instructions from the Royal Marsden Hospital were to call Maryland two weeks before each dose. "It will be flown out to you at no cost and the local doctors would manage it for you".

That was the sum total of information with which I returned home!

I was to have a rude awakening!

I contacted the only oncologist in South Africa in the early 70s. He would not have an extended discussion with me over the telephone. He insisted I had to see him in his rooms in Johannesburg. While Gill was still around to look after Wilfred, I could steal a day off.

I caught the newly initiated flight from Nelspruit to Johannesburg, only a six-seater Cherokee, but an improvement on Echo Romeo Charlie.

As I was leaving the house, I received a call from Doctor Ray Dimbleby at the oncologist's rooms. His secretary said, "Please ensure you wear trousers to the meeting today."

I was so taken aback, I forgot to ask why. I felt too embarrassed to call back. Time was running out for me to catch my flight so I changed into trousers and drove to the airport.

I couldn't begin to imagine how his strange request tied in with my meeting. Oh my goodness! Did he think I was the patient? Did I somehow forget to clarify that I was the partner? Would I have to have tests? Could he have some strange fetish about women in trousers? He was very friendly on the telephone, perhaps even a bit familiar. I began to feel uneasy.

I arrived at the consulting rooms and was shown into his office.

A short and stocky fair-haired man held out his hand and shook mine warmly." I knew you'd be good looking," he said. "really, hows that ?" I asked. "Your voice gave me a picture," he said nonchalantly. His wicked grin and sparkling eyes made me relax.

I sat down to discuss the chemotherapy drug, CCNU with him. This was the first inkling I got that this drug was universally unregistered and as yet, untried in South Africa.

Wilfred had been selected as a trial patient. No one had asked if he chose to be "on trial".

Dr Dimbleby and anyone else in South Africa was forbidden by law to prescribe or use it! We could not just stop using the drug. He would have died. Dimbleby realized he had to help us and was rather appalled at the lack of forethought on the part of the Royal Marsden Hospital, so he devised what he felt would be a technically admissable solution.

We would become friends. We would lunch whenever I needed to.

He seemed to sense I really needed to pour out all my doubts and fears. He himself was keen to see the workings of CCNU and was well read on the subject. Based in Africa, he was also a long way from world trials going on at this time. In a sense, Wilfred was becoming his guinea pig as well! He was not allowed to prescribe it or manage it.

He would listen to me, suggest routes to go, and tell me when I needed to call Maryland USA for help. If necessary, he would see Wilfred as an oncologist from time to time, to check him out in general terms.

I realised he was my only available *ally* in this cure on CCNU and I desperately needed his help and co-operation. I was the only person who had seen the drug in action and watched the daily management of the cortisone. I could not call the USA daily and wait long periods on the telephone for some foreign doctor to answer my questions, as they could not see the effects on Wilfred. I was on the spot and I could gauge what was happening. This forced me to be the person responsible for checking his platelet count every day at the laboratory. Then I had to make a decision whether to move the dosage up or down. I needed Dr Ray to second my decisions and to watch over his progress in case of haemorrhage. This smacked of science fiction. I felt like I was taking his life in my hands each day, and each time I altered the dose, I prayed it was the right thing to do.

I agreed to Dr Ray's plan. I had no other option. But I was still intrigued as to why I needed trousers.

He collected his briefcase, told his secretary we were going to lunch and we made our way to the lift.

I realised this was my first day away from Wilfred in nine months. I felt as if I had been in exile from reality for a long long time.

We reached the basement where I presumed we would pick up his car. I couldn't believe I was going to spend the day eating at an expensive restaurant if my life was quite normal. He turned to me with the most mischievous smile and with a broad gesture of his hand he said "Our transport madame!"

Standing before me was his huge black high wheeled motorbike!

I laughed out loud. "You're not serious?" "Yes," he said, "we're going into the country. It's a gorgeous day, you need to lighten up and remember 'life' and you need fresh air and professional advice, remember?"

I was gobsmacked! I hesitated only a moment—then I donned the helmet, bravely blanked out my fears and climbed on. I had survived everything I needed to do so far in this miserable adventure of life.

Why not something intriguing and uplifting.

My hair flew like a kite following us. I clasped his waist tightly and we took off!

To ride a motorbike had never really been a major ambition of mine, but experiencing it was great. My Dad had had a Harley Davidson in his younger days and I imagined my mom clinging to his waist as they rode the highways in "the old days."

We arrived at a wonderful restaurant near the Hartebeestpoort River. The table looked out over the peaceful, soft ebbing water. Brown sludgy hippos lounged around, peeping indolently out of the swells.

For the first time in all these months I breathed deeply and I ate with an appetite.

For the first time in all these months he helped me to face the fact that the chemotherapy was an uncharted road. He made me talk about what *could* happen. He alerted me to the unstable pattern of chemotherapy and how I should adapt our lives.

We discussed how best to handle all the side-effects. He tried to explain the significance of the platelet count to me so that I could make the best decision on a daily basis.

The methodology of CCNU was to attack the blood cells. This created an effect similar to leukaemia except it supposedly attacked only the rascal cells, hard for a non-medical person to comprehend! To control the side-effects we would have to heighten the cortisone dosage for two weeks.

Wilfed grew energised and ate voraciously again, then the chemo would start kicking in and he'd be really sick for two weeks. He'd vomit and he became aggressive and unpleasant and very hard to deal with. This was extremely difficult for the children, who were too young to understand what was going on. The complete change in personality confused them.

One day I came into the lounge to investigate the trauma I heard from the kitchen. Wilf had little Tirza standing in the middle of the large round dining room table. She was yelling in fear as he repeatedly told her to "say hello" to his friend. I grabbed her off the table and apologised to the friend.

After a few rough incidents, I realised he no longer had what I would term reasonable judgement in dealing with them. I vowed never to leave him alone with the children. The middle weeks would be maintained by the cortisone. During the last two weeks the treatment would plateau, and peace would reign for a short respite.

Week three and four of the treatment was so hard to bear, that when week five and six came our coping skills were frazzled. Wilfred lay quietly in bed with no interest in much around him. We geared ourselves up for the next dose, becoming familiar with the pattern that began all over again.

This made my life extremely tense. I had no family to call on.nearby No-one to help me. JP had insisted we go back to living in White River, and my life was profoundly distressing.

Months turned into years, he lived in this twilight world, living only two weeks out of every six. I wondered if this was ever going to get better.

Each day at noon I would hire a teacher on leave to come into the house for half-an-hour to look after Wilfred while I fetched the children from nursery school. I wanted to call for them myself. I was trying desperately to introduce some normality into their lives. I wanted to be there to fetch them as the other moms were.

Daniel was still at home and accompanied me on this important daily outing.

At school I would leave him in the car and dash out to get Tirza and Alissa . It was a small country town and we were very casual about things.

One day I came back to the car and Daniel was standing excitedly on the back seat. As I opened the door he gladly told me "Ma, a man came and asked for your bag and I gave it to him." He was so proud that he had been able to handle this on his own, I couldn't disillusion him, but it was a lesson well learned. I always carried him with me after that incident.

The six capsules of CCNU were flown at no charge from the USA but no one had considered the fact that we lived in the Lowveld, and they had to be transported from Johannesburg to White River and then immediately placed in the freezer. This cost me a fortune, as I had to hire a courier to fly them down to me and I had to drive onto the tarmac to receive them.

Once again, because they were not registered drugs, no-one could be seen to receive them except me.

Dr Ray was true to his word. He became a valued friend. He was always at the end of the telephone when I needed him. If he had started out with any ulterior motive, and I tend to think this was just his easy manner, it soon became a working relationship. He helped me to take on the huge responsibility with the confidence that he was there for me.

He was interested in painting and his daughter was studying painting, so whenever I needed to see him I talked him into riding down to the Lowveld on his bike, or bring his family with him, rather than my going up to Johannesburg. That way he got to see Wilfred first hand.

After the first wave of adventure had passed, I lost my cool going out on the fast track!

My weeks now consisted of driving Wilfred to the laboratory in Nelspruit four times per week for blood tests. This involved getting him up and dressed which was sometimes very complicated and took two or three hours if he didn't want to go. He had become obsessional about washing and had a ritual which took ages, and he could not be organised to miss any part of it. It became so bad that I was forced to build a second bathroom so that we could sometimes have the use of the facilities while he was keeping it eternally engaged.

The focus of my life became his daily platelet count. I wasn't allowed to ask for any medical help locally.

At times it was so disconcerting, trying to decide whether I had to reduce or increase his doseage, knowing the consequences of doing this. His moods were altered by the drug dosage, and we feared the next outbreak of unreasonable behaviour.

The children and I coped. We became a little unit. They knew when to shout and when to play silently. It became a lifestyle, a lonely and empty existence on a farm, far from other adults with whom I could commune, living amongst a community where I could not relate to the people.

From loneliness to love.
from joy to gratitude,
From pain to compassion,
And grief to understanding.

37
CHARLIE AND DAVID

I shudder still as I remember the years that followed.
I'm not sure how we survived and the children became reasonable
adults, but each of us found our own way of relating to each other.
Wilf became almost permanently catatonic.

The weeks in between treatment rolled into one another until most
of the time he lay listlessly staring out of the window as if the sight of
Legogote mountain was so far away he had to keep trying to see it.

We are not given a course in being parents. We become parents
overnight and we do the best we can to make correct decisions, depending
on our own life experiences and whatever we can find to read and relate
to on the subject.

I encouraged the children to share whatever they needed to with
Wilf. They would run into the room to show him their new shoes or
jump on the bed on return from nursery and sing him the latest song
they had learnt. I suppose the fact that they got no response may not
have worried them as much as it should because, in their experience
with him, this was the norm. I kept hoping that one day he'd give us a
surprise and respond.

I also believed we should keep the daily noise of life around him,
encouraging him and making him want to take part.

The empty blankness was agony for me.

I never knew how he felt or IF he felt. His platelet count became
permanently low, akin to leukaemia, except I knew it was artificially
brought on by the chemotherapy.

Where was this leading us? Was this all he could expect from his
life from here on?

JP had almost abandoned us.

As long as we were in White River, out of sight, no-one needed to
acknowledge what was going on. I called Dr Ray constantly, but as he

reminded me, we had no history of this drug to refer to and I had no practicing physician to help me make any of the decisions.

It was my habit to lie in the bath until the water grew cold. This was my think tank. This particular night I lay there until long after the bath water had run away and after assessing all the facts I had been able to research, I realized once again his life was in my hands, a terrifying thought but one I could not run away from. If we stopped the chemotherapy, his platelet count would rise and he'd have the energy to get up and perhaps take part in life around him. This might encourage the tumor to grow but it would give him some quality of life. If we didn't stop the chemo, his platelet level would cause his demise in the near future so the end result might be the same but along the way he could have some quality of life.

It was late at night.

I called Dr Ray. He was distant and cautious. He reserved his judgment "These are uncharted waters, Hilary" he said, "I can't advise you".

I called the Royal Marsden in London who gave me virtually the same answer and so I prayed to G-d, who I no longer believed in, to help me and guide me. When I had worked it all through in my mind, I turned over and drifted into a deep sleep.

In the morning I arose and I tried to tell him we were going to stop the pills,that I wanted him to feel better and swim and pick oranges in the garden again. He stared at me uncomprehendingly.

That day I upped the cortisone to cover the effects and I slowly withdrew the chemotherapy.

I found myself unconsciously praying as I walked around hoping I was doing the right thing. I annoyed myself in doing this. G-d had long forsaken me, why did I keep talking to him?

Guess I didn't know anyone else to lean on at that point.

Wlfred became less listless but it took me a few months to realize that his personality had changed irretrievably and he was very much in a world of his own. His obsessive compulsive behavior became heightened. This made life in the house very stressful and his management almost nigh impossible.

His day consisted of shaving, showering and dressing, and this took up most of the day. He would wrap his hair, which was long and wild, in plastic to start, and then commence the operation of dressing himself by tearing squares of loo paper and setting them out in readiness for shaving.

Eventually I came to realize that I had to leave him to it, but the process of coming to this realization was a period of angst and frustration for both the children and me.

Around this time I learnt that JP had once promised his English counterpart in the timber business that their sons would be welcome to come out to South Africa and learn the business.

No-one had thought to let them know that Wilfred was in no position to teach them anything. JP simply informed me that they would be arriving by the weekend. He still refused to face the reality.

I was aghast. I'd been going to the factory on a regular basis to assist with decisions that Wilfred would normally have made.

I sent Edward, our driver, to fetch them and two bouncy young lads got out of the car, excited at the prospect of living in the African Lowveld.

David was red-haired, freckled, with a wide and wicked grin. He had seventies boots with spurs on and immediately got out and picked Daniel up in his arms.

Charlie was less outgoing, a "lange lokshen", with long blonde hair and a cockney accent.

The girls were so excited at having visitors. Our social life had become non-existent .They ran forward, took his hand on either side and we went inside to sit on the stoep.

Fresh scones with our home grown strawberries arrived and I wondered what to say to them.

I tried to explain our situation. I took them to the room to meet Wilf. He barely looked at them and we returned to the stoep.

They looked at each other in horror.

If they returned to the UK, they would have to do military training

They definitely didn't fancy that.

We talked a long time and they begged me not to call their fathers and discuss it with them.

They would keep themselves busy, explore South Africa and learn what they could in the factory. When it was time to go back they would have benefited by their trip, they assured me in beseeching tones.

"I've got the rest of my life to learn the business", grumbled David. "I m gonna be in it forever ………."

I was torn between parental duty, wondering what their fathers would think and yet felt that, as they were my age, I should be in cahoots with them, should understand the situation.

I realized how lonely I was, how much fun I was having talking to them. I watched how much the kids were enjoying their attention.

I was 25 years old and it wasn't really my doing!

I allowed them to stay.

Life became bearable. We played squash every day.

They sat in the kids' Wendy house and were served tea and mulberries by the little misses. They gave Dan piggy rides and we walked down the path towards Legogote to the African stall that sold Mapani worms, a great delicacy in the Lowveld and eaten by the local Africans as food and notable as an aphrodisiac.

Charlie bet David he could eat them too and so began a daily exercise where we traipsed down the hill, with the kids on their bikes. They bought the Mopani worms and them tried to eat them but could not swallow.

The kids would shriek with laughter at them trying to down the dried worms with beer but neither managed to actually swallow a mouthful.

We were all three avid readers and we discussed books at great length.

I began to take more interest in the meals and we'd sit at the table and talk. Eventually they helped Wilf walk to the stoep and we made him a boerewors barbeque. He ate slowly, savouring each mouthful, and watched us intensely as if he were trying to remember who we were.

I began to hope I had done the right thing by withdrawing the chemotherapy.

One weekend we loaded up our station wagon and Charlie and David drove us into the Kruger National Park nearby.

One is not allowed to get out of the car once you are in the reserve. The threat of lions pouncing and elephants trampling you was real, but so were three little souls who wanted to pee at regular intervals, so we would have to keep stopping put the potty in the back. The intending *pisher* would perform and then one of us would have to open the back door while the others kept watch and empty the potty quickly.

This happened so often it took over the whole journey and David and Charlie told me it put them off having kids forever.

David and Charlie stayed the full six months. I never knew what their fathers thought they learnt but it was a great experience for all of us.

David continued to write me long detailed letters for many years after that and we always exchanged Christmas cards. Eventually, he sent us pictures of his marriage and to my great relief his first child, a gorgeous red haired freckled clone of David.

Financial survival was becoming more and more difficult. Wilf ceased to get an income from the factory and whenever I tried to take temporary work, he would make life at home for the servants so impossible that they would telephone me to come home on the threat of leaving him alone.

Tirza was experiencing extreme severe asthma; something that began in Port Elizabeth when we were away, and doctors told me she had to leave the Lowveld to improve. Even her beloved ballet became too much for her as she struggled to breathe day in and day out.

I was at a point where I couldn't bear the loneliness much longer. I knew that if I lived in a Jewish community I would have a better chance of integrating the children into schools and with friends. I was also facing the looming decision of Tikkele beginning school. In the Lowveld she would be schooled in Afrikaans. In Johannesburg she would be schooled in English—our home language. I'd be able to get help to look after Wilf and I'd be able to sell my art work from home on a market that I could be in touch with.

After a particularly bad month where Tirza was in and out of hospital needing oxygen, I resolved to pack up our lives and make a new start in Johannesburg.

At this time I experienced the death of someone close to me for the first time My beloved gynaecologist James had been accustomed to travel to Swaziland each month to attend to local obstetrics One evening obviously overtired from long hours of labor, he accidentally drove over the Piggs peak mountain on the steep road home. The telephone rang at 4 a.m in the morning and I rushed out to be with his wife and family. He was only in his early forties. My deep heartbreak was the last straw when one morning I awoke to find myself sitting bolt upright at the telephone calling his number in my sleep with tears pouring down my face! It had become too hard to remain in the Lowveld.

As you can imagine, this would mean relatives in Johannesburg and family and friends would all be confronted with what had really become of Wilfred.

An enraged JP threatened to cut us off without any support but I'd been managing knowing I could not rely on him for so long this didn't phase me.

I had a friend who was looking for a house-sitter for a few months in Johannesburg. She would let us stay in her house rent free.

I put on my armor, took up my sword and moved forward into battle.

We loaded the two cars, Edward the driver and I, with as much of our worldly goods as we could fit in, including Gingy the cat and Brady the Labrador. Gladys the nanny was to ride with the children and me. Wilf would ride with Edward as we drove in convoy to Johannesburg. As we were leaving, I gave one last look at my favourite windmill. It wound slowly round on its axle. It made me mindful of the fact that life takes its course and we have to go with the flow. Birth is a beginning and life a journey.........

The kids wept at leaving. They *needed* their Wendy house. They couldn't go with out it "That's where we LIVE ", TIrza told me. Alissa nodded very emphatically, holding Tikkie's hand and agreeing with her representation.

I promised faithfully that I would arrange for it to come to Johannesburg as soon as we were settled.

RALEIGH STREET SYNAGOGUE,
now a Museum
PORT ELIZABETH
SOUTH AFRICA

PART THREE
Scattered Lives,
Connecting the pieces

PART THREE
Contents

38.
CLUB SHULMAN

The value of property in Johannesburg was much higher than that in the Lowveld. Our six acres of farm land would not buy us much of a house there.

I had put an "X "on the map of where I wanted to live in Johannesburg because I wanted my children to go to the Rosebank School. In the 70s you had to live in a particular catchment area to attend a government school.

We drove around the area with Maureen and I laughed out loud at the house prices I saw.

As we turned the car to return home we saw a "For sale" sign on a house on show for the day.

"Just stop and let me have a peek inside" I entreated Maureen.

"OK", she said. "It's my cousin Rina's company and she is probably sitting on duty at the Show House today."

My eyes lit up as we entered the beautiful Herbert Baker house. I had always dreamed of an elegant curved staircase.It flowed down a mahogany bannister into a double height hallway. Hallways have always been important to me. They were the meeting and greeting place where first impressions took place. They gave you time to look your guest over and to warm to each other.

I was always particular about hallways. The rooms downstairs were airy and spacious. Elegant chandeliers prismed colourfully in the sunlight and large French doors onto the garden revealed an acre of smooth well-kept lawn. An Olympic sized pool was set beside the tennis court. One could certainly keep fit in there!

We wandered around the garden and there, to my astonishment, was a bowling green, surrounded by four garages. I laughed with delight at this beautiful house. "Only a princess should live here," I thought.

Satiated but reluctant to leave, I went inside to thank Rina for allowing us to look around.

She questioned me as to my household needs. I smiled as I told her I had sold my house for so little I couldn't possibly make an offer, but I wanted to satisfy my curiosity about living in a house such as this!

She looked at Maureen who had obviously had a word with her while I was out of the room.

"Hilary" she said "this is a deceased estate sale. The court wants it sold and you have twenty-four hours to make an offer!"

Then she lowered her voice and said, "I did NOT tell you this, yours will be the only offer that's been made."

Maureen's eyes said—"Do it".

She took my shaking hand, she guided me through the written contract.

I made an offer based on the price of my White River House and I signed my name in a state of whirling confusion.

I felt completely delirious as I walked out to the car. I could not even imagine it ever coming true. It was like taking a lottery ticket—something I never did.

Usually, for the small price of the ticket, one was free to dream.

I told no-one. I didn't want to get the kids' hopes up.

Wilf had no interest or idea that we needed to find a permanent home.

I lost weight—I lost sleep—I couldn't even read coherently, but I was determined not to even think about asking G -d for any favors.

I bided my time.

Six weeks later the court ruled to accept my offer.

The magnificent castle was all mine.

I collected my two little princesses and my sturdy prince, Gladys the nanny, Wilfred, Brady and Gingy, and I drove them to our new home.

My reward was a notable reaction from Wilfred. What a win!

He looked at the tennis court and bowling green and he smiled at me.

He never asked me how I had bought a house five times the price of our farm because he never had any responsible consciousness about any of these things.

Welcome to "Club Shulman", I said grandly as we got out. Brady barked and the children dashed off, looking into every room, slipping up and down the stairs.

The main bedroom had a little Romeo and Juliet balcony overlooking the pool and tennis court. No sooner had we moved in when the door bell rang. I opened it wondering who could know we were here, and there stood a most welcome sight. My new neighbour Penelope, with a plant in hand had come to offer an invitation to tea.

I had made the right decision. We were going to have a more normal life and I inadvertently thanked G-d, but then took it back again a few minutes later when I looked at Wilfred, staring into space as I tried to introduce Penny.

The children began school. Tirza attended Rosebank Primary, she was fast becoming an admirable ballerina. Alissa and Dan were at the local nursery.

Lissi was a sweet pretty child who made friends easily and soon I had mothers ringing to ask her round to play and I began to make some new friends.

One of the little girls who invited us for tea was the daughter of a journalist for the local newspaper. Lissi was later roped in to give her opinion of "Mom" on a mother's day article. I awoke one Sunday morning to be greeted with Lissi's picture in the Sunday Times reporting that her mother always burnt the rice! I couldn't even deny it.

Wilf became more active in a removed sort of way. He became physically more mobile and seemed stronger. I hoped a healing process had begun.

He kept his own counsel, his own programme, and lived a symbiotic life around us, but never with us.

At this point I had a major altercation with JP. As we could no longer afford a driver for Wilfred, I had to let Edward the driver return to White River. We were all very sad as he'd grown so fond of the children. Incredible as it sounds, JP went out and bought Wilf a car, despite the fact that Dr Rosen had told him Wilfred should never drive again.

Part of me now realizes he just could not come to terms with the permanence of Wilfred's condition, but at the time I felt he was endangering our children's lives and those of other children on the road.

I attempted to get doctors to speak to JP and tried to get the law to prevent Wilf driving. I came to understand that the only way to do this was to have Wilfred's mental capability assessed by a psychiatrist.

I wasn't ready for that yet.

So I resolved never to allow the children in the car with him and never to allow them to play in the front yard where he drove into the property. They seemed to accept this with their more than mature understanding of Wilfred's situation.

I lost count of the times he didn't stop before he reached our wonderful Doric columns at the entrance to our stoep. I kept having the front wall repaired. Our builder knew as soon as he heard my voice it was time to come and rebuild the front wall again.

Despite this fact, life still had its humorous side. I was never allowed to complain. The children in total faithfulness to their father would remind me about the one and only time I was extremely pre- menstrual, agitated and aggravated. I reversed out of the main gate hitting the gate post. Dan was standing at the back of the car and from this little man I heard "Oh Shit". I turned around to make sure he had said it and his eyes sparkled with the excitement of it all.

I had to laugh out loud. At least my son was expressive and at the time this seemed so much more important than appropriateness.I worried about the effect that his father was so non- communicating.

We settled into our castle well. It was the perfect house for birthday parties, On one occasion, we had an egg and spoon race on the bowling green where everyone cheated and held onto their eggs! They could ride their bikes, play hide and seek in a wide green space with trees to climb, and swim in the huge pool every day.

Alissa had a Hawaiian party one summer; everyone in grass skirts and flowers in their hair and all the excitement a birthday party creates, despite the fact that their father was a little strange He'd be there in person, but not really part of what was happening at any given time. As the Hawaiian birthday cake came out with candles he proceeded to get into the pool and swim up and down, oblivious to the fact that we were blowing out candles and singing happy birthday. But the children had learnt to live with his inappropriate actions, and barely noticed, although I felt sad at not being able to share the moment with him.

As the years passed, this pattern became more and more exacerbated.

One day I encourage Dan to play in the father and son soccer match with him.

We all piled into the car excitedly, and drove off to the match. Dan was captain of the under- 9s soccer team at the time and he was very intense about it all. I felt bad about Dan's anger and embarrassment when Wilf kicked a goal into the wrong side's posts near the end of the match. He walked off to change without a glance at anyone. This was my first realization that the process of growing up with a brain-damaged father was much harder for him than it was for the girls. Sometimes I couldn't decide what the correct thing to do was .Should I allow nature to take its course and just let the distance grow? Should I try to keep them in touch with him despite the lack of response and reaction time and again? I vacillated between the two wishing for a magic day when Wilf would be excited by something going on around him.

39
A DECADE OF CREATIVITY

Thereafter followed a period when I could not allow myself thinking time. Only survival counted.

I began to sell paintings for an international South African artist.

In the late 70s and early 80s, Johannesburg was a vibrant and growing business community. People had disposable income and this propped up the art market.

I had to make it my business to harness every possible sale in the new office blocks going up overnight.

Galleries opened on every street. The Goodman Gallery was at its peak, selling my paintings on a regular basis. A café society with cultural advantages to explore, expanded and gave rise to opportunity for evolving artists.

I needed to mix in this very artificial circle. While I didn't have the means to buy the outfits, thanks to gramps, I had the talent to make them. I went out there, dressed to kill—and I sold paintings.

On average, I sold a large painting a day, sometimes two.

Thomas, an international artist whose paintings I sold, began to depend on me more and more. This left him free to paint while I managed the business side of things.

He spent a lot of time in our home and grew close to Wilfred who liked having him there because he was prepared to play bowls or tennis with him whenever Wilf felt up to it.

Wilfred would have been a springbok rugby player had he not been crocked in the knee, but sport was his life. In his reduced state of mobility and concentration he was left as a mediocre player but still managed to work up a sweat and present as a reasonable opponent.

These weekly combats were Wilf 's saving grace because Thomas was a lousy sportsman, but he made a big issue out of trying to beat

Wilf, sometimes allowing him to win, and this would please Wilfred immensely.

Thomas was very generous in helping me to look after my family. About four times a year he asked me to go to Zurich to organize his exhibitions.

During this time the "patron saint of husband-less-mothers" came to the fore in our lives in the form of Audrey and Ellen.

My friend Audrey had left her husband in White River about the same time that we had come to Johannesburg. She had brought her three small children, who were the same age as mine, to live with her mother Ellen, whom we all called "Gaga."

At these times Thomas allowed me to hire Audrey and her mother Ellen to come and baby-sit Wilfred and our children to enable me to travel with confidence to Switzerland, knowing they were superbly cared for as Audrey was a highly trained nursing sister. This was a good income for them and an opportunity for me to see the European world of art. Thomas was very generous in paying me for my trips and matched whatever I made in Europe, which went into his Swiss bank account, to an amount which he paid me in South Africa.

Considering the exchange rate, this allowed me to pay our mortgage and costs for at least six months at a time. In addition, it meant I didn't have to work every day of the week. I was free to fetch and carry my children, look after Wilfred and, at the same time, learn the ropes of international art dealing.

Because I already had had to survive the trauma of leaving my children, I was better prepared for these absences than I might have been without the previous trip to London with Wilf, but it never took away the constant nervousness and ache I had of being separated from them.

Thomas allowed me to call them every day and I existed from call to call.

Nearly two decades later, as I sit here now in the 'plane flying back to London from Lithuania, I realize that this was the origin of my now daily and neurotic calls to my children. The habit has remained and must have been established them. I wonder if perhaps one day when they have their own children, they will begin to understand?

Every day I talked to each one separately. Each day I heard Audrey and Ellen tell me I was a saint to survive Wilfred's habits ....

After one of the evening calls, I realized Audrey had not put Daniel on the telephone for two days.

I called back and said "I didn't speak to Dan, what's cooking?"

She admitted he had a bad dose of measles and had elected not to worry me.

I was on the next 'plane home filled with anxiety, traumatized at the long haul home. My babies needed me. I needed them.

Needless to say, by the time I got back to Johannesburg, the crisis was almost over and I had to sit and watch the concert all six kids had rehearsed as they always did for my home-coming.

Dan was always the cowboy and Donty was always the crook. Tishy was the funny part of the show and dearest Nix always oversaw the production and kept everyone in control. It was so amusing to watch their endeavors that tired as I was from traveling through the night, it always gave me pleasure.

We considered Audrey's kids almost as our cousins. We supported each other as family as we didn't seem to have many cousins around.

Socially, people were wary of inviting me round with Wilf. He wasn't always appropriately behaved and there were times when I went on my own as an easy solution.

I always felt out of place and people treated me as if I was a peculiarity.

I made a lot of money during this period. I was very successful but the hours were long and hard and I was working without fulfilling any creative ability of my own. This was rusting my soul.

Wilf was stable, slow and kind of blocked. He just lived through everything at a simple separated pace of his own.

For me, his management remained very complex. He'd often fall out of bed. He'd wake up at four in the morning and wake the children for school. I'd scream with frustration "It's only four in the morning." He'd look at me in confusion and then get back into bed and I'd have to put everyone to sleep all over again. By the time I got to lie down it was time to get up!

He would not allow the house maids to do anything for him and as soon as I left the house he became quite unmanageable, letting the bath water run over, burning things and eventually, each time I was out for any length of time, I'd inevitably get a call from the maid saying "Please come home, we can't cope". With the help of therapy, I understood that this was Wilf's way of holding on to me.

One day, after another long lie-in bath, my body said NO MORE. I physically just could not do the extended hours any longer.

I longed to be creative and expressive in my own right, to find some satisfaction in my daily life.

I applied to a ceramic college to become a ceramist. Clay had always been my first love. My portfolio was accepted but I did not have my own kiln – a prerequisite of entering the course!

A few weeks earlier I'd seen an advert in The Times for a Lingerie Designer. I dug it out of my archive where I stored bits of paper, and I answered the ad. It was for a company that sold naughty underwear! Repulsive work, but I resolved that if I did a giant commission for a giant fee, I'd be able to buy my kiln and we'd all be better off forever.

I spent six grinding weeks designing panties with zips and fluff in every conceivable combination. Sometimes I would laugh to myself, thinking this is all just a means to an end.

Triumphantly, I handed the completed job over. I collected my cheque and rushed off to purchase my first ceramic kiln. I'd spent every night looking at catalogues and I knew exactly what I wanted.

Thereafter, I took a year off life.

I remained in my pyjamas most days. I taught myself ceramics by experimenting with my kiln, and firing at night when the family were asleep.

The advantage of teaching myself was that I came up with a unique production that was entirely my own, although not without many ruinous experiments along the way!

In the early days in White River, I had been preparing an avocado one night, when to my horror the knife slipped and I sliced the tendon between my thumb and finger on the right hand.

This left me without full use of my hand. I was four months pregnant with Tirza and therefore I could not have surgery, and neglected to have it thereafter. There never seemed a time when I could have surgery with all my single responsibilities.

So here I was, a one-handed potter, making slightly crooked porcelain pieces which people loved.

I became known. My work sold in galleries. Many buyers came to my studio. We began to survive.

But the children were growing up. Their expenses were increasing. They needed sports equipment and holidays, shoes and clothes, and I realized I was always just short of providing what we needed.

I determined that we might be able to subdivide this wonderful property and set about going through the civic motions.

Two harrowing years and twenty thousand Rand down the line, we became the first property to gain subdivision rights in Fourteenth Avenue, Houghton.

I searched for a building company that would fit my budget but eventually had to admit to myself that an architect was out of the question.

I decided it couldn't be that different to making a clothing pattern, so I drew the house I wanted to build on my subdivision. Once that was built, I would sell our wonderful castle and we'd become kings of a smaller and more practical castle, where my teenagers would be more secure and more independent.

I took my drawing to a builder who was building standard houses to a simple design. He was quite open to my suggestion and together we decided we could make this budget house where I would hand-make all the basins, tiles and murals in the bathrooms. He would get the plans passed and he advised me that it would take him six weeks to build with a complete team on site.

It was exactly six weeks to my 35th birthday.

I invited my friends to a party around my new pool, in my new house. Everyone winked, thinking "she's hallucinating."

Each morning I stood on the Romeo and Juliet balcony of my current bedroom facing the subdivision, shouting encouragement to the builders. I made sure they had chocolate biscuits for tea every afternoon. We worked Saturdays and Sundays.

I did any unskilled labor I was capable of, and, in exactly six weeks my new house was completed. The bathroom boasted black and red ceramic tiles, a jaccuzzi surrounded by a ceramic tree in vibrant red oxide glaze with moulded blossoms standing away from the wall as if waiting to be picked. A water feature in the garden and an eat-in kitchen, tiled in terracotta completed the living area. Large sliding doors opened onto the garden. This was where the former large old Olympic sized pool had stood. We had filled it in with builders' rubble and built a smaller, more modern pool complete with drawings that Tirza , Alissa and Dan had done onto tiles. These hand drawn tiles were incorporated into the sides of the pool.

On my birthday, friends called to ask where they should meet for the celebration.

"At my pool" I replied. No-one believed me—but there it was!

We ate the boerewors, a South African delicacy and we swam in the cool blue pool.

The garden was an extension of my old garden, so it was already established "Bob's your Uncle!"—I had a wonderful new state of the art home.

I'd managed to sell the big house and tomorrow morning we would move all our clothes and possessions across the lawn and settle in.

Champagne glasses were raised.

«Hilary, you are something else!» they all admitted.

40

THE INVADERS

Crime was at its height in South Africa at this time.

After a burglary one felt soiled, your personal space had been trashed by some unknown stranger and it gave you a feeling of revulsion and rejection towards your formerly special space.

By this time, after several burglaries, I kept my small 2.2 Astra, the little gun I'd been trained to use in White River, next to my bed. Our home also had electrified fencing, and an armed response company patrolling the area twenty-four hours a day. This was the norm.

One Saturday morning I decided we badly needed a new lawnmower and as I returned to the house with my purchase, I turned into our driveway and paused at the electric gate. It took all of one minute to grind its way open. As I opened my window to push the control inside my car, four youths leapt out of the shadowy foliage of the tree growing just outside our gate. One held a knife to my throat through the open window and rasped, "Take us inside or you're dead," while the others dashed inside the gate and up the garden.

My sweet and thoughtful Alissa had come running to the door to help me carry the lawnmower when she saw the intruders. She doubled back to the bedroom to push the alarm button, only to be pursued by one of the burglars who shoved her onto the floor and proceeded to hold the knife at her throat.

I heard her shouting "Don't kill me, don't kill me!"

I ran, mad with trepidation, down the passage pursued by the other three and, unthinking, was about to grab him when he raised his knife away from her face and allowed her to stand up. They herded us together and into the bathroom. Alissa was pale and shocked. By now, they had rounded up my sister who was on a rare visit from Cape Town and my niece, who had been asleep and was therefore not fully attired. We were terrified of her vulnerable position, as rape in burglary was very common.

Lizzie, the trusty old maid, was also wrenched into the room where she was roughly shoved into the bath with us.

They instructed us to switch on the hot water tap and stand in the bath, obviously trying to intimidate us further.

These youths could not have been older than sixteen or seventeen. They were very nervous, with the knives wavering shakily in their hands. They kept asking "Where is the boy?" I said, very emphatically, "THERE IS NO BOY. You can see,there is no boy".

I was petrified of Daniel coming out of his cottage in the garden. They would have felt threatened by him and hurt him.

This alerted me to the fact that this was not some random burglary but one where they knew who lived here.

Had they been watching us?

Perhaps I handled all this without any noticeable trauma present because I was completely and emotionally drained after spending the week with Wilfred who had just had a devastating stroke. I felt psychologically blank and afterwards I could not recall their faces or anything about them at all.

Waggling the knife in my face, they asked "Where's the money? Where's the money?"

While I tried to keep my cool and explain that we didn't keep money at home, I was astonished to hear Lizzie chipping in with "the jewelry is in that cupboard", pointing to the bathroom cupboard where she knew I kept my jewelry roll, filled with bits of heirlooms from my mother and grandmother. I was a bit taken aback but absolutely rigid with fear as I knew my gun had been carelessly stuck into the towels inside the cupboard earlier that morning before I went out. Who knew how they would react with a weapon in their hands?

I can only say this was the one time, my wholesale untidiness saved our lives.

They pulled open the cupboard and spotted the jewelry roll, which they grabbed and put it in a pillowcase they had emptied. Taken aback at the sight of bathroom lotions, sanitary pads, cotton wool, tissues and boxes of pills—all manner of stuff one collects in one's bathroom—unceremoniously stuffed into the cupboard in a mangled jumble, they closed the door and moved on. I thanked G-d silently. What were a few precious jewels in the face of this adversity?

They were becoming more jittery and didn't really know what to do with us.

Lizzie was murmuring soft words of calm and I tried to cover my niece with towels. They pushed and shoved us down the passage and into the next bedroom. Here they proceeded to tear clothing and tie our hands behind our back, while the other two guarded us threateningly. Then they shoved us unceremoniously into an empty cupboard, all elbows and shoulders, bent and squashed into each other. We heard the burglars pushing beds and heavy drawers up against the cupboard.

We remained silent, holding onto each other, listening to the sounds of them shouting from room to room while methodically dragging our worldly belongings out of the cupboards. They seemed unhurried as we heard them laughing and discussing the goods in South Sotho, their African language. We kept silent lest we annoyed the young men. We calmed each other quietly, as if unaware of our spatial disadvantage. I prayed with all my heart that Dan would not hear them and come into the house.

After what seemed like an eternity, but turned out to be two hours, we heard my car being started. Of course! My keys were still in the ignition. This was followed by a long empty silence. We waited a while to be sure there was no one there. I wiggled and turned so that Lizzie could try to loosen my ties in this limited space where we could not really move a limb. My knees began to tremble.

Then we leaned all our weight on the doors and heaved, to try to move the furniture away. As it slipped forward, we fell out of the doors, feeling awkward and disorientated. Dan came bursting into the room shouting "Oh my G-d—Jeez—what's going on?" He began to shake with rage and fear. He grabbed us and helped my sister out of the cupboard.

I was so stiff I couldn't move. We needed to rub each others' arms and hands. We moved stealthily out into the hall and there, in total disarray, lay all our worldly goods—well those they had left behind—scattered over the floor and lying ragged over the garden, leading to the glaringly open gate!

We hugged each other in thankfulness. We were unharmed.

My sister swore never EVER to come to Johannesburg again!

The reason for her visit had been to dance in a festival that night at the city hall and to her broken-hearted consternation, they had stolen their costumes and her antique flute. She wept in anger and traumatized disbelief.

Lizzie tried to calm us down. She made tea while we wandered aimlessly around picking our way through the debris, discovering moment by moment, some other treasure we had been relieved of.

We called the Flying Squad and sat down to wait for them. It seemed we were each in an unreal trance. How could we make sense of it all?

41
MAKING SENSE OF IT ALL

Tirza had left for synagogue very early on this morning. On her return she turned into our street, and she slowed down at the gate. To her astonishment she was suddenly surrounded by police cars screaming to a halt with flashing lights and sirens all trying to turn into our driveway as well.

She panicked—parked her car and ran inside shouting "What's wrong? What's wrong?"

As she came through the gate, her jaw dropped at the sight of the household debris shredded across the lawn. She noted our shaky expressions and she knew.

They'd got us again!

We all spoke at once. We tried to make sense of it all. Dan was most upset as he felt he should have come out to wrestle with them,but I was so grateful he'd not come out sooner as one young man against those four scoundrels of no morals, would have been too terrible to contemplate.

As we went over the facts, Daniel remembered seeing four youths sitting on the pavement a few days in a row. At the time he'd felt them watching him turn into the driveway. So—they had been casing the joint!

Trying to get the facts straight, Tirza asked why Lizzie had told them where the jewelry was kept?

Yes, we'd all wondered at that. Was she trying to distract them giving them something worthwhile to keep them from hurting us?

It was common knowledge at the time that intruders sometimes used the domestic worker to get information threatening them with dire consequences if they did not co-operate. Lizzie had remained remarkably calm throughout, but everyday life in Soweto was filled with violent robbery so perhaps she was not as frightened as we were. We also acknowledged that to us, they were black intruders, people we did not come close to very often. Foreign, unknown and disturbing. To her, they might have been naughty young black teenagers from her own familiar location.

Questions filled my mind, but I was thoroughly reproached by all three children. "Ma, how can you even think she was involved, she's so loyal".

"People are people," I said. "We're all vulnerable."

As we were talking, I developed a cold chill down my spine. I walked quickly towards the dining room, thinking "PLEASE no—please no, not my Lithuanian brass Samovar." I pushed open the door, held my breath and then I saw it, standing tall at its usual post atop the liquor cabinet. It looked unpolished and unloved. They probably didn't know what it was. I ran to pick it up, hugged it like a baby and resolved to hide it away in future.

On the following Saturday morning, at exactly 11.37 a.m. Lizzie brought out a tray of tea. "What's this for?" we asked.

"We are all going to remember last Saturday" she said, trying to be cheery, "and then attempt to find out if all five of us can get back into the cupboard." We had to hand it to her! When we stood in front of the cupboard we could not believe we'd all fitted into it.

The next few weeks were spent finding what we had lost.

It rained. I found I had no raincoat, nor did I have my leather coat or my fur coat, purchased when I sold my first piece of ceramic art. Alissa's favorite Nikes, Dan's racing bike, all our electrical goods, as well as the strangest things; treasures which I had accumulated for twenty years, my collection of crystal glasses, our silver water jug and the silver tray Uncle Albert had given me as a wedding gift. Many things were irreplaceable. Dan joked that they obviously "had no taste in the arts," as they had not stolen any of my own art work, exhibited all over the house. My heart was so heavy, I couldn't even raise a laugh.

Jewelry which Wilfred had bought me had been stolen. A coral and cultured pearl necklace which my father had commissioned for me was missing—forever lost. A pendant my mother-in-law had given me with eleven diamonds and a ruby on it. One could not replace these things because their intrinsic value to me was encapsulated by the person who had given them to me.

I became an insomniac. I couldn't sleep at night, despite the fact that we invested in Oscar the Doberman. We had a dog trainer teaching him how to guard each of us and the property. I'd never been a "dog person" but I grew to accept that Oscar liked sleeping on the electric hot blanket of my bed as much as I did and I compromised. It made me feel secure.

We wasted weeks of good time where we had to list goods, meet insurance brokers and police officers investigating. All this was in vain as they never caught anyone, although my car was found burnt out in the grounds of a school in Soweto. It made us re- assess our values.

We kept going back to the fact that we were not harmed and they were only *things*. These were inanimate objects that were mostly of decorative and surplus value.

We could live without them and maybe this was an indication that the time had come to dis-invest ourselves of goods and make a new simple life for ourselves, in a country where we might own nothing, but we could close both eyes when we slept at night.

Alissa decided to go off to London on a two year working holiday. I was anxious at the thought of her being so far away but, on the other hand, relieved she would get away from the memory of this very traumatic event.

In her usual loving way, she put all her thoughts at leaving home into a little sunflower drawing she produced, which she left for me to find after she had gone.

My days of being a full time mother were drawing to a close. The chickens were hatching out and I had to take stock of my own life! Perhaps we would have to face the answer to the question we had debated at many family dinners.

Was it time to leave our South African roots and re-invent ourselves?

What kind of life did we envisage in the future?

42
WILFRED

The years had passed quickly. Tirza , Alissa and Dan were now almost grown up, in chronological age, that is. As decision-makers, they had become mature and responsible. Despite this fact, as a mother I had to keep reminding myself to acknowledge this.

Each had developed into a really well-rounded strong person with their own views on the world and a tremendous loyalty to each other. The headmaster at school told me that he had rarely seen the likes of such family bonding, but I guess when you had to learn to deal with the emotional hardships that my children had faced in understanding their father's limitations, and our family difficulties with his parents, it was natural that you would develop a mature attitude earlier and find ways to cope.

Each family finds the norm to their own peculiarities and we were no different in this regard.

I considered it a priority that, as the mother of these three children, I had to endeavor to make their lives as near to normal as possible, despite having a non-functional father.

In so many ways, consciously and unconsciously, I tried to be a mother and father, but more than that, I tried to be true to myself, and who I was, and to incorporate all this into my mothering plan. They regarded me as funky, whatever that may mean.....I hoped I was open minded! It was at this time I realized I had begun to suffer from what is known as "anticipatory grief".

I was afraid of so many things, of unexpected problems cropping up and fear that I would not know how to handle them, or have the financial means to do what had to be done. I kept going through a process of mourning and grief before things happened, almost as if I was rehearsing so that when the time came I would cope. I prepared myself for any eventuality long before it happened, or didn't! This pattern was to last for the rest of my life and became a limiting factor for me in so many areas of endeavor. I learned to deal with my fears through therapy but became a frightened person with many neuroses that I hid quite well outwardly, unless you knew me well, as my children did, but, in the dark of the night, I suffered bitterly.

I endeavored to carry on with our daily family activities. I watched cricket and netball and I went to every soccer match. Dan was the captain of the soccer team and played exceptionally well. I was always relieved to come home knowing I had controlled myself in the stands and not yelled "Don't push him"at the opposition!!

Within myself, I had an inexplicable concern that being alone with me on Shabbat evening at the supper table was not special for the children. I always made a point of inviting people round to join us. The table was filled with interesting friends and entertaining people and often guests who had nowhere to go themselves. It covered the missing conversation between Wilfred and the family. If he joined us, he concentrated on his food, concerned with cutting his vegetables and spooning them into his mouth, oblivious of the surrounding chatter, or social niceties. Wilfred had relatives in town, but they never came to spend any time with him,and no-one really gave us any support in terms of helping to look after Wilf , except Thomas.

In the years to come, when Tirza grew up and entertained relentlessly in her own home, as if it was the normal thing to do, I wondered if my plan had backfired somewhat, but nevertheless, during these teenage years we had a full and noisy household, always filled with young people, who knew they were welcome. I was called *Mom* by many and I recall quite a few nights when I sat with troubled youngsters listening to their difficulties which they felt they could not discuss with their parents.

While the kids were at university, we received a notification that White River was intending to honor Wilfred for his contribution to the development of the town of White River by naming a street after him.

It came to my notice that JP had responded to the letter and accepted the honor, and so the street came to be called after JP.

I was filled with rage at this, knowing it was Wilfred's sacrifice, his hard work, his vision and his kind *tzedakah* – charity—that was to be lauded. In conversation with White River officials, they acknowledged it was intended to be for Wilfred. Perhaps my father–in law was embarrassed at Wilfred's condition and so chose to publicly accept the honor himself.

I gave him the benefit of the doubt, but I insisted the street was to be in Wilfred's name.

When the time came to go to White River, I urged JP to purchase air tickets and not to drive as he intended to do.

He and Wilfred set out together and Shulman Street was ceremoniously named.

JP returned to Port Elizabeth, leaving Wilfred in White River with his former managers for a few days. I was concerned about this.I felt he needed supervision when out of his normal environment, as he often became confused. On the day he was due to fly back to Johannesburg I called White River.

Unable to connect with him, I called the factory, only to be told that Wilfred had lost his air ticket and decided to DRIVE HIMSELF home—a five hour car journey!

I returned to the TV room where the children were sitting and explained the situation. We all looked at each other dumbfounded!

How could the factory manager have let him hire a car, and drive all that way home when he might not find the route or stay awake?

I tried to calm them down, but I felt rising panic within myself.

We tried to keep busy. We ate. We watched TV, mostly in solid silence each one coping with their thoughts and analyzing their own knowledge of his capabilities.

The ringing of the telephone seemed unreasonably loud. Each jangling tone made us jump, only to find it was a social call.

Darkness fell.

We moved out to the stoep, eager to see the light of the car as he turned into the gateway.

We waited.

Time stood still.

We prayed.

About ten hours after he had left White River we called the traffic patrols. No accidents reported on this route. Perhaps he had stopped for the night and forgotten to let us know.

We called each hotel along the way. Brits—no. Ogies—no. Witbank – no, Holiday Inn – no-one by that name.

It was the same problem I had faced for over twenty years. No-one close to him would acknowledge that he needed help in decision making.

They all found it too hard to confront him with the truth. More so his co-workers, who still regarded him as The Boss. In view of this, they allowed him to drive himself home, aware he was not supposed to handle a car, and certainly not on this long and treacherous road, which had now turned dark.

The police would not go out and look for him because he was not a missing person. He'd never mastered modern technology and did not have a mobile telephone.

Finally, at midnight, Dan picked up his keys. I said hysterically "where are YOU going?"

He said "Ma I can't just SIT here, he may be stuck somewhere, he may be hurt. I have to go and look for him".

"Dan", I said, "promise me you will drive slowly. Take my gun for protection, and call every half hour".

"Yeah", he said, although I knew he was apprehensive. "I'll be fine".

I had no choice but to let him go. The girls and I huddled together. He began by scouring all the roads leading into Johannesburg and Pretoria.

Two hours passed and he had found nothing. He kept going. He called us periodically to keep in touch.

He turned onto the highway and drove along cautiously, looking at both sides and trying to see into the dark open spaces beyond.

We sat at home quietly, not speaking, just hoping that both of them would be safe.

At three o clock he called. "Ma" he said quietly, "I've found him!"

"Is he alive?" I asked.

"Yes, I found him off the road, parked in a *donga,* a ditch. He was asleep at the wheel and the front of the car is battered, so he could have hit something, but the side of the car is also badly dented, so who knows what could have happened!

"He does not remember anything and says he lost his way!"

"Leave the other car there Dan, and bring him home. Well done, my darling I'm very proud of you," I said, my heart in my mouth. "Can you get him into your car?"

"Yes," he said, "I'll help him over. He seems very far away, almost dreamy."

"Let him sit in the back and sleep and drive home carefully, Daniel."

I regretted letting Dan go alone, he'd only recently got his driving license, but thank G-d Wilfred was not hurt, as far as we knew.

Two hours later the driveway lit up and we ran to the car. Daniel looked ashen with exhaustion and Wilfred looked frail and shaky. He seemed not to acknowledge our presence.

We had to haul him out of the car and drag him into the house, half carrying him, half lifting him as much as we could.

I led him to his bed and he passively allowed me to undress him without a word.

I could see no obvious injury, but I knew he was not himself.

In the morning he was no better and towards lunch time I called a doctor to check him out. After a long examination, he closed the bedroom door quietly and came to sit with us.

"It looks like he has had a slight stroke", he said sadly. "This could have been due to a bump, or it could be what caused him to go off the road. We do not know which came first. We will watch him for 24 hours and possibly admit him to check head injuries."

We were shocked at this new disadvantage. I felt very angry that JP had not stayed with him until he was safely home. He, of all people, had the most difficulty in confronting Wilfred's condition and elected to continue pretending that he was still able to look after himself.

I called the rental hire and asked them to collect the car.

I didn't trust myself to speak to JP.

By the next day he had had a second stroke and we knew he was in trouble.

He never really improved from there. His concentration became very hazy and he needed constant care.

A year down the line, we were becoming concerned about Wilf's state of health. All the years of drugs had taken their toll and as one of the side-effects he seemed to be developing Parkinson's disease. We had hired full time carers and I spent many hours wondering how I could find a way to access his emotions and thoughts. It almost seemed as if he didn't have any. The emptiness of his expressions irked me.

For some years I had been trained as a hospice counselor. I was used in the capacity of advising brain tumor families. I discussed with them how to adapt their daily lives, and I supported the partner of the patient in any way I could.

I found it rewarding—perhaps I found it distracting. I was able to communicate with other people in this situation in a way I could not reach Wilfred.

In the meantime life at No, 3A was hectic.

We tried to maintain some semblance of normality. We were all extremely nervous coming into the house after the burglary and I forced the children (who gave me much *flak*) to call as they were approaching the house so that Oscar the Doberman could be at the gate. We tried to forget the things we'd lost to Soweto. I did not replace any of the goods with the substantial bank cheque we received from insurance. I paid it all towards our mortgage, still maintaining the thought in the back of my mind that we might choose to leave this country someday soon.

The new house was a marvelous home for entertaining, the eat-in kitchen and the large covered patio off the pool were ideal for Tirza's twenty-first birthday, for pool parties, and late night suppers. We sat many a night discussing the state of the world around our tiled kitchen table. Each of the children was passing through undergraduate courses at tertiary education institutes and making their way towards post graduate degrees.

They worked hard and led very busy lives. Naturally, as with all well-balanced teenagers, this did not leave much time for the parents.

In this case, although they tried to spend time with Wilf, it wasn't always easy to arrange. He had disappeared into his own protected world over the years. We had learned to get on with our daily lives as far as we could although I called home incessantly to ensure I was not needed.

By now he was having small regular strokes, and had lost his ability to speak properly. This was very distressing for all of us.

We felt we could no longer reach him or exchange much in the way of any communication with him. As he deteriorated, he needed 24 hour monitoring and I could not lift him alone.

He was looked after by two amazing loving and dedicated ladies who treated him with such kindness and understanding that I will love them forever.

After a series of setbacks, he could no longer move himself and seemed to be encapsulated in a world of his own.

It broke my heart and I found it so hard to accept that I would never ever be able to communicate with him and know his thoughts on our children, events in the family, or actions taken by the Shulman family on his behalf. He had never been a particularly garrulous communicator, but I felt I was the one person who had lived with him as a confidant, and as an adult. When we were first married we talked a lot about his family relationships and I know how he felt about so many private things in his life. I believed I was the only person who really knew what his personal attitudes were.

One morning Rebecca, his carer, called me to say "Hilary, he wants to tell you something but we can't work out what it is. He keeps pointing to the phone asking us to call you and saying your name".

I hurried over and I took his hand. I looked into his eyes and I tried so, patiently to encourage him.

"Tell me what it is, Wilf. Try to tell me.......... Take your time and I will help you."

"Hil -ll lary, Hill- Hillary", he just kept trying.

Sadly I'll never know, because shortly after that afternoon, he had a massive stroke and died. Just before he died he asked for a piece of paper and in his shaky, stroke-hampered hand, he wrote "Daniel", and his brother Barry's name!

Even in his faraway state, he was concerned for his son. This made me wonder how much he had really understood over the years. How lonely it must have been, locked inside himself, unable to speak and yet, having thoughts he needed to share. I knew in my heart he must be so angry at some of the things that his family had done in his name. Things that were contrary to his nature and his beliefs as I knew him.

The children and I were stunned.

After all these years of coming close to death and then rallying so often, we'd become conditioned to him surviving the crisis each time.

He had lived 26 years beyond the physicians' expectations.

A psychologist friend once told me how he watched Wilf communicating. He maintained that when I came into a room his eyes followed me everywhere and one could not distract him in order to connect with him until I had left the room. This man was of the opinion that he understood when we spoke to him even though he was not able to respond.

Over the last few months I had seen the look he gave me when Rebbeca had to wash out his mouth or move him around or take him to the toilet. The eyes said "I can't bear this" and those last few months I hated the way he had to live, maybe as much as he did.

His death was a great sadness to all of us. We finally had to acknowledge the wasted life span of a formally handsome vigorous young man who had only just reached the successes he had worked so hard to achieve when he was struck down with this bad luck. My children remain a tribute to his kind nature and his genes.

To my surprise, the strongest feeling I felt for months afterwards was a kind of deep and concluded peace. It overwhelmed me and I became a different person. I still worried every day out of habit. I still went to the phone, and then remembered….. Inside my head I never knew how much the terrible state that he had to live in had affected me all these years. I only came to acknowledge this after extended psychotherapy. My tool for coping was to shut off my feelings about him completely. For twenty-six years, I made it my focus to forge forcefully forward with practical things. I never allowed myself the time to mourn the loss of our relationship, or to present the appearance of being needy. It was not my nature. I didn't know how to be sad at what happened to my tall dark lover with smiley turquoise eyes.

To feel at peace with myself was unusual. I appreciated the calm that had come over me. I seemed almost tranquil—as windless as a sailboat floating on a glass lake. I lay on my bed for many days looking out at the blue sky and the Jacaranda trees and thinking about *"where to"* from here?

43
MEMORIES .

I remember warming my hands on the mug of tea, musing at how a totally non-beverage person had been converted to an inveterate tea drinker by this fascinating nation of time-wasting tea drinkers.

My cup of cha was only Rooibos Tea, considered by the Brits as a token tea, but perhaps my concession held the taste of home, wherever that was for me now.

I sat at my desk, glancing out at the wan grey sky.

I delighted in the wispy white snow, capping the top of every branch like an iced doughnut.

As an artist I always subconsciously took note of where the light was coming from. With the snow on the trees, along the roof and on the top of dustbin lids, the white was a total contrast to the red brick house in which we lived. This made it easy to identify the contrast of light and dark from where I sat. I doodled on the envelope lying on my desk. Roof triangles amidst elongated skeleton trees.

I had parked here at my desk through the prolonged night, and now it was morning. I was finally reaching a point of cohesive expression.

For days my mind had been racing with images I couldn't bear to remember. My heart filled with trepidation and fearfulness.

I'd call my thirty-year-old children at work to ensure they had arrived safely.

The wry answer would be, "why wouldn't we?"

How could they know?

I was shaky and weepy. I panicked at the door bell and I ate box after box of chocolates.

I was sleepless in Edgware.

My mind hopped back and forth to images of forgotten places, terrifying events, my first visit to London when I lost Wilfred in Oxford Street and had to mobilize the London Bobbies to help me find him wandering mindlessly around Bond Street.

I had e-mailed the first tentative pages of the story to my kids.

I was attempting to write our story, unconsciously wanting to feel their reaction to a story we all knew so well.

They had all e-mailed back. That was a first!

"Why are you doing this?" was the thrice asked question.

"Is it to make your million?" asked my son.

"Are you trying to come to terms?" inquired my psychologist daughter.

"Not only did I have to live it, you now want me to read it!" commented my eldest daughter

Yes to all of these and more.

Through my long forgotten trauma I, too, was wrangling with these thoughts. In the wee hours of the night I had thought I had dealt with it all, that I was done. I thought I had packed up and left it behind. But a year after arriving in Britain, while I was sitting in a class of hopeful Booker prize winners, I realized it was not possible to write this story in the third person, or to make it move over there to the distance, to give it to some other voice to act out, because I realized I had not yet acted it out myself. Was my intention honorable? Was it fair to tell this story? Or was it vengeance I sought?

I agonized that this was MY LIFE. It had a value. I wanted my grandchildren and great grandchildren to hear the facts—to understand. To appreciate how valuable it was to document all this, and not lose it in the generations, as we had lost our geographical validity and forbears.

I wanted my own children to understand how it had all evolved. I hoped my grandchildren would be privileged to live their whole lives in the country of their birth

I yearned to know that they would not have to go through the agony of annual foreign applications to remain on in the U.K .or elsewhere. I did not want them to be plagued by the nightly terror of your passport being refused, because the government had been voted out and the new leaders had moved the goal posts. This could happen despite having fulfilled all the original criteria you came into the country with, and despite paying taxes, stringently obeying all the laws, you could still fall short of the qualifying pointers demanded by the home office..No thought to your family being split up, or your talents being used would come into consideration. There was no one you could appeal to except to make a gross journey to stand at Lunar House, better known as" Looney House" from 5 a.m. in the morning. Standing out in the dark cold queue you would be confronted by harsh immigration officers who only worked to a formula and had no opportunity to view you as a human being .

I feared my descendants having to pack up and find another parking place for their lives. My children were too young to remember most of our story. How different their lives might have been had I been an ordinary stay- at- home mother as opposed to funky and fortune hunting!(to quote Alissa).

They'd wished for a traditional Mom, often reminding me not to arrive at school covered in clay. Most of the time, I barely noticed my attire.

I had so often wished for an ordinary life. I envied ordinary people. I still do. Perhaps I lament of it all too often when I hear TIrza my eldest snap "You've been trying for 30 years and you're still nutty so give up and just be A Nut!"

Today, while still sitting at my desk, my South African passport arrived at the door stamped with my permission to remain in Britain indefinitely.

I very nearly kissed the postman. The four required years of anxiety, of uncertainty, were over. My alien status was a thing of the past, a discomfort to be forgotten, to be written into my journey. I swore my allegiance to Queen Elizabeth II with solid sincerity.

Birth is a beginning, and life a journey.

I celebrated with a cup of English breakfast tea, and a cream scone.

Four years ago I arrived at Heathrow Airport penniless. I had checked in through Customs, as was required.

I then determined it would be wise to return home to have a hysterectomy, which would simplify the safety of my estrogen needs. I did not feel confident at the idea of having a major operation in a foreign country yet.

Once again I ignored medical advice out of necessity. Immediately after the surgery, I packed up the house telling myself I had no other option. I was to pay dearly for this unwise obstinacy in my medical future.

Returning weeks later, as I left the house with my suitcases in hand, the sale of my house fell through.

To access my special visa as an artist & writer I had to be back in the UK by morning.

There was no going back.

I locked the door and rode out to the airport. My dear friends Heather and Roger stuffed my oversized luggage into all the crevices of their car, complaining bitterly at the weight of my possessions.

I closed the door to my former life and I didn't allow myself any questions.

44
An Immigrant in London

I couldn't afford bus fare so I walked..
I couldn't really afford food, so I ate sparingly.I slept on the floor of my daughter's bedsitter and I explored, looked, watched, listened to strange people talking at bus stops.I walked around the area in the evenings trying to imagine how I would ever call this home. I looked at the neat little front gardens with pert nodding daffodils and tulips planted in stiff rows .Would I ever be able to enjoy the pleasure of gardening again.Would I ever own a spot I could call my own?

I could not visualize this happening in my future as it looked at this moment.

When I rode on the tube for the first time in rush hour, I understood how it must have been for our African woman coming to work at four in the morning on over- crowded trains, with bodies packed tightly against you and tension heightened by fear of attack or bag snatchers. I felt deep regret that I had not treated my maid with more understanding when she arrived late in the early hours of the morning.This was simply because I had no knowledge of how treacherous her journey might have been. As white South Africans we had never traveled by bus or train, our parents had driven us to our schools and sporting activities.

As I sat in the tube, I wondered if all the London city firms insisted on employees everyone wearing black as if it was a uniform and why no one made eye contact. I tried to do the same but found it very uncomfortable.

I was Mute and Stunned -

But I was here, in the UK.

If I believe in anything, I believe in the body's natural capacity to adjust. If we take note, we are directed by nature. One morning, months later, I couldn't get off the bus. My knees were so swollen I couldn't maneuver myself down the platform. The kindly bus driver got out of his seat, came round the bus to the door and helped me down to the pavement. "Let me help you my dear," he said "you are a bit young to be hobbling," he smiled amusedly.

I acknowledged then that I needed to seek help. I went from GP to orthopedic surgeon in unusually quick succession. The Orthopod looked at me, asked me a myriad of questions, listened to my history and then leaned back in his chair thoughtfully.

"I don't touch you until you've had psychotherapy" he said. In my temporary disdain for doctors I thought "What a nudnik! It's my knees that need attention not my head!"

The sometimes wonderful NHS was free. I was at a time of life where free was great, so I went along with the hurriedly made appointment the GP had organized for me with Jo, the local National Health psychologist.

Jo appeared as an angel dressed up as a councilor. She was large and free, wore long pink socks with open toe sandals under voluminous skirts with oddments of tops which she wore short ones over long ones. -Very funky. She was clever, insightful and funny.

On our first session there was so much to tell her, I promised her it would take forever.

She made me laugh at my telling .She made me laugh so much I began to cry.

And I cried.

I cried so hard, day after day week after week, I shed all the tears that had I had saved up for twenty six years. The natural tears of my harsh and battered life cycle, dammed up for so long, just burst their banks and disappeared into boxes of special offer Kleenex. As I let go, day by day regaling Jo with my oft harsh descriptions of how I had overcome the obstacles of life, my knees began to shrink.

I had six months of weekly laughter, hilarious raucous shared laughter. Jo and I had the same sense of humor and with her I could tell it like it was.

As I described some of the things I had had to do to survive and some of the things I had spat at my harsh critics at times of crisis, I laughed at myself for the first time, instead of viewing them with all the anger I had held onto, believing I could make myself inviolate by not giving in. I acknowledged my heartbreak over Wilfred, and I understood I was vulnerable and needy in all the normal senses of the word. I wanted to be secure and loved and fulfill my ideals without the daily fear of death and debt.

Finally one day, when I think she couldn't afford the rate I was using tissues any longer she asked me if I thought I could manage on my own.

That day, I walked out into the London Street without crutches, either wooden or imagined.

I began my new life, in a new place, with a much clearer vision of who I was.

I hired an apartment with my small savings account realizing it would last me six months at the most.

I had to find a way to earn a living. I had come from a very judgmental society in South Africa where the car you drove and the position you held, classed you on one side of town or the other.

I loved the feeling that I found here in Britain that, as long as you did a good days work you were contributing to society. Whatever you did was acceptable.

I offered babysitting. I tried dog walking. I even offered to clean and to my surprise a lady in a large house in Golders Green asked me to come for an interview.

I faced the reality of this situation with some humor as I had never cleaned a toilet, much less used a Hoover, and I d certainly never attempted to iron a shirt. In South Africa we had always had housemaids to do this, but on the plus side, I'd written seven cook books. That made me sound like a worthwhile proposition ....almost as if I could cook!

I went along in what I thought was suitable attire for a domestic job, sensible shoes and an over large bag for my cleaning gear.

We took tea in the drawing room and I felt obligated to tell her I wasn't very experienced and I didn't do ironing.

The conversation was more like a social occasion because in truth I didn't really know how to behave as if I was applying for a cleaning job although I did remember not to talk with my mouth full of cake!

She was very kind and polite and assured me I would hear from her.

A week later she responded, apologetically saying she wouldn't be offering me a job, but her brother was newly divorced and would I consider having dinner with him? So much for my culinary skills!

As I sat on the plane flying back to London, my mind took me back over all the times I've had to pick up the pieces of my life and knit them together again. I am left handed. No one at school could ever teach me to knit properly. Perhaps this could be the reason for so many holes in my cardigan of life.

45
DISCOVERY 1998

The worst part of leaving your home to emigrate is the beloved people you have to leave behind. At least I knew my son Daniel would be joining us by the end of the year when he graduated, only six months away, but my parents were too elderly to travel.

The worrying factor was who knew when I would next have the means to come back and see them. It was a choice I had to make, a very hard choice as the eldest daughter.

So many years before my younger sister Jinny had emigrated to Canada but the folks had been younger then and traveled regularly each year to see her.

I had to be in the U.K before I reached the cut-off point. The final age of immigration acceptance was 50. This was almost upon me. My only choice was to leave for London immediately or to risk never being able to settle near my children and be a "six week per year grandma".

The thought of that scenario was the deciding factor in my decision making. My Mom had never been a babysitter for my children. She'd never been there to help me. For me personally, if there was to be purpose in my old age, this is what I wanted it to be, to be in a position to give my grandchildren quality time. To teach them all the things busy mothers don't have time to share, to give them the wonderful bits of our heritage that their daily lives would not provide. With this in mind, I made my peace with myself. I made the decision to go before I turned fifty years old, knowing Dan would follow at the end of the year. This would set the platform for my future near my children and grandchildren.

At this time in South African history, most parents with children in their twenties could not guarantee on which continent each sibling would end up living.

It was not unusual for South African parents to travel between Australia, Canada and Britain or Israel to see their offspring. I was only too aware that I would not have the means to travel and I had to do my very best to put myself in a position where I could be accessible to all of them.

To my parents' credit they did not discourage me in any way and wished me well, although they didn't really understand the need to make a new start. At this point I only saw them annually so I hoped I would find a way to see them equally as often, even from Britain.

When you have grown up as separated and distant as I was from my parents, it is hard to ask them to discuss with you when they think their time to leave earthly pursuits is near, so that you may have the opportunity to say goodbye.

As Mom had always been a hypochondriac, we tended not to notice if she complained endlessly, but over the last few months she began writing me long letters giving me her family history and letting me know family details she'd never talked about before. I sensed that she thought she was nearing the end of her life, and I would keep asking whether I should come home to see her.

We all know we have to die, yet making a timetable for such a non concrete thing is difficult. I kept thinking "Maybe I'll go next month". I thought I had time to see her.

I am left with a feeling of such incompleteness, knowing that despite all the training and experience I had as a hospice counselor, I was unable to utilize my knowledge in my own loss. I thought about all the times I had sat with families, helping them to accept and prepare themselves in saying goodbye properly. I did not have the opportunity to do so with my own mother. I understood that a large part of this was her inability to relate to me, or me to her. I tried very hard to accept this angst as something that could not be altered and should be accepted as such; our relationship was too damaged, too fraught with horrid memories.

When Dad finally called me, his words to me were "Hilary, I'm widowed", not "Your Mom has passed away", or even as if it had anything to do with me!

Over the weeks before she died, I had constantly called him to ask if I should come home and the answer had always been "no, she does not want you to come." Perhaps her acceptance of our relationship had been easier than mine.

To the bitter end she wanted him to herself preferring to be just "them" rather than "us."

Much later, I learned from him that she had been falling for a while and he could not pick her up on his own, so between Miriam, our trusty old maid, the neighbor and himself, they'd had to drag her up the stairs and try to put her on the bed.

My heart broke at the knowledge that we were not there for them but I knew it was her choice.

On hearing the news, I called my daughter Alissa.

She arrived full of love and tenderness. How lucky I was. She arranged for Friends of South Africa to get me on a flight and escort me from Johannesburg to the Port Elizabeth air connection. I felt incapable of doing anything rational until I saw my father.

My mind was blank. I left for Port Elizabeth knowing gratefully that Jinny, who lived in South Africa, was already there with him.

Who would ever have thought Mom would go first?

Charlotte—her proper name—had been a much loved person in the town and her friends rallied round. Dad was OK. In his dignified way he did whatever he had to do and I realized that for a long time before this had happened, he and Miriam had held the fort.

She had already sorted her cupboards. Her papers were all in order.

To my amazement, in her cupboard I found every cutting, newspaper article and photo I'd ever sent her about my career. All those years of never acknowledging any of them, she had indeed received them! According to her friends, she had proudly shared them. Sadly she felt unable to acknowledge her pride to me. She regularly berated me for being constantly featured in the newspaper.

Perhaps the neat pile that she left me was a final acknowledgement.

Alternatively, it was a final message of "here—you can take these all back now." I'll never know!

Jinny, Dad and I spent the first few days trying to sort out Mom's things. Jen and I were very panicky about Dad. We never ever imagined we would have to look after him alone.

For the 57 years of their marriage he had never had to make himself a cup of tea and now he'd have to fend for himself. Jen had to go back to work, I had to return to London and we had only this one chance to re-settle him safely.

In our haste to help him, we got going. We hurried him through the decision to move, with no alternative. In retrospect, it was too soon, but at least it kept him occupied.

The three of us had a good laugh as we opened the cupboard that all our life Dad had called the "penicillin cupboard." Mom had always put her best things away for a special occasion until eventually they'd go off or we'd outgrow them.

What would we find in here? Most of her clothes she had already given away and much of the linen was worn and faded. She had only one photo album of her youth and no photographs of her parents or family as they'd been lost in a fire when she was a child. Jinny stayed as long as she was able and I took 6 weeks leave, preparing to help him adjust to his new status.

We arranged that I would stay with Dad and shut down their apartment and then bring him to Cape Town to live with her in her family home.

Johnson, Jinny's's husband was generously open to this idea and I was eternally grateful to him for this.

It is hard to describe this period of time. I got to know my father by direct contact. I was allowed close to him for the first time, to talk to him and hear about his life. I learned his vulnerabilities. I enjoyed his brilliant dry sense of humor which Dan had inherited. We walked, we talked. We ate onions. My mother had never allowed him to eat onions—she couldn't stand the smell.

I learned that the last decade with her had been hard. I didn't know, because he chose not to tell us, that her triple bypass had been a failure and he knew she would not be well and strong.

When the breast cancer attacked her remaining breast he didn't tell her that either and he bore the burden on his own. In retrospect, I began to understand the first few weeks after her death were a relief before the reality of being without her set in.

We never gave him a choice about packing up their home. There wasn't a soul left in town who could look after him Our only remaining relatives who had been so good to my parents in our absence, were themselves ailing and we could not ask them to take on the responsibility. There was no suitable aged home for him to go to—not that we even broached the subject.

Their lovely sunny apartment had been impeccably kept. For 57 years they had sat together on the stoep looking out over the sea and being ideal companions. Only someone who has grown up with a beloved nanny in South African apartheid could understand the poignancy of Miriam and Mom watching the soaps together every evening. In so doing Miriam never ventured into the lounge, always bringing herself a chair at the door. This was Miriam's choice, not Mom's. It was part of the natural respect of her tribe and the distance maintained between madam and maid which we grew up with.

It would be impossible to replace this standard of living, but Dad could not live alone. Only the bribe of living with Jen and her grandson would make him agree to move. He was very vulnerable and we arranged what we thought was the happiest solution.

We set about emptying the cupboards and making the arrangements.

Miriam was also completely floored by the whole process. She'd looked after them for 44 years and was pleased to be able to retire but fearful of leaving "Her Jacob."

I thought of all the times she'd got me out of trouble when we were kids, covered for us when we bunked out. How she'd cleaned the kitchen from floor to ceiling before my parents arrived home after I tried my hand at cooking and nearly burnt the house down, and many other unmentionable escapades.

Miriam had given birth to her four children in our kitchen with the help of my father, always distrustful of the hospital and always waiting long enough to announce the birth was imminent, making a rush to the hospital impossible.

Mom and Dad had purchased a home for her in her ancestral home in the Eastern Cape, at Debenek and that's where she wanted to live at this stage of her life.

We sat on Dad's bed and opened the tin box with rusty old keys. Inside the box was the document my father had told me about years before. I'd nagged endlessly to see it, but he always said he didn't know where it was. Now it appeared—Daniel Levinthal's ticket out from Lithuania to Port Elizabeth, on the Galeka in 1906, for which he paid the princely sum of eleven guineas!

I took it with shaking hands. I looked at his signature. My Gramps. His rusty old bunch of Ramsay Avenue house keys were still in there too. I held the keys and I longed to see Grampa smile with all my heart.

All the sadness of the day—Mom, Grampa, the remainder of jewelry that she'd made into two little bags, one for each of us—took hold of us and we held each other and cried.

Inside the box were the brown faded title deeds of Mackay Street, the original house my Grandpa had owned. I could remember Dad and Mom collecting the rent for all those years.

Those were the days we always stopped at Trompaitzkys for iced doughnuts

"Is it still there Dad? " I asked.

"What", he said "the bakery?

"I don't know", he mused. "Let's drive that way and look and perhaps I can show you Mackay Street."

He perked up at this idea and we took off on a reminiscent tour of my childhood city, something I knew so little about.

We trawled up the steep hill into Russell Road and round the corner into Mackay Street.

Next door to each other stood two very well kept little 1820 houses.

Over the years, Daniel had built a cottage to rent at the back of each house, bringing him in a tidy sum. An entrepreneur, my Grandpa!

The tin roof had been replaced with tiles but otherwise they were much the same. We found the bakery but now it smelled of fish and chips and sported large coke ads and tables and chairs.

We sat down to have tea and a doughnut.

"He was only a tailor. How did he manage to buy so much property?" I asked.

Dad smiled at my question. "He was *THE* tailor Hilary. I was always the envy of young people as I wore superbly made trousers and jackets". (My mom had secretly confided in me that they had called him "Fancy Pants" in those days). "Daniel Levinthal came to this country carrying his inheritance", said Dad. For the first time in all my 50 years, he told me the story of how Grandpa had brought a bed roll with him, that had turned out to hold his mother's (Gittel) jewels. She, in turn, had inherited these from her father.

When Dad asked Mom to marry him, they had known each other for only a week. He was drafted to leave for the Second World War within the next week. During that week her father Herrmann died in Cape Town and, not wanting to go to war without marrying her, he asked

Tuvia and Dan to make hasty arrangements for a wedding in the Raleigh Street Shul in Port Elizabeth.

Grampa revealed to Jacob that the remaining diamond had been left for him in the crown of the Chuppah which, by now, had graced many of the marriages in Raleigh Street Shul.

Dad had rushed off to the shul and made a request to borrow the chuppah from the Shamus, ostensibly to "get it cleaned for the impending simcha!"

"Oh no", said the Shamus, "it never leaves the Synagogue and it's never allowed to get dusty!"

Dad got quite agitated. "It's MY family heritage and we want to check it for Halachic reasons before we get married. It came from my grandfather, a Litvak Rabbi", he argued. Eventually, as he could not question the source of Dad's information, the Shamus allowed him to borrow the Chuppah and to take it home to Ramsay Avenue.

There Grandpa, Dan and Jacob cut the hidden diamond out of the crown where it had lain since1914. Dan stitched the crown together again adding little threads of gold woven through the stitches to remind us under the Chuppah of what had been there. They returned the Chuppah to Raleigh Street and Jacob ran to Uncle Albert's jewelry shop and entreated him to make his bride, Charlotte, a diamond ring before he left for the war.

Perhaps this opened a window for me as to why my Mom had hijacked my wedding as her own. She had dreamt all these years of all the things she really wanted at her own wedding. I wished she had been able to share this with me. In fact I realized that I knew nothing at all about her wedding.

"Is the Raleigh Street Shul still standing? " I asked Dad.

"Why, yes", he said with enthusiasm, "it's just been re-opened as a museum. Would you like to see it? It's just round the corner".

He hurried me along the road excitedly. We came to an elegant old building with an Art Deco front. Along the way he showed me his music teacher's house and the open lot where he had played football.

I wondered why as children we had never ever been shown these precious places. I thought that perhaps Mom had resented them as part of Dad's happy childhood, while hers had been not all that happy as the ninth child of elderly parents.

The door of the museum opened and there I recognized Auntie Etty. She had been in labor when I was born and her son Dennis was an old friend of mine. We had played together as children.

She was the new curator of the museum. She was also the daughter -in-law of a well known protagonist of civil reform and a revered Mayor of Port Elizabeth. She had taken on the job of restoring this museum to its former glory, collecting any historical documentation she could.

It was an amazing revelation to me, a time I knew nothing about. I was excited to be introduced to an era of our past that I had no knowledge of.

All the war time wedding photos of people I had grown up knowing, a photograph of my Dad in the barmitzvah class with all his old mates whom I'd known only as adults.

At this point Sam joined us. Sam was my Dad's bowling chum, working with Etty to put it all together. He was happy to show us around.

We climbed onto the high wooden Bimah, the central dais from which the service was conducted. I stood there imagining how the rising murmur of praying men must have sounded. He took me to the still shiny brass plates where my grandparents' names were engraved. Morris and Dorah Nurek, proudly displayed with Daniel Levinthal's seat next to Morris. I sat down in their seats to get a clearer vision of their view.

To my amused delight, he pointed out how the back of Granny Dorah's seat was slightly set back behind her shoulders. This was because the" big machers", the committee members in the women's league, expected to wear large hats and needed extra space to sit upright in them. This painted such a fabulous picture of who Dorah Nurek was. She was known for her kindness and generosity to the needy. She was also known for calling a spade a spade!

Sam couldn't believe I'd never seen a photograph of her. He took my hand and led me onto the Bimah. There, in a dusty plastic cover was the Lithuanian travel document of Dorah Nurek, documenting her arrival in 1901, listed as *Lithuanian by birth and by marriage* .

I could not believe my eyes. As a new convert to genealogy—one would kill for this!

"Where did you get it?" I screeched.

"Your Dad gave it to us", he replied.

I looked at Dad and he knew I was going to throw an apoplectic fit!

Sam told us that they were beginning to seek any old relics of the Raleigh Street Shul. The building had been used for other purposes during wartime and the new Western Road shul had been used as a synagogue. Recently they had found the Menorah in good condition in a city dump that was being excavated for 1920 relics in the east of the city. Somehow a layer of pre war remainders were appearing, dumped on top of the 1920 relics and people were rushing to find souvenirs.

"What about the old Chuppah?" I asked.

"We are hoping to find all the old artifacts in the same dump", he told us.

"Wouldn't you like to join us in the dig?" said Sam suspecting my interest.

Dad shook his head and answered laughingly on my behalf, "All that dust, all those old things? I've got enough old things already!"

I stood tight-lipped. I kept silent.

While we were on this journey of reminiscence and discovery for me, I asked my father if he'd like to drive past Ramsay Avenue, Grandpa's former home.

He nodded, with a forlorn look of faraway memories. When we parked outside the door we both knew we had to go in.

Nothing outside the house had changed. The palm tree stood strong in the garden, the loquat tree was heavy with fruit. The stairs of the stoep were still highly polished in red. Even the gate creaked the same way. I knocked tentatively on the door.

An elegant black lady opened the door and for a moment I was awakened to the fact that this was the new South Africa for me. I could not tell if she was the owner of the property, or the domestic help.

I told her this was our former home and we were visiting from the UK.

"We'd love to just have a quick peek inside." I held my breath

She stepped back and welcomed us warmly inside.

Memory is such a precious thing. We hold onto the images that brought us childhood happiness and we keep them hidden until something triggers the memory for us to enjoy all over again. The parquet floors where we had played hop scotch was still just as shiny. The front room, although filled with modern furniture, looked the same to me. Perhaps I saw only the former lumpy couch with low cushions and the polished roll of the wooden arms in my mind. The bathrooms had been totally modernized. Tuvia would have adored them.

I walked into the kitchen. In my mind I saw Dan sitting at the table, napkin tucked into his chin and Tuvia rolling the dough. I smelt the chicken soup. I tasted the *tzimmes* on my tongue, and I remembered waiting for the crusty piece of the aromatic lokshen pudding. The Aga was long gone and a modern washup stood in its place. I remembered Jen standing on a chair to wash the dishes. Tears ran down my face.

Dad and I held hands as we walked to the tailoring room.

The beautiful wooden floor had been well looked after. I remembered sitting there with the chalk and a piece of suiting. Gramps was always so patient with us. I looked out over the park. We had peddled our bikes along the pathways happily whiling away the afternoons as part of the "exciting eight," our cycling group.

I thought about the day Mom pointed out the handsomest boy in the world AND, I remembered my reaction! In the back of my mind I heard them speaking Yiddish to each other over the sewing machines. I marveled how it had never seemed like a foreign language to me. It was just the familiar sound that I accepted when my grandparents spoke to each other.

Finally, she ushered us into the dining room. As we walked in Dad s jaw dropped. There stood an old pianola.

"Where did you get that?" he asked.

"From an antique dealer", she replied

"Who plays?" I asked.

"My son plays" she told us.

"Would you mind if I looked inside the back?" my Dad asked. I looked at him in surprise. He was so animated

"Not at all", she answered.

He lifted the back flap and there, just visible, was the name D. Levinthal 1924 scratched into the wood.

"My father decided to sell it", he explained to us, and now, this same pianola had returned home to the SAME house .That really made Dad's day!

With that, we thanked her profusely for allowing us in to see the house, and made our way home.

What a day of discovery!

We went to bed early. Dad was exhausted and beginning to miss my Mother.

Miriam had made fish cakes doused in Worcester sauce, as usual, to keep him happy. I never knew how he survived the same regular diet for 57 years but that's what he enjoyed, as I was to learn when I tried to make him other interesting foods.

I never closed my eyes. I went over all the details of the day, what we'd seen and how it all tied together. I switched on the light to re-examine Grandpa's ticket again. I'd been asking for it for as long as I could remember.

Early the next morning, Sam called to see how Dad was doing. He asked me if I'd like to come with him to the dig to see what was going on. He knew I was absolutely hooked. Dad was feeling very frail and told me I should go with Sam. He wanted to stay in bed.

We walked over the sandy dune. The windy city, true to its name, was blowing a gale. Many people of all shapes and sizes were carefully extracting pieces and parcels, each digger being careful to extract what they had found without damaging any of it.

It was an unusual sight for me. l longed to have a go, to put my fingers in the soil and the dust and wish for a surprise. We spoke to several people. They told us how each sector revealed objects from a similar epoch, so they were able to date the time of the dumping levels.

We found an official city digger, someone who was working in the area of a later dumping created just after the war.

We told him we were looking for a piece of velvet, embroidered with Hebrew. He looked at us wide-eyed, stood rigid for a moment, and then beckoned us towards black bag lying near by.

"I extracted this late yesterday", he said. "Any idea what it could be?"

He opened the black bag to reveal a mouldy yellowed cloth. Inside the cloth, wrapped up tightly in a plastic tablecloth, was an old dusty maroon velvet with gilt embroidered letters, the lions and crown just visible. Sam held on to my arm very tightly.

"Don't say too much", he cautioned me.

I would have screamed and ripped the bag open, but the pressure on my arm told me to let him speak.

"Yes", said Sam quietly, "this could be of interest."

"Could we take it away and let you know if it is what we think it is?"

"By all means", said the official relaxedly. "Help yourself."

I could barely walk. It was heavy and full of sand. We put it into the boot and I thought seriously about getting into the boot myself!

Sam drove me home but on the way he explained that the chuppah belonged to Raleigh Street Museum and he had to take it back to the museum.

I could not come to terms with this.

I got back into the car with him and I said "Let's go and see Auntie Etty."

At the museum we took out the Chuppah. It was a bit moth eaten in parts. Some of the edges were frayed but, on the whole, the plastic tablecloth had kept it safe from water and it could be saved.

Never before have I tried to use my persuasive powers with such intent. I culminated my argument by using my creative ability to its ultimate climax in the conversation that followed. I explained to them I was making a study of my family roots. I wanted to have the passport which was my family document. I argued that Dad was not interested in these things but I felt they were my FEW bits of heritage. I wanted to keep them.

I promised Sam and Etty I would make as generous a donation to the museum as I could. In my mother's name I would hand-paint them a modern full size Chuppah with beautiful poles. It would tell the story of how the museum came to be situated in Raleigh Street.

I'd tell the story of how they had run up the hill with the Siddurim, all the prayer books. I would restore the original chuppah and look after it.

They could see I was genuine and very intense about it all. They were aware the Museum was very short of funds and had more important projects to concentrate on.

Both Sam and Etty had been fond of Mom and, all in all, with my determination they didn't have a hope in hell!

I walked away with my family possessions, passport and Chuppah.

Dad was not pleased at what I'd taken.

"What do you want with all this?" he said. "They are dead and gone. Why do you want them?"

I couldn't argue over the 'dead and gone' bit at that point. I knew he was feeling very fragile and that everyone who counted was dead and gone but for me they were precious and priceless and I felt intensely possessive of them.

Talking to him over the next few weeks I realized why he felt the way he did about it all. He'd fought in the World War II. The holocaust was not a newspaper article for him, it was a real experience. He'd been a captain in the army in Italy. He'd photographed Mussolini being hung upside down outside his headquarters. He'd run out to drag my mother's young brother Jackie back after being shot. Sadly, he had died there. He'd sat waiting in the desert for orders for weeks on end, with no communication to the outside world. He'd been there—done that.

After the war he'd returned to life as a young married man and worked hard to build a normal life in a young country. Originally he'd qualified at 19 years old, too young to practice as a lawyer, and had had to wait to be called to the bar. Over the years he'd worked extremely hard and had built a solid reputation as a criminal lawyer, as well as being Chairman of the School Board. In my schooldays this had given me quite a pulling power with the teachers and I always took full advantage of it!

He didn't want to be associated with Lithuania and all the images that Eastern Europe imposed. Most young people after the war wanted to be South African and they became integrated and harnessed life with gusto.

My parents as young 30-year olds had a good life.

The suburb we lived in was made up of young newly married families who'd built their houses and established a bonded society. They threw fancy dress parties and dinner parties. We went on picnics with other families. .At The Willows, we fished for goldfish with safety pins and ate watermelon, collecting the seeds to grow Jack in the Beanstalk in cotton wool. We had lift schemes to school and lift schemes to cheder. We played tennis on Sundays and we watched Charlie Chaplin movies on Sunday nights at the Tennis Club. We practiced our Judaism openly without any evidence of anti- Semitism

I had taken all this for granted, but perhaps he did not.

As soon as I arrived back in London I made a very good scanned copy of the passport—one would have had difficulty telling which was the original—and I sent it to back to Etty. Then I set about painting a maroon velvet Chuppah, complete with the picture story of the Raleigh street museum and the dates of Daniel and Tuvia's wedding as well as dedicating it to my mother Lotte.

The museum was pleased with it and it stands there proudly today.

During my last week in Port Elizabeth Miriam tried to teach me to polish the silver which Dad and Mom had bought on honeymoon 57 years ago and used every Friday for all those years. She told me it HAD to be polished every week whether it was used or not! It had 18 place settings and every piece from pickle forks to teaspoons was all there, beautifully maintained. I knew I could never look after it the way she did, but I hoped I'd be able to try.

Dad settled in at Jinny's in Cape Town and I returned to London.

The night before I left, he took us out for dinner.

At the table he took out two boxes. From the first he gave me Mom's original diamond ring which she had left me in her will.

"If this is Mom's engagement ring, then it must be Gittel's diamond" I asked?.

"It is Gittel's diamond, all the way from Linkuva"

"Where is Linkuva?" I asked.

"Somewhere in *drerd afen dek*" he smiled, meaning "to hell and gone".

46
LISSI'S DREAM COMES TRUE

I had already made my plans to emigrate to the UK in the foreseeable future, when I returned to London to see Alissa again. I took as large a suitcase and as much as I could carry, particularly concentrating on our many certificates, papers and family heirlooms. What do you do with the nursery school certificates, the ballet exams, the first piece of pottery. As a mother you cannot throw them away. One of the reasons for traveling at this point was to meet the special young man that Lissi had met.

When Joseph called to introduce himself on the telephone I couldn't believe the hot potato accent. I thought perhaps Prince Charles had called me!

Alissa had found the most wonderful bright and interesting young Englishman, (much more exciting than Prince Charles.) He was empathetic and caring and turned out to be an outstanding son in law. But that day as I walked through the Heathrow Concorde I caught sight of my Alissa in a "pooh bear hat" and a young blonde man with his arm around her shoulder. They were waiting to greet me.

We chatted politely until we came to his car and then we all three realized my suitcases would not fit into his car!

Thank goodness in years to come he never held it against me!

Not only had Alissa found a very special love, but he brought to the relationship his parents who were to become my solid friends—often my anchor in London.

They were warm and welcoming. They opened their home to me, were always there for me. In the years that followed we shared our grandchildren and had many happy Shabbat laughs together. It was a genuine relationship where we could criticize each other with the confidence of life long friends.

Months later, at a time when I was fairly low, and had had a really bad experience with an English rogue posing as a gentleman, Joseph's mother, Julie, called me to say she had arranged for me to meet "a friend of a friend." I really wasn't interested and told her so, but Julie was a force to be reckoned with and she went right ahead insisting I keep this dinner date.

So early one cold British evening I got into my standard "thin" outfit, and I was duly collected. I had found no plausible excuse for not desiring to go along.

We joined 6 other couples at dinner in the home of an ex -South African friend of Julie. I'd hardly made an effort, but wanted to be polite. The hostess was a cousin of Alon and she had generously arranged the dinner through a friend of hers. All these ex South Africans had our welfare in mind.

The others diners were all married couples. We had a wonderful meal and they were all interesting and pleasant to meet. I glanced around the room trying to assess who belonged to whom, and which one "He" could be.

I raised my eyebrow at Julie and she nodded unobtrusively towards a gentleman sitting in the far half of the room.

He later told me he positioned himself there so as to look at me first!

All I could see was two very long thighs sticking out of the chair.

Well, so far so good! Then I reminded myself I wasn't really interested in making this work anyway.

Eventually the long legs rose up. A man like a cedar. He probably shopped at Large and Tall. He ambled over, shook my hand, looking me in the eye, and then sat down and continued his conversation with someone else.

At dinner we were seated next to each other but apart from "pass the salt please" he did not take much notice of me and at the end of the evening he shook my hand with a cursory "nice to meet you."

"Well", we all said on the way home, "it was a pleasant evening and we've had a good dinner."

Secretly, I went to bed with a feeling that I might like to get to know him. He felt solid and strong and dependable. I knew he'd lost his wife many years ago and maybe the similar experiences we'd had would help us to relate to each other.

Weeks passed and I heard nothing. I didn't wait at the telephone. Via the grapevine, Julie reported he was interested in seeing me again.

About four weeks later I was surprised to hear a very nervous male voice call me up. It was Alon of the long thighs. He invited me to come to a quiz in three weeks time. I absolutely loathed all quizzes. I never knew any of the answers and I was lousy at playing games. It was likely to kill any potential this friendship might have!

My natural chutzpah took over." Why do I have to wait three weeks for a date?" I asked him. "Wouldn't you like to go for a walk tomorrow?"

He was quite taken aback, not used to casual dates or forward chicks.….. . He'd been taking out a variety of woman for so long, but always to an organized dinner or dance or formal occasion.

"Well" he drawled a bit uncertainly " that sounds good."

He collected me the following afternoon. I opened the door and his huge sheep dog bounced through the door in front of him.

I should have noted then that he preferred animals to people, but I was delighted to see him. It was a gorgeous day and we drove off to Hampstead Heath.

We walked for hours. We had so much to talk about, so much to share in all the similarities in our lives and neither of us had done much sharing in a long while. He had lost his wife many years before and had found it hard to begin a new relationship.

Later in the afternoon it turned cold and wet and walking in the mud was slippery. Over a treacherous bit of path under a low branched tree he took my hand to help me and he just kept holding my hand for the rest of the walk. It felt warm and good. His hands were large and muscular and they enveloped my hand like a glove. All this as I was busy telling him I wasn't looking for a relationship!

He just smiled.

When I remind him of all this today, he denies he was brave enough to hold my hand on that first date, but he obviously felt at ease.

Charlie the sheep dog bounced around us and all too soon we were on the way home.

"Cheers, I'll call you", he said, and I wondered.

I dreaded the quiz.

I didn't know what to wear, I wasn't familiar with the habits of British society yet, but I need not have worried.

Alon knew all the answers. He was a wizard at quizzes, and I just pretended to be the score keeper and kept busy.

It was a lovely evening except for the inconsequential discomfort of being aware that there were various women glaring at me. Apparently he was much in demand around Edgware.

Two weeks passed and I heard nothing.

One morning I was working at home when the telephone rang. There was no one there.

Curious, I dialed 1471, a telephone recall system and it was Alon's number. Strange—had he called me?

I dialed the number back and a croaky cockney lady answered the phone.

Oi vey- I thought, he had a lady friend there.

"Yes" she barked.

"You have just called my number so I was checking to see who called me", I replied.

"Hold on" she barked again.

After a few minutes she returned to the phone to tell me she was Dr Rubin's housekeeper and as he had lost his voice and could not speak, he requested I give her my e mail number.

I was intrigued.

She wrote it down very carefully, obviously unfamiliar with e-mail addresses, and then thanked me and put down the phone.

A little later I opened my e-mail to find a message from Dr Rubin.

He had severe laryngitis and couldn't speak. He also had an automatic dialing system on his phone. My number was listed (well, that was good!). He claimed he'd pushed the wrong button and the phone had automatically called me.

I was not to know at that stage that he was an electronic gimmick fanatic so I pondered on the authenticity of this explanation ....

We communicated by emailing each other a few times during that day, and the next, and the next. The e- mails surrreptiously transformed into loving notelets.

A few days later I e-mailed him asking if he needed anything as he was still voiceless.

He invited me over to his house and I walked down into Edgware to the address he had given me.

Dorcas, the housekeeper opened the door.

She didn't seem particularly friendly and grabbed the basket of oranges I had brought with me "I'll take these" she said, jerking her finger upstairs "he's up there."

I called up and he croaked that I should come upstairs.

The house seemed old and dark, the carpet on the stairs was worn, and I sensed no woman's wand had touched this house in a while.

I sat primly on the bed and tried to chat, but he really could not talk.

Every five minutes Dorcas popped in to check me out. She seemed very unhappy to see me sitting on the bed, and then decided to sweep the passage outside his room so she could hear what we were saying. I gathered that even if he was pleased to see me, she wasn't.

In the days that followed we began to say good morning on e mail, good night on e -mail and somehow, not being face to face, this shy wonderful man felt he could express himself more openly. Our friendship grew and still I kept telling him I did not want any intense involvement. He was patient and caring.

I felt he was a man of principle and he lived by those principles.

Our grown up children met each other and they got on well. His daughter was the same age as mine and they all seemed quite amicable to come together for Shabbat suppers.

One day I was at home, doing battle with the heavy mirrored bedroom cupboard doors, when one door came out of its mooring and fell on my foot. It crushed the bone in three places.

I crumpled into a dead faint and came too, lying haphazardly on the bed dangling just off the floor, unable to move my leg. My first instinct was to call Alon. I leaned over to the mobile, feeling very fuzzy headed. I must have felt I could rely on him, and luckily it was a Sunday. He came flying over.

He scooped me up and laid me on the bed.

I always maintain I was still in a state of unconsciousness, but I put my arms around him and pulled him amorously to me. I felt unhitched, almost mindless.

We kissed tenderly. He imagined he was comforting me. I grasped him more engagingly than I had before. I felt as if I was transported to another state of being, in cerebral Disney world, swinging freely round the wheel of fortune and down the dizzy slope. Desire stilled the agony. The pain felt celestial, like stars exploding in a universe I could not touch, distant and unrelated to me. My body waned from reality. My nerve centre seemed on leave to NASA.

I didn't want to let him go but eventually we had to go to the hospital and get my foot x-rayed.

This development seemed to cement our relationship.

We e-mailed our thoughts, our feelings, our ideas. I could not wait to open my e-mail each day, knowing he would have left me a message before he went to work very early in the morning.

We began to socialize together introducing, our friends and to support each other. When he invited me to be his partner at his daughter's wedding I was encouraged. I felt this was an acknowledgment that he trusted me to be his partner on such an important occasion.

47
THE JOY OF SIMCHA

Today I was so excited. Jinny and I had decided Dad was able to travel to the U.K on his own. We were so frightened that he would get onto the wrong flight or lose his ticket, so we decided to pre-empt any incident by arranging for him to be escorted to the plane. Needless to say this very elegantly attired grey haired man told the stewardess "he'd escort her before she escorted him," and he marched onto the plane himself. He slept well all the way extremely excited at his first long haul flight for a very long time.

He was 83 years old.

I had also arranged for him to be escorted out on arrival. By morning he was very tired and more "manageable." He allowed British Airways to bring him through on a wheel chair but he leapt out of it as soon as he saw me.

Oh Pops, I felt so sad that my Mom could not share this wonderful occasion but I was happy to have the privilege of him being with us.

He fitted into all our pre-wedding planning, taking an interest in everything that was going on He was amazing, muddled but amazing. Tirza arranged for us to go to a specialized yoga session as one of Lissi's pre-wedding relaxation treats.

It entailed lying on the floor and we thought perhaps he'd better give it a miss. He was totally insulted. "You'd have thought I didn't sleep on the floor in the desert " he asked us tetchily? "O.K Pops," I said "put on your track suit".

He donned his gear in double quick time and off we went. He actually took part in the whole thing although at the end of the lesson when we all lay relaxing,he fell into an exhausted sleep and snored so loudly the whole class roared with laughter.

He was an absolute star!

By now Dan was qualified and working in the U.K. He drove him around to see the sights. They were like two peas in a pod. Had the same good looks and sense of humor and obviously shared a lot of empathy with each other.

We girls got ready for the wedding. We partook in all the excitement and ritual that went with it. Tikkele and I accompanied Lissi to the Mikveh. The tradition of the ritual bath had fallen by the wayside in our family as a regular event, but doing it the night before your wedding as required in Orthodoxy made her transition to bride all the more meaningful.

I didn't pressurize Joseph and Lissi to use the Chuppah from Zagare. It needed a lot of renovation and I d already promised them a modern painted Chuppah with a *Tree of life* at Joe's request.

This was almost finished. Dad watched me paint, silently amused at the strange modern concept of my making a personalized Chuppah.

Alissa now had a Masters degree in education. She had done very well in her field. She was a kind gentle and loving child, still my "gold star child" according to the ragging we got from Tikkele and Daniel but always well behaved and reliable. I kept saying I was still waiting for her teenage rebellion to come about, but we were all surprised when it came in the form of a bridal overdose! Initially I showed Alissa my wedding dress packed away in a trunk in the loft. I had not been able to abandon it when I left South Africa. She told me in no uncertain terms that she wanted a modern dress. Each weekend she would go to the West End searching for this dress of her dreams. She would call us frantically from a bridal store.

"Come now, right now, as I'm standing in it and if I take it off someone else will buy it."Dan and I would leap onto a tube and run all the way down Bond Street to find her standing in the store like a statue, staring at herself in the mirror. The image of a fairy queen stared back. Dan would smile in wonder at the vision of his sister and then give his respected opinion. As she discovered what was available, she became more and more frustrated. One day she shyly asked me for another look at *That Old Dress.* We hauled it out and although it would need taking in a size, she decided the design was absolutely perfect. I couldn't believe that my unconscious dream to see my daughter wear it for her own wedding was about to become a reality.

This understated young lady must have read too many bridal magazines. She wanted every bridal accessory there was to be had.

I was very wary of just being there to provide back-up and not impose my wedding dreams on her in the way I myself had experienced. When the hairdresser had completed her hair, our bride came to the top of the stairs and yelled down "Where's my tiara, I want my tiara NOW."

The whole house filled with bridesmaids and flower girls. They just hooted with laughter at what had become of our sensible balanced Alissa?

"The Wedding" was a weekend of ultimate happiness in every way.

Friends and relatives—the weather—the venue, all turned out perfectly.

Dad stood on the bimah, the central podium, with the wedding party throughout the ceremony. He led her to the Chuppah with Dan. As I looked at the two special men in my life walking this fairy bride down the aisle, I swelled with motherly pride. I looked at Tirza in attendance. Her thick blonde hair glowed, radiantly elegant in the dress of pale blue and dark blue that I had made her. She was so elegant, so together, a queen hidden in a beautiful package. I was so grateful for the genuine happiness I saw around me. Here we were, emigrants in the UK, holding a wedding with three wonderful children of whom I was immensely proud, not only their achievements, but the kind of person each one had grown up to be, with all the right values and each their own virtue. We were blessed with a Rabbi who knew our family, was originally from South Africa and was aware of the difficulties of relocating. We felt he was speaking from the heart rather than a standard few words which the Rabbi gives under the Chuppah.

As Joseph smashed the glass,the sound of "L' Chaim "filled the shul. Rabbi Levy put his arm around Jacob Levinthal as once they must have done in Zagare, and danced him round the Chuppah. All the men joined hands and began to sway. The woman circled them and the joy and happiness of our simcha filled the synagogue.

The reception took place in the Rose Garden of an old 18th century hotel.

Alissa and Joseph walked into this gorgeous cream draped marquee, her bridal train in her hand, as she skipped happily along the petal scattered pathway, both showing all their inner radiance and WE CELEBRATED ! Happiness filled my heart.

Dad was impatient with the separate dancing. Men danced with men and women danced with women as long as the Rabbis were present. This was not something he was accustomed to in South Africa. He was a superb ballroom dancer and wanted to get out there and waltz.

I couldn't match my mother as his partner and when we finally got out onto the dance floor he *kvetched* and moaned at my clumsiness and it made him miss my mother all the more. At 2 a.m. my new son in law called me to say thank you for all we had done to make the wedding so wonderful, but also to inform me that Lissi would not take off her tiara as she didn't want the day to end!

That said it all.

A week after the wedding when we had recovered from all the excitement, I invited Alon to come for Shabbat supper and to have some quality time with Dad.

I wanted Pop's impression.

I baked and cooked all day, trying to make most of Dad's favorites. Sweet and sour cabbage rolls with minced lamb, chicken soup with kneidel and stewed guavas just like Charlotte used to make.

We reminisced at the memory of poor Mom who had tried all her married life to get the cabbage rolls as good as Tuvia's and to keep them together she had to use tooth picks and we'd teased her mercilessly.

I made apple kugel and fresh ground coffee which he loved and I knew Alon enjoyed too.

They got on famously although I did see Dad looking a bit askew at Alon's collar not properly turned down and his shirt not tucked in straight but then Dad was the son of a tailor till the end.

I was taking a long time to get the supper together when Alon shouted.

"*Gib zich a shockel*" towards the kitchen, meaning "get a move on already"

At this Dad burst into loud raucous laughter!

I came through to the dining room and asked "What's so funny— what does it mean?" Alon looked sheepish.

"Well", said Dad, "it means hurry up, but that's exactly what Grandpa Daniel used to shout at Tuvia when he was waiting for his meals. I haven't thought of it in all these years."

At that moment I looked at Alon with a new vision, and I knew I wanted to complete the circle of my Litvak origins.

We were *Beshiert. We were meant to be.*

48
SAYING GOODBYE

Dad returned home to Cape Town. I missed him every day. Jinny felt he never really settled down again .He missed Mom and he was aging visibly. He fell badly, he lost his appetite and nothing we did seemed to help.

Daniel had returned to Cape Town for a while to change career direction. He decided that a medical career was not, after all, fulfillng enough for him, and he needed to pursue his other love – animation.

I was pleased with this direction as I knew it was an opportunity to fulfill his creativity and talent and certainly one of the technical directions of the future at this time.

He was studying animation and I climbed great *"nachus"* pleasure, watching him acknowledge his emerging talent to himself.

Dad loved being with Dan. They were both quiet funny and succinct.

He'd take him to movies and take him shopping. Each night I'd call him from London and chat to him trying hard to keep the contact we'd established in London going.

He was always pleasant and never complained, but I knew he was miserable.

He asked about Alon and I sensed he hoped something more would come of our relationship. He was still of the old school who believed I needed a man to keep me safe!

At the old age home he'd met a lady quite a lot younger than himself and they'd become friends. She'd make him come to the bridge afternoons and she took him out to tea. He was reticent but grateful to have her company and we were pleased she was around to keep him occupied.

One night, without warning, she died of asthma and he was absolutely devastated.

I guess he hadn't really mourned my mother properly. We'd whipped him out of Port Elizabeth too quickly and this brought death back to him with a great anguish.

Dad died as he had lived, like a gentleman. The night nurse had chatted to him at 12 a.m. and when she popped in at 3 a.m. he had passed away.

She called me very early in the morning, and I felt so grateful for the long chat we had managed to have the night before, where our parting words were "I love you."

I arrived in Cape Town. Jinny had not yet arrived back from the country trip she had been away on that night.

I walked into his room and sat on his bed. We had packed up his life before his move and his few sparse things were all neatly packed in his bureau.

I opened his bedside draw and there placed carefully in full view waiting to be found was the silver and gold ring he'd bought Mom for their fiftieth wedding anniversary and had worn since her death. I slid it slowly onto my finger. I held it there with aching anguish and I said the prayer for the departed to myself quietly vowing to wear the ring and to remember them with it.

Jinny was not a collector of "emotional mementoes" as I was. I knew she would not mind my having it.

Dan arrived then and I showed him the ring.

We tidied the last of Dad's things and left to make funeral arrangements.

When you have to fly long haul to parents' funerals and then hurry back to your life in another country one does not find a peaceful place to mourn properly. Moving from A to B, transporting the loss with you, makes the connection feel remote.

I hadn't really mourned my mother yet and now I had both of them gone. However old one is, being an orphan is still difficult to come to terms with and still today, years later I have difficulty with it.

I returned to London feeling very used up. As well, in my usual clumsy style, I'd tripped over a stone in the garden and broken my ankle .

I seemed to have lost the plot. I felt aimless and had great difficulty sleeping.

Alon was so patient, so supportive.

Our children were all getting to know each other and forming a friendship.

Alon's daughter Rosalind was soon to be getting married. I knew it was difficult for him on his own. When he invited me to be his partner at the wedding I offered to help in any way I could, hobbling around on one crutch.

I was very surprised to meet Rosalind's in laws.

They turned out to be the couple originally from Bloemfontein that I had met at Raleigh Street Shul with Dad a few years ago. It seemed G-d had this wide plan.

Alon was grateful for the help as he could not take time off from his practice.

I gently worked towards suggesting that if I was going to prepare the Friday night dinner for all the guests at his home maybe we should brighten up the house a bit. He was very wary of my taking over and when I suggested starting with giving the toilet a coat of paint myself he seemed cautiously O.K. with that.

"Will you give me Carte Blanche?" I asked him.

"*Oi vey*", he said nervously, "what are your intentions?"

"Trust me" I said and he giggled nervously.

I set to work and he went off to do his chores. Rosalind was pleased with the idea of renovation as she shared my view.

As he arrived home he came bounding up the stairs to see the toilet. At that moment the doorbell rang. It was Ros arriving to view the improvements.

As she came through the door she hopped up and down and said excitedly "I hope it's a bright color."

Hearing this, Alon came to the top of the stairs and said wryly, "Ros you don't have to worry, it's a VERY bright color".

I'd painted the loo a brilliant peacock with a few gold leaves here and there. It was bold and strong but it went down well.

The Wedding was a great success. Rosalind looked too wonderful. Her little waist shown off by the beautiful designer dress, complete with matching stole embroidered with little pearls. The music and dancing were very vocal, enjoyed by all the guests and I felt Alon and I were good back up for each other.

For the first time in a long, long time I felt comfortable and connected to someone. We were soul mates and we understood each other.

We were growing closer, we began to need each other. My instinct alerted me to question where we were going and if I could really commit myself to this amount of emotional responsibility again.

49
THE BREAKTHROUGH

I was settling into the British way of life. Long hours on the tube, learning the bus routes—Alon maintained I'd win any quiz on bus routes! I'd expereinced the peculiar English custom of people moving their chairs and tables into the street to partry with unknown neighbours!!

I was becoming solvent, but I needed to work very long hours each day and I wasn't sure I could handle a relationship and all that went with it. My career was taking off.

I went back to Jo, my councilor for a while, explaining to her how I had struggled with emotional involvement during the intense parts of my life. I believed I could either be a successful artist, committed to my career and concentrating on it 100 percent, or I could be in love—that too 100 %. I had not mastered the art of doing both in a complete way, simultaneously. I always felt I had to choose.

If I was to decide on living a life with Alon, how would I operate within the boundaries I had always set myself? I was very afraid of this choice as it was very foreign to me.

I'd never really had a "present" husband, one who made demands on me or needed partnering. I'd always made my own way and own decisions.

After spending 365 days a year for the last thirty years, trying to russle up something interesting and enticing for all to eat each night, I had reached a point where it didn't matter if I ate cereal alone every night.

I relished in the freedom of no decision. Just pouring it out of the box and scoffing it in front of the TV. Did I still want to be washing someone's socks and folding the laundry? I thought not.

Taking stock I realized I was exhausted from the girls' weddings, from constant long hours of moving all the furniture back and forth in my house to turn it into a studio where I taught textile painting. Most of my pupils seemed to be ex- South Africans. This was wonderful for me as at least they understood my accent. They became my friends and my loyal followers in the exhibitions to come. In addition I had found a niche market where more and more weddings were being held in venues, rather than in synagogues and I evolved a business where I rented out chuppot, the Jewish wedding canopy for the day. These were hand painted modern chuppah and were becoming fashionable in the new decade .This rental business entailed my carrying all the equipment, poles, chuppah etc to the venue, setting it up, waiting around for hours until the wedding was over and then taking a taxi home with all my paraphenalia. I did not feel confident enough to drive into central London. At times the taxi took all my profits but slowly the business grew and I was able to pay my bills.

Still I had not touched the old chuppah I brought from Port Elizabeth. Now and then I took it out to look at and ponder over.

Living permanently in a country where the majority of people spoke differently to you, their terms of reference foreign to you, and their humour different to yours, was not easy. I found it hard to make real friends.

This led me to spend satisfying time on searching for the Daniel Levinthal connections in Lithuania. The researcher I was using in Vilnius had shown my work to the director of art and culture in Vilnius. He was in the process of re-opening a new Jewish Museum in the old Yiddish theatre there.

He invited me to come to Vilnius to see the project and to produce a mural for the entrance to the theatre.

I was intrigued. I never ever imagined going there, but with this invitation I acknowledged to myself that I really longed to solve all the questions in my head. I wanted to answer all the queries that I had never asked Grandpa Daniel when I sat next to him at the weekly Shabbat table.

The East European Cultural Forum eventually agreed to cover the cost of my fare and all the materials I would need.

I had to pay my own accommodation but I found a sculpture foundation who offered me reasonable board as a residency if I would give some lectures on textile art. This I agreed to do and set about getting my visa.

I knew I needed a break and I needed to think through my

relationship with Alon. Where were we going? Did I want to take on a life of domestic responsibility again as well as having the enlarged family we would have with our shared offspring?

I felt I'd done my season and was now free to pursue my art and travel. On the other hand, I was becoming fond of him and looked forward to seeing him at the end of the day. He was "gruff and gentle" all at once and I felt so comfortable with him.

How had I let this happen? It wasn't part of my five year plan!

Within weeks I was ready to go. Alon was somewhat surprised, but very supportive.

In the interim years we had remained close to our Johannesburg neighbour Penny. Their daughters had come to live in London and we kept in touch.

One evening Shera, their daughter, called to say she wanted to introduce Tirza to a friend. Zizi was not keen but was persuaded to accept the invitation. The said gentleman was in London from Israel for the day. However, to my motherly disappointment, on the agreed evening she was in bed with 'flu. The next day Richard called to say he had half an hour before his flight. "Would she still like to meet for coffee?"

In true "Tikkele style" she was twenty minutes late which gave them ten minutes together. When she arrived back home she made no comment.

In my evaluation of the date, that was a great improvement on the usual "yuck—cut me out! "

Richard came to London twice after that and still she made absolutely no comment after her evenings out with him. I didn't dare ask and kept my questions to myself. When he started coming regularly I was eventually allowed to meet this tall impressive young man. He maintained a strong presence but remained distant and private. As I got to know him better I realized he was quite shy. As an anthropologist he was enormously well travelled and informed about world affairs. I marvelled at how, on different continents, at the right time in their lives, the forces of nature had led them to each other. They were amazingly well suited to each other, intellectually, spiritually and even physically. They looked wonderful together. They were both fair haired and seemed "matched" in body and mind. To my delight not only did they have so much common ground but Richard had been to Lithuania and knew exactly where his family came from.

In the interim my search had revealed that my great grandmother Dorah Nurek had come from Shadowa and I had intended to go there en route to Zagare.

Richard's great grandmother also came from Shadowa and as the relationship grew, I became convinced that somewhere along the line they had must have sat together in shul in the late 1800s and made this match.

It is said that forty days before you are born G-d organises your mate.

These two *balabustas* must have been heavenly assistants.

Within a short time I was ready to go, but still Rachel, the researcher had found no trace of Daniel Levinthal.

On the night before I was due to leave, feeling very despondent at knowing I had no leads to follow, I woke up at three in the morning with a start.

It was all so obvious!

From the reading I'd been doing I'd missed the fact that Daniel had run away in the revolution of 1905. He was only 17 so he hadn't owned property or a business yet and moreover I realised that from all the reticence I d experienced from my grandparents when talking about home, as well as my Dad constantly telling me to "forget it" when I wanted to look into things, I assumed that Daniel Levinthal may not have ever been registered in order to hide him from the Russian conscription. I crept into my office. I connected the internet to the All Lithuanian Data Base.

My hands were shaking, I kept hitting the wrong keys.

I sought the tax lists of 1899.

I typed in *Reb Shlomo Ben Zalkind Levinthal* and

THERE ....

I found my family!

My Roots. My great Grandpa Shlomo, whose photo I had carried around with me for all these years! He was listed as "a man of means" as opposed to "bourgeoisie", with a wooden house, wife Gittel. Address; Zagare in Province of Shavli .

At a time like this I sincerely wished I was able to enjoy a stiff drink.

I ached to call my children there and then at 3 a.m. in the morning.

As it was, I called them at 7 a.m. in the morning and I gabbled my excitement out so fast it was all jumbled up.

"Ma, we don't know WHAT you're talking about.

Oh well, they never did!

I e-mailed Rachel and Alon drove me to the airport

I took Dorah's passport and my photograph of Shlomo and Gittel with me and I flew to Vilnius to begin my adventure.

50
Lithuania : Lost in the Forest

At the last minute I had lugged a six foot velvet wall hanging with me onto the aircraft. It illustrated the Trance Dancers that centred around the myths of the Koi San bushmen of the Kalahari desert. I didn't really have a plan as to what I would do with it but decided I needed something of my work that I could show along this journey.

My host had assured me I would not need to bring anything with me as all the materials I needed could be purchased there?

Luckily, I had decided to bring my most valuable tools with me because he failed to enlighten me(probably because he didn't realize) that there were absolutely no 20th century art materials in Lithuania yet !!!I did not realize at the time that Kaunus was one of the foremost European Textile Art centres.

My arrival at Vilnius airport with a six foot wall hanging led customs to question me at great length. Apparently at the time the government were trying to stop antiquities leaving the country They were very suspicious of my intentions albeit I was entering not leaving .

My host was waiting at the arrivals hall.

I greeted him with great excitement and he shook my hand gravely, unsmiling and the we walked to the car without a word.

What was wrong? Maybe he thought I was too young to be giving lectures, or maybe he didn't speak English. As the long journey began, I asked questions, tried to make conversation, but got only monosyllabic nods of the head.

Maybe the problem was being Jewish? But, he knew that from my original correspondence where I said I wanted to see Jewish landmarks and museums.

I felt very uncomfortable.

I felt more uncomfortable when I found that I'd not been informed that I would be based miles from civilization. The nearest bus stop was a three mile walk through the dense forest.

We drove into the sculpture park which was an endless vision of stern unwavering pine trees. In each clearing between the thick trees I saw enormous steel sculptures located around water features and exotic plants.

I was shown to my room in this newly built wooden construction. The room was a little space in the attic with a minute spotless bathroom, with a little bed under the slanting window. You had to be careful not to bump your head when getting off the bed.

Not another soul in sight.

I sat down on the bed and wondered what to do next.

I crept down the stairs and found a kitchen and a dining room and the cook could not speak English but indicated I should sit down to eat.

She was very welcoming and we tried to communicate that I had a special diet.

I need'nt have worried as the daily diet didn't vary at all.

So much for the *"all meals provided"* promise.

Eggs for breakfast—I didn't eat the toast.

Watery vegetable soup was served for lunch and rice and fruit for supper.

And I imagined I was going to have kugel and lokshen pudding

Where was my head!

For days I waited for Mr Sharkes to approach me or seek me out!

I waited in vain. No one came near me .I explored the surrounding forest fearful of predators, never straying too far from the homestead.

The electricity went off at nine and apart from my torch I was in total darkness up in my little attic.

I had always been nervous of the dark but now I was scared of the unknown as well.

The only other occupants were the sculpture makers.I could hear them talking at night so they must have been in the building, but I didn't know their proximity.

Eventually I found his wife in an adjacent building and I communicated that I was very,very angry and wanted to speak to him.

She shrugged uncomprehendingly and I stormed out of the room.

The worst part of this scenario was that there was no telephone communication as there was no satellite in the area.

Me, the neurotic telephonic caller could not call a soul! It was a sobering experience.

I had to walk the three miles to the nearest bus stop,get onto a little local bus and go to the nearby supply store who had a call box that sometimes worked.

After I had dealt with my hysteria,I seemed to get into some sort of routine.

I slept a lot. I lay in my narrow cot looking out of my slanted window and thought about my Dad and Mom. I examined the processes of our relationship and how grateful I was, despite the sadness, that I d had this time with Dad.

I cried a lot and I was free to just feel my sadness. It was ultimately very healing.

I realized that I needed this time, this isolation and once again I questioned whether it was G-ds plan,or natures plan. Was there was a difference?

So despite my anger and my anguish I felt I used the time in a positive way

At night I pushed my suitcase and all the furniture such as it was, up against the door so I could actually fall asleep and feel safe.

On the fourth day I was expecting Rachel the genealogy researcher to come out and see me. I had arranged this prior to knowing what my geographical situation would be.

I walked down towards the bus, embarrassed that she would have to walk so far to get to me, failing to appreciate this was the norm for a Lithuanian society.

I waited at the bus stop watching the simple village life carry on around me.Dogs barked, a sheep baa'd.

A young woman got off the bus dressed in stylish peasant clothes with her thick red hair in braids.She walked purposely towards me.

"Hello Rachel " I put out my hand she stopped and said surprised" how do you know I' m Rachel?"

"You look like your emails "I said

"What do you mean" she asked and we both laughed

Over the next few weeks she kept asking me how I had known it was her and I could not give her a concrete reason. She just had her own style

We got on so well and I grew to love her and her family.

We sat under the trees and I poured out the story of my disappointment in the sculpture park and surroundings to her. She promised to see what she could do and we arranged to meet again.

She was delighted with the development of finding Shlomo Ben Zalkind and left to find out more information from the archive at Kovno.

Two days later she came all the way back by bus to fetch me.

She had made some enquiries and found that I wasn't the first person to be duped by Sharkes promises of exhibitions, workshops and lectures.

Apparently he got government funding for inviting foreigners to boost cultural activities but he had made out as if I was going to be exchanging ideas with artists from all over the world.

The last one had had the same experience as I did, and in fact on my return to London, I managed to make contact with an American and an Indian whose experiences had been a total waste of time, so I could consider myself lucky that actually, the genealogical side of my trip was successful and much more important to me.

I was very angry and resolved not to do more than the pending press talk Sharkes had arranged for me the following day.

Rachel took me to the city and left me in the main street of Vilnius.

I had instructions on where to meet the Minister of Culture and she gave me directions and left me to it.

I arrived at the building in the centre of the old town.

The old city of Vilnius was stone and grey, but gracious. In Gediminio Street I entered a very austere looking building to be faced with heavily armed guards.

I later learned this had been communist headquarters. It felt to me as if it still was!

I was thoroughly searched (by men in dark suits.)They took my passport away and told me to wait. Not even a bench to sit on. I looked at the tall concrete columns and the severe undecorated walls and I shivered at the silence.

After an interminably long time ,two armed men came to collect me and I felt I was being marched down one long corridor after another.

Again, I was told to "wait here."

Another hour passed and then a short and jovial man popped into the office shook my hand vigorously and asked me if I wanted a drink?

Zimanulus was the Lithuanian Minister of Culture. A Litvak by birth

He was also a master of seven languages, one of them Yiddish and had degrees from many European Universities.

He looked at my portfolio told me how excited he was with my work

He explained the whole project to me, and I absorbed his excitement.

At the same time he loaded up his plate and mine with apple tart and patisserie crème and two vodkas.

I was embarrassed. I couldnt eat the apple tart or drink the vodka,but he was unphased. He just drank my vodka and ate my apple tart.

He was the kind of associate I loved working with .Wasted no time or words. Before I knew it I was frog marched back out of the building and Shurina, the architect of the new museum was waiting downstairs in a car with a driver to take me top the site.

We drove to the museum building which was still in its early stages of building renovation, but I could see the European elegance evolving,

We were joined on the roof terrace but Violesa a lovely Lithuanian woman who spoke some English.She was going to be my translator.

We struggled with signs and with only a few words we began to understand each other. I felt their excitement and their hope. I was privileged to be part of this emerging renewal.

When we had finished our discussion.I invited them to have coffee with me and they shyly agreed.

We walked around the corner past the shops where my eyes boggled

The shops were so bare, so simple, no décor mostly no rails, just goods out on a table. No Marks and Spencer, no Woolworths! How did they survive?

We sat down in an elegant new coffee shop which had just opened, evidence of all the regrowth taking place .

Over the weeks that I got to know them, I realized coffee shops were not normally in their budget and I spoke quite openly to them saying if I invited them for coffee they were my guests, and they needn't just order a glass of water.

They eventually became relaxed about this and I think they really enjoyed the treat. Our regular coffee circle grew and I like to think it was not because I was buying coffee, but because they were really interested in what I could share of the west and more importantly my tales of normal Jewish life. They made me describe exactly the rituals of how we celebrated Pesach and Shabbat and what we ate. When a new woman joined the circle they'd make me tell it all over again. Each of them had had one Jewish parent, although this was totally unacknowledged, forbidden information during the communist era. In most cases they had only confirmed this information after the fall of communism.

Violesa told me how she remembered her Mother always being on diet at the same time of the year and not eating bread, and this must have been Pesach.

Shurina told me how she remembered going in the dark of the night to a secret cellar once a year where they ate what could only have been what we know as teigelach.

With Violesa's help to interpret, we began to talk, as woman do, slowly unfolding our life stories. We developed such an empathy and a valued friendship.

In my eyes they were each admirable woman. My mind was opened at the quality of life they had created for themselves and their strength and vigor at achieving their goals despite huge adversity ,and such paucity of available funding and material.

We refilled our coffee cups many times and then they called the interior designer to come and join us.

Lexia was immediately recognisable as a designer.

She had close cropped hair, wore her simple beautiful cloak with an air of grace and revealed a wonderful handcrafted necklace that she wore, to be one of her own designs.

We mapped out the details of what I was going to make and I discussed my isolation and disappointment at the forest venue with them.

I decided I would need space to make the mural and I'd use Sharkes place to begin making the base.

When I could sensibly move the work I d find somewhere else to stay.

Each one offered me a bed.I marveled at their open generosity.

I caught the bus back to the forest. It was crowded dirty and very bumpy. I sat among chickens, ducks, a goat and some very toothy gentleman all looking at me as if I was exhibit A!

It was getting dark as I walked the three miles to Parkes Palace, as I had began to call it in my mind.

I thought of how interesting it was that, put in an arkward situation for a while, we adjust ,our perimeters shrink, we get used to our new space, however sparse or lonely it can be.

When I reached my little attic room it almost felt like home and I got into bed and slept well for the first time.

Early the next morning I came downstairs, ate the same watery half boiled egg and set to work.

I ignored all stares and took over one of the steel workers tables in the large outdoor studio where they worked. As we could not converse due to the language barrier, I didn't bother. I set out my tool s and materials and got to work

I went into the kitchen, pointed at a plastic bowl and some bleach, the cook shrugged her shoulders shaking her head .I picked up the plastic bowl and bleach and appropriated it to my table.

The workers kept coming by to look at what I was doing.

But I was oblivious of anything around me. Today I was a force to be reckoned with!

Eventually that miserable coward Sharkes came to see proof of what had been filtered through to him .

He asked what I was doing. I shook my head as if I didn't understand his question.

In three days I had the basis of my mural ready to move into more detailed work which I could do indoors.

By now the atmosphere between Sharkes and I was silently building up for thunder.

I went to his wife and suggested that I would be going back to the UK to report to the newspapers as to the conditions under which they had pretended to invite me to exhibit.

I thought I would wait until just before I left to announce my intention to demand my refund which he had been prepaid for my accommodation.

I walked the three miles to the end of the woods and called Shurina

"I need a really big favor " I told her.

"I will help you if I can "she said kindly.

"Then arrange for your Minister of Culture to send his car and a driver to collect me in two hours exactly.

If they do not let you in to the forest , bring a government letterhead to show you have urgent business with me."

"I will be ready and packed and when I see you coming up the drive. I will announce I am leaving ,demand my money and come out with my things. "

I will wait here at the call box while you call the minister!"

In less than 5 minutes she called back to say the car would be leaving in half an hour.

I walked quickly back to the house.

I encountered the Shark on the stairs. Well, it was now or never .

"I ve come to collect my refund. I m leaving,"I said.

He ignored me and turned away.

His wife heard my voice and opened the door.

She sullenly asked me to wait. She prepared the refund and silently handed me the envelope.

I rushed off to my room, threw my things into the case.

I rolled up my velvet mural, my new unfinished work and their plastic bowl.

I dragged it all down the back stairs just as the long black government vehicle pulled into the driveway

Shurina climbed out of the car. Angel!! She d had come along to ensure I was O.K.

We piled into the car and rode off with official flag flying in antagonistic triumph in the wind!

As I glanced back I saw surprised faces at the window. Perhaps wondering how I got an official Lithuanian minsterial car to collect me?

She took me into the old city where she had arranged for a new hotel which was still incomplete to give me a suite.

"It will be noisy but you are in the centre of the old town and one block from us at the Jewish centre. They will charge you a minimal rate as the building is not yet complete. "

It sounded like Buckingham Palace.

A TV, a Telephone, and clean sheets, room service and smelly soaps replaced everyday.

How I appreciated my Western standards that day.

I called Alon

I told him how much I missed him. How much I realized he meant to me and how I looked forward to coming home as soon as I had completed my mission at the museum.

I called each one of my children and caught up on all their news. I felt whole again with a telephone hitched to my ear.

·

51
EN ROUTE BACK TO ZAGARE

U p to this point in my eastern European travel, one would have thought there had never been Jews in Lithuania. I came across no evidence or information, no acknowledgement in any area of history or culture.

The young ladies of Lithuania that I spoke to working at the Sculpture Park had no knowledge of the Holocaust. They had been born into communism and told me they were completely forbidden, even in the privacy of their own homes, to discuss, or to learn anything about pre-communist rule. Freedom of speech is a privilege we demanded in our society. The concept of controlled conversation in the privacy of your own home was something that took a lot of explanation. These young ladies accepted it as the *norm* that they had known.

I became angry and more and more astounded.

A week or two later, after I moved into the old city, I met my new friend Violesa through the museum and the Jewish Community Centre.

She was a Lithuanian poet and because she could offer some cultural prestige to the communists, she was allowed extra privilege. She had a communist allotted two bedroom apartment. She was permitted to travel to linguistic seminars and poetry readings out of the country and they produced her many volumes of poems, all paid for by the party. Now that the communist era was over, she had freedom of choice, but no government publisher, no income. She had, though, been allowed to keep her home.

To earn her keep she worked at the museum which she said was endlessly depressing because they had no heating and very little in the way of exhibits to show the increasing number of visitors who began to come to Vilnius to find their roots.

Here, at the center, I found the library and the museum, young peoples organizations, study groups, all with such limited resources I could only admire their courage and tenacity in the face of the hopeless prospect of funding.

The museum had a few interesting pieces to show, but no real treasures of any significance were left.

The local Women's Zionist Group were meeting the next day and I agreed to go along and give a talk and show them my portfolio, which I did with great humility.

They were all highly educated woman and so appreciative of seeing my work.

Every woman had a question and they were genuinely intrigued by all I could tell them about the West and about modern Judaic Art, of which they had seen very little in the eastern countries. I felt such a connection with them I stayed all afternoon.

They gave me a space to work at the Community Centre and I took time to make friends with everyone there.

In the afternoons I wandered around the city, into the former ghettos and along the narrow streets. I peered into gated courtyards, remembering the tales I had read about life in the passages and pathways during the war. On Shabbat I went to The Choral Synagogue in the centre of town, the only one still standing. The taxi driver in the area was unfamiliar with the building and when I finally found it for him from my map, he asked me what kind of building it was, so obviously it was not a building the public had much of a consciousness of.

It was a high turreted old building, large and draughty, with the Hebrew lettering just visible over the arched entrance. Inside, the Aron Kodesh, the ark were astounding and one of the visual highlights of my trip.

Burnished and gilded, it enveloped baroque and rococo coils and swirls, the gilded pillars were inset turquoise from floor to ceiling. They were absolutely astounding in the midst of all that was so austere in Vilnius.

A few men were dovening and praying downstairs. As men and woman are separated, I crept up the back stairs to the women's gallery.

There I met with a real eye-opener. Only two bare wooden benches completed the barren décor.

I sat down gingerly on the one and peered over the banisters at the service.

The sound filled my ears, although I could hardly follow the service, until they sang *L'Cha dodi* ...The familiar melody filled my head and took me back to my childhood.

Now I was irrefutably sure I was of Lithuanian descent. They sang the songs exactly as Grandpa Dan had sung them, and as they were sung in the Synagogue in Port Elizabeth.

Shortly after I sat down, a youngish woman in jeans wandered cautiously into the women's area. She sat down tentatively beside me.

She was an American called Scott Davis, looking for her roots and soon we were exchanging genealogical research details.

After the service, she was going on to a dinner at the Community Centre arranged by the Yiddish Society.

"Do you speak Yiddish?" she asked.

"Unfortunately not," I answered.

"Never mind, come along, it's free and you'll meet some of the people here for the Yiddish course."

I had nothing better to do, so for fun and out of curiosity I went along with her.

Contrary to my expectations, I had the most enlightening experience. The whole evening was completely in Yiddish. About 50 Americans had come to Vilnius to do a course and to my absolute amazement I understood 75% of what was being said. I could get along in Yiddish and I had never envisaged that I could understand it! The sound was so familiar. The words were often words I knew and the intonations and expressions one could guess. I'd been brought up with the sound in my ear, in that little sewing room all those years ago.

Oh how I longed for Alon! He spokeYiddish. He would have been in his element here.

The mural for the museum was developing well. Lexia and Shurina were excited by the progress and I decided I would take a week off and go to Zagare with Rachel.

We plotted our trip to include Shadowa and Ponevys, from where Alon's family had originated. Close to Shadowa was Keidania, where my friend Barbara's father had been brought up.

I was excited and eager to explore. We traveled by bus to Kovno.

We walked around the town and Rachel showed me the sites of all the old Jewish buildings. The shuls, the orphanage, the Beit Midrash, house of study.

We had made an appointment at the Kovno Archives. All government buildings are run-down but this one was in exceptionally good condition. We climbed up seven flights of steps and were ushered into a room furnished with heavy wooden pews. We were told to wait.

Everyone spoke in a quiet whisper. Just audible, Rachel spoke on my behalf. She gave in the names and dates we were looking for and from the attitude of the researcher I gathered Rachel was known here. She requested papers relating to ShlomoBen Zalkind Levinthal and the Nurek family.

We waited patiently until the door dragging along the old wooden floor heralded the arrival of the researcher bearing two large and obviously very old record books. She placed them gingerly on the table, reminding us to use them carefully. We were asked to put on gloves so as not to damage the pages.

Rachel sat down next to me and I felt a sense of great history, a feeling of awe as I opened the pages to see the spindly old fashioned writing obviously written with a quill pen, in an ordinary exercise page. We were directed to the pages relevant to our query and I could not believe I was looking at the actual entries the Rabbis had made in 1901 in their shtetl communities. At the time they had to record taxes, land tax and candle tax, as well as property, births, marriages and deaths.

Gingerly, and with great reverence, Rachel helped me search the pages, translating easier than I could as it was all written in Yiddish. To my excitement we found an entry showing the signature of Morris Nurek's older brother. But the piece de resistance to my exhilarating surprise were entries in the hand of Shlomo ben Zalkind. Entries showing donations made to the shul in Alt Zhagare, obviously on *Yarhtzeits* anniversaries of family deaths. Now I was more certain than ever that I was on the right track. I obtained a copy of the signatures and I found myself staring at his handwriting as the only way I could physically connect with him.

I marveled at the fact that Grandpa Dan had never ever given me any negative impression of his homeland, only regaled me with the details he remembered with longing and delight. Part of me felt sad that I never had the opportunity to discuss any of his experiences with him and I mused over whether my father had ever had any enlightening conversation about Zagare with him.

I left the archives in a daze and we walked along the now modern main mall. We came to the only shul left operative there and she caught sight of her friend Chaim.

"We are about to doven Maairev, the evening service. Come in," he said.

"Do you want to go in and see their chuppah?" Rachel asked me.

"Definitely" I wanted to go inside.

The required ten men were making a minyan, a quorum. They all stopped as we entered the darkened shul.

They asked her in Yiddish "Who is this?"

"A Yiddishe meidel visiting Kovno, looking for her roots" she replied.

"A Yiddishe meidle? She doesn't look Yiddishe", they said. "Why is she blonde?"

Rachel laughed heartily, and translated for me. She spoke to them, trying to convince them I was Jewish. I was very tempted to say "just look at my Bobba's boobs for proof", but I worried they would not appreciate my brand of African humor.

Eventually they grudgingly took her word for it and came forward to shake my hand. Once I was accepted they wanted Rachel to take photos of them standing with me.

I learned then, that they were sponsored and assisted to keep the shul going by a group of men from Cape Town.

They hauled out their chuppah, a simple velvet square with a Magen David, a star of David, embroidered in the middle. They were very amused at the thought of my making individual chuppot. Theirs had been in use since 1929. This synagogue was even more decorative than the Vilnius shul.

The Aron Chodesh was the size of a smallish room and heavily gilded in a myriad of fluted columns and plaited curves embossed with bright molten gold. The fittings were heavy black carved wood and marble. Inside this spiritual enclosure they had a very valuable collection of Torah.

I told Rachel wanted to book into a hotel with swimming pool as I needed to exercise.

She laughed and said "Hilary, this is not Jo'burg, it's Kovno. If there is a pool it will be so small we'll have to get in individually."

I was adamant, I needed to move my limbs, so we arranged that I would stall the receptionist while she dashed into the back and looked at the pool. If she winked I should register, if not we should seek some other pool.

She came out winking and we checked in and changed into our costumes.

We had to wait while they opened and warmed the pool. It was so rarely used but we swam together. She was so excited at this unexpected treat and I was so happy I could treat her to it. I looked the other way when she kept putting the food from the buffet into her bag, not sure why she did it but I did not want to embarrass her. In retrospect she didn't really care. She wasn't embarrassed about her need to survive. She did what she had to do and I so admired her for it.

We swam a few times before we picked up our driver in the morning. He was to drive us north to Zagare.

The road was long and straight. Not a hill in sight.

I asked about the rows of corn growing along the road and the driver laughed. He told me through Rachel, that the communists had ordered various crops to be planted. They did not bother to be informed as to the suitability of their crops and the commandants, who checked out that the farmers were obeying orders, only drove along the roads. They never came into the properties so the farmers would plant the corn along the road and behind the corn, their chosen crops. Over the years since then the corn had been left to grow.

The roads were fairly good although most cars we passed were really old. The distances between shtetls seemed endless.

I had a lot of thinking time and felt so privileged that I had had this lucky opportunity to come and find not only myself, my priorities, but a people that I really felt such empathy with.

As we turned into the entrance to Shadowa I hooted with laughter. There under the board showing the name of the town was a huge colorful sculpture of a toothy crocodile.

"Do you have crocodiles here?" I asked Rachel puzzled.

"No" she grinned, "it's to welcome all of you South Africans home!"

I had to have a photograph of myself standing at the croc under the sign for Shadowa.

In my notebook I had the address of my cousin Alain's grandmother's house in Shadowa. She was a Levinthal and had left Lithuania at the turn of the century.We parked and walked around the narrow streets until sure enough we found number 16 Gediminio Street (all the main streets seemed to be called Gediminio).

She had said it was opposite the Post Office, but I guess in 100 years the Post Office had relocated because it was opposite the fire station.

An old couple on a horse and cart passed by. We examined each other in great detail.They smiled and waved. Imagine still traveling by horse and cart in 2001! The area of Shadowa was owned by property magnate of that time, and a lot of development had taken place outside of Shadowa . We stopped for lunch at a lovely restaurant overlooking the lake It was a pleasant time to chat and enjoy the local speciality of veal. I had this weird feeling I might bump into someone I knew!

After lunch we drove to the cemetery and Rachel walked through the over grown grass reading occasional scripts that one could still see .We came to the taller stones in the front of the grave and she explained to me that these were the Cohenim.I knew that Dorah Nurek s maiden name had been Cohen and I stood for a while wondering if these were family of hers and therefore mine.

I was anxious to get to Zagare now and we continued our long drive north.

We passed through Linkuva where I wanted to see the Shul I had heard about.High on the front lintel of the shul was the date 1561.Still standing, as if waiting for our return, although no longer any Jews to attend I was reminded that my diamond, or Gittel's diamond, had come from this very area.

Hours later we saw the sign and I absolutely had to stop and take a photograph to prove I'd been to Zagare. Rachel explained the history of this town, how it had been renown for Torah study and many well known Rabbonim, very learned men had originated from this area. We went straight to the cemetery.It was well kept although many of the stones had fallen and broken over the years. Much of the engraving was so worn it was impossible to read. We had stopped at many cemeteries along the way and some of the time I wondered why, as Jews, we needed to travel halfway around the world and stand in cemeteries where we can't identify the names. But standing in the cemetery at Zagare I felt such a strong presence, I felt as if I might faint. Tears poured down my face and I wanted time to sit and feel. So far back, so long ago. Yet, I felt them around me so strongly I could not deny the aura of someone close to me touching my head. Rachel gave me space. I wanted to hold onto the feeling for a while. Sadly we could not identify any grave but she decided we needed to seek the last Jew in Zagare.

Izak Mendelsohn had just had a stroke. We helped him out of the house and bundled him into the car.Yes, he remembered my great grandfather Reb Shlomo ben Zalkind. He remembered going there for Shabbat dinner when he was a very little boy, and he remembered the HOUSE!

Oi vey! I was trembling shaking as we drove over the hill and into an area where the houses were larger and the plots more luscious.

Grandpa Dan had always told me he lived alongside the big shul and was regularly compelled to make up a minyan when they were short of the ten men required for a service, when reading the Torah .He had also told me many tales of how he had skated to school.

The house had been bombed in 1944 but part of it still stood. Izak wanted to get out of the car. I helped him out and stood holding his hand as we looked at the scene before us. Alongside the pathway the large imposing shul stood intact!

I wept. I wept with my whole body. I couldn't cry any harder. Izak put his arm around me and picked up a stone from Great grandpa s house for me to keep and remember.

"You must show me the school" I begged

"Over the river that way," he pointed.

So he HAD skated to school. The river still flowed.

"This was the Levintahl house", using the yiddish pronounciation, "then the Gordon's house, and then the other Levintahl brother lived in the far house. It had a long verandah and a large dinner table for all to sit at," he told us.

On the other side of the river was Neue Zhagere and Izak regaled us with stories of how the community was split by the young renegades who wanted their Judaism modernized. They would not even attend each others simchas and the *veribbles* their squabbles, were always the talk of Shabbat mornings .

Izak recalled that Reb Shlomo ben Zalkind was one of the few members of the Alt Zhagere whom was respected by the Neue side and sometimes invited to give a *drosha*.

I was standing here in Granpa Dan's childhood home, breathing in the same air he had breathed, looking at the same view he had looked at.

I could not have expected the fervid emotionality I felt. I can not elucidate the experience. Could my father Jacob have understood? Was this something I wanted to relate to essentially because I had loved Grandpa Dan so much?

As long as I live, I will remember the feeling I had, standing on the corner, facing the shul and looking back over the river .A moment in time, held for eternity.

We treated Izak to tea at the local pub and onlookers were very curious as to who we were. Time and again he had to explain to each new person who came into the tea house why we were here and who we were.

Isak wanted to take us to Narishkin Park. I had read Rose Zwi's book but somehow at the time I hadn't made the connection to Zagare and I didn't really take much notice.

He had been a teenager when picked up by Lithuanian police and herded into the park on Yom Kippur 1941 with all the other Jews.

Made to dig their own trenches and watch their family being shot into the graves before their own turn came. Izak sobbed still today, as he told me the story. He was secretly in love with a young non-Jewish Lithuanian girl.

Her house bordered on the park and he managed to crawl through the fence unobserved and run to her house where she hid him until he escaped to Riga under cover of the dark night—one of only three men who escaped the annihilation of all the Jews of Zagare!

Lithuanian Police confiscated their goods and their houses and are still living in them today. Izak felt compelled to come back after the war and marry his young lady who had waited years for him. He looked after the cemetery and kept the unused shul neat and safe.

It was getting dark and we had to make our way to Kovno.

I hugged him with promises of coming back with my family one day

I felt as if my own being had been verified and my longing for my grandparents had, been satisfied in some minor way.

52
OPENING A NEW DOOR

As the plane landed I felt my excitement rise. I finally knew where I wanted my life to go. This gave me a feeling of heightened libidinous courage, a wondrous exciting direction.

I collected my Lithuanian cloth witch, my parcels, my bags and I sallied forth.

It always pleases me to come through arrivals and see Alon, a mountain among men. He always stood back unassumingly waiting for me to find him.

When he enveloped me with his broad shoulders and his arms, I knew where home was.

I opened myself to a new era in my life without the fear of being limited by what I wanted to do. I knew we were both mature enough to give each other the freedom to live as we desired to live, and to share the things we chose to share.

We went home and prepared to move into his home together.

Dorcas the housekeeper was devastated and set about being as obstructive as she could.

I set myself a personal goal to overcome this barrier and make it my "*mitzvah*" in life to cope with her onslaught .I reasoned that my life was getting better and she would be the loser, so I owed her some leeway.

On the hard days I gritted my teeth, and yelled at Alon as he came through the door after work, but he took it all in his broad shouldered nonchalant stride.

It was soon to be Rosh Hashana, the Jewish New Year.

We pooled our silver and set about polishing our joint wares to embellish our table. We would celebrate this happy family occasion a Yomtov with all our children around us. When I was a young girl all I ever envisaged of my life was to be seated at a full Shabbat table with children and grandchildren around us. Thirty-three years later I was to fulfill my wish with his children and mine. Thirty-three had always been my lucky number!

We had not much time to linger over our decision as we were presented with the fabulous joyous news that Richard and Tirza had decided to be married.

The Wedding was to be in Israel in the very near future. I gently suggested that they could consider marrying under the antique chuppah, but at this stage it looked like an old *lappie a*nd I was vehemently informed that this was a contemporary wedding and everything was to be ultra modern!

I remembered my determination not to intrude in their bridal dreams.

Despite the intifada, which gave me many sleepless nights worrying about the safety of our guests, we began preparing with great excitement and joy.

Tikkele requested that I make the Chuppah in a see-through material so she could see the sky. This was to incorporate the promise made to Abraham that "your descendants will be as numerous as the stars in the sky". Since every Jewish marriage is a continuation of Abraham's progeny, she wanted to be able to see the stars.

I made up the sides of the canopy with velvet, decorated in a design of orange and pink flowers. The canopy section over the top was transparent voile, embossed with pearls and appliquéd flowers. The family names were painted on the inside flap and in this way we felt the memory of Wilfred could be present.

I could not believe my eldest child who favored beige and grey was to be married in orange and pink. She had chosen these colors because she knew that the orange and pink bougainvillea of her childhood home would be in full bloom in Caesarea, in Israel. This was her meaningful way of connecting the wedding venue with home.

The wedding dress was my personal nightmare!

I reluctantly agreed to make it. We fought like wild cats as it progressed.

I unpicked it *"over countable"* times but, when I saw her standing in it on the wedding day, every moment had been worthwhile. The stretched fluted edge of the orange and pink layers peeked out under the pure silk off white skirt as she walked. Her perfect figure filled the little bodice encrusted with pearls and the veil was covered in pink and orange ribbon roses.

To our great joy, so many of her friends from South Africa, Australia and London, flew to Israel for the wedding.

We hired a large house near to the Ruins of Caeserea. Everyone brought with them a mattress and sleeping bag. Best of all, Alon agreed to share the experience with me and Ros, Alon's daughter, her husband Milton and young son Joe were to share it all with us. Joey was the daily centre of attraction. His antics intrigued everyone and he was "borrowed to play babies" and held by all. His presence proved to encourage all the young couples around us to think about babies.

Tirza's special friend Shirley travelled three days from Australia to get to the wedding. She was our domestic goddess and went straight into the kitchen and to cook. She made us amazing *Pesedicke* (passover) meals in the days that followed the wedding .

It was strange that all our family events seem to have taken place over Pesach! Daniel's barmitzvah, Wilfred's death and, now, Tirza's wedding. We were destined always to be wandering Jews!

It was a house filled with laughter and celebration and sharing.

Alissa and I accompanied Tikky to the mikveh. We drove through the strange Israeli countryside feeling as if we were driving back through time, until we came to the mikveh in a wooden clearing on the edge of a kibbutz settlement. It was again a night of quiet contemplation and ritual preparation for the forthcoming nuptials. The three of us bonded quietly together, before she became the participant of her new unit with Richard.

Just before the Sabbath, Tirza's associates from the Rabbinic school turned our hired house into a shul. I was privileged to have the Sefer Torah carefully placed in my cupboard and like a baby I kept checking it to see it remained undisturbed.

Both Richard and Tirza had studied the Torah for their coming ceremony and on the Shabbat morning we celebrated Richard's " *aufruff*" This is when the groom is called up to the central Bimah in shul and reads from the ancient text in Hebrew. This is no easy task and calls for dedicated learning. We all walked home together in the warm Mediterranean sun, singing songs of joy. We prepared for Zizi's turn to read from the Torah in the afternoon.

Not many brides are able to do this and I was very proud of her.

In ancient times it was not considered proper for woman to touch the Torah. This was because they were considered impure at menstruation but today in the 21st Century this thought is being adapted in some modern communities so as to allow woman to read from the Torah.

On Saturday evening we all traipsed up to the ruins for a last minute check on where we would be holding the wedding.

We were almost submerged.

The wind blew a gale, the giant waves came over the wall gushing over our shoes, our hair stuck to our head in matted lumps and we wondered what we'd all look like tomorrow under the Chuppah.

Later that evening I told Tirza that I wanted to give her something lasting and meaningful for her wedding gift.I'd decided that as she was named after Tuvia I would like then to have one of my most precious possessions as my gift to last a lifetime. I entertained visions of Tirza and Richard serving English tea with cream scones and little rounds of cake on a Sunday afternoon.I had wrapped the brass samovar in a huge box with loads of pink and orange tissue paper and placed it in their home to find on their return I hoped they would value it and keep it polished..

At exactly five o'clock the next evening, as the princess in her orange pink and white silk dress stepped out of the bridal "Bus "as it were, G-d in his wisdom stilled the wind. A perfect evening began with a magical walk down the ancient tunnels of the ruins, the first wedding held here in 2000 years. They walked through the long shadows of the old stones into the natural light of the amphitheatre where an excited Richard was bouncing from foot to foot, waiting to welcome her under the chuppah, as if, into his home, to be his bride.

My joy could not have been greater as I watched my daughter circle her future husband in the traditional wedding ceremony. This was to signify she would make him the centre of her world.

Then, to the mirth of everyone in true feminist style, she made him circle her in the same way.

As Richard completed the blessings required of the groom, he stamped healthily on the glass. We break the glass to remind us of the destruction of the second temple.

Cheers of "MAZELTOV, mazeltov" rose through the amphitheatre. The Holy One, ever present, caused the natural light to fade at the very moment the glass broke, and the electric lights in the amphitheatre went on in dramatic theatrical style.

It was a perfect climax to a perfect moment in time. One we would hold precious in our minds, as Richard and Tirza held each other in a circle of love and tears. We all wished for Wilfred's presence under the chuppah

It was romantic and lively. The young people sang and danced leading the bridal couple towards the ruins of the old city.

There, drinks and snacks had been laid out. Little two seater couches had been placed around and thanks to Richard's parent's thoughtfulness, blankets had been provided for the sea air. They had thought of everything. Little mounds of watermelon balanced daintily on lettuce baskets,and litchis marinated in coconut juice, sugared with whiskey were handed out on sticks. It was an enchanted evening made all the more successful by their generosity and their desire to make this such a special event

My happiness for my daughter and a wish for a good partner for her had all come to a rounded fruition. Now I could relax and enjoy the wedding.

Alon and I wondered down to the waters edge. Born and bred a beachcomber, I took off my shoes hitched up my elegant skirt and sat down on the sand.

He followed suit somewhat dubiously.

He put his arm around me and I leaned my head against his broad chest.

The sound of the sea made me think of my parents. How I'd missed them tonight. "That was so magical Alon, I feel so happy for her."

"Yes" he said "it was one of the most beautiful weddings I've been to".

"I hope it was her dream come true", I sighed. "She is such a generous person to other people. I hope this is her gift in life."

"Yes" he nodded quietly," and then enquired "and what would make your dream come true?"

"To marry you under the open sky in our garden" I said dreamily without consciously thinking about what I was saying.

Oh VEY!!! I couldn't believe my ears. Had I just said that? Had I proposed to HIM!

I couldn't take it back now.

"Do I get a choice of Chuppah?" he asked smiling.

"I can't believe I said that" I stammered.

At that moment Tikkele and Richard summoned us to come back to the party and I didn't know whether it was a yes or a no!

53
UNDER THE CHUPPAH

Nothing spurs an artist to spring cleaning like a white canvas—any excuse to avoid starting a new work. I tidied my studio, I catalogued my bottles of silk paint in groups of reds, blues and yellows. I cleaned my brushes and re-arranged my collection of threads, fingering and winding them delicately round the bobbins while I remembered where I had found each treasure.

Finally, one morning there were no chores left to do.

I took out Doniyel's antique Chuppah and I spread it over my work table in my London studio. I ran my hand lovingly over the velvet pile of the cloth, still smooth and rich. I felt it speak to me. I had washed it by hand and the velvet pile had come up soft and springy. The stale smell of being in plastic had dissipated. How on earth had Gittel made this vibrant rose color?

I cut a dozen pieces of silk into squares and tried various experiments with color. I knew I had to match the color exactly to mend the few worn areas which had been affected by being in the ground. I mixed carmine with turquoise. That sometimes gave a vibrant wine colour but it was too purple. I tried medium blue with magenta but that was too dark. I tried traditional red /blue combination but that was even further from the color.

I was at a dead end.

Per chance over Pesach, I learned from Sephardi friends that they cooked their eggs in red onion skins and it turned the shells a deep maroon.

Of course! That was it! How short-sighted of me. Gittel hadn't had the Hobby Craft shop to rely on, so she had used nature's color from vegetables.

I sped off to my studio. I cooked up the red skin of the onions. In my veggie bin. I spied fresh beetroot. I made a separate pot of beetroot skins mixed with the onions and—Voila! I had the exact colour.

I dipped the new virginal white silk velvet that I intended to patch with, into the pot. While I stirred I closed my eyes and thought of Gramps—his heavy watch swinging from his pocket, his long white curls at seventy, the tales of Zagare where a large bag of grapes only cost him a penny. I smiled when I remembered how he sucked the sugar cube.

I sat at my studio table and unpicked the worn bits stitch by stitch. I would have to hand stitch them back on, in order to be sure everything was well aligned. I walked my fingers hands over the embroidered stitches of the crown and lions. They were so sophisticated I did not know how to achieve these couched knots. But, next door, my dear neighbour Hettie was an expert with the embroidery needle. I wondered if she would help me to repair the Chuppah.

I invited her over and she examined the cloth that I had told her about on my return from Port Elizabeth

"Well" she mused "it will be a laborious process, but I do know these stitches."

So, to my delight, Hettie agreed to add her skill to the chuppah.

While I tacked the newly cut velvet edges, she whirled and twirled her needle with gold and silver thread. It took us weeks and many cups of coffee, always accompanied with a slab of chocolate. It reminded me of how Grandpa Daniel used to secretly creep into the spare bedroom to pinch a piece of chocolate out of Gran's stock as soon as he knew his diabetic urine test was clear.

We reconstructed this beautiful Chuppah cover, renovating it section by section, trying hard to preserve every stitch carefully.

One fine summer day, just as the daffodils were fading, we had completed the project. We both stood back in awe of this marvellous piece of artwork, our efforts joined to Gittel's original effort.

"What are you going to do with it?" Alon asked me.

"Oh, probably exhibit it in an appropriate place" I shrugged.

He looked at me questioningly.

Nothing more had been said about my suggestion of marriage since Tirza's wedding. We'd studiously avoided the subject although both very conscious of the conversation having taken place.

I vacillated between thinking I wanted to marry this man, tall as Mount Lebanon, and rueing the day I got involved . "*Oi vey*," I thought, he's more untidy than I am, with more bits of paper in organized piles in every room, and that's saying something. He throws newspapers on the floor all weekend until one can't find a path back to your bed for newsprint, and mostly, he hadn't even read them.

I couldn't *stand* people who read Sunday newspapers on Monday.

He wore two dozen pairs of socks a week! How many feet did he have?

He clomped around the room in the early morning like a dinosaur romping in a forest.

I knew I d have to live with the parrrot, the dog and Dorcas!

What was I thinking...............

There were days when I knew he was thinking the same.

Oi shlect !!!!

I've lived happily on macaroni cheese for all these years. Why do I have to eat this healthy nouvelle cuisine, such small portions, and so many vegetables. They were coming out of my ears! I never ate them as a child why should I be subjected to them now?

As for the amount of loo paper she uses to clean her make-up off. Formerly 12 rolls had lasted for months. And, worst of all, poor Charlie the dog was no longer allowed to sleep on the bed. We were no longer allowed to leave used tea bags piling up next to the kettle. She said it was a dirty "English habit" and could she "*Hak n dir a tsheinik* (do my head in) when I wore black pants with a blue jacket!

It was *Meshuggah* ,a madness, at this stage in my used life!

At the beginning of the summer Alon and I went to Portugal on holiday. We sat on Estoril beach watching the sunset, my head on his shoulder, our feet waiting for the tide to tickle our toes."*Nu* "said Alon "so when are we going to put the chuppah to its proper use?"

"Well" I smiled up at him, "I'm waiting for you to propose to me!"

"But I thought you already did," he asked confusedly,

"Oh no," I proclaimed very definitely," that was just a suggestion! I want the real 'down on one knee' proposal before I can even consider it."

"*A nechtiker tog* "he laughed, "forget it!"

I felt relieved. I told myself I was too old to make such a change.

Later that night we sat together, our appetites sated with the fish bones around us .We had polished off the wonderful fish stew I'd made from a large freshly caught Dorado, purchased at the market. Alon was handy with a carving knife. He cleaned the fish for me and I sauté`ed it gently in white wine with fresh herbs and mushrooms.

While we were sitting at the table enjoying the quiet of the warm evening, I knocked over the glass of wine. Alon rushed to the kitchen to get a cloth. He knelt down to mop it all up, and then with a broad smile he looked up at me mischievously and said "and while I'm down here in this uncomfortable position, will you marry me?"

I was flabbergasted, but the question needed an answer.

"I will, I will", I said and got down onto the floor and put my arms around his neck. It was a moment of awkward old bones entwined together in happy oblivion.

He couldn't have known that my dad had told me about Dan proposing to Tuvia in the same way in 1914!

We would have to use Tuvia's tea cups for the wedding feast.

Now all we had to do was break the news to our children.We called them in London. They all thought it was quite cute and preparations began in earnest!

As the day approached, I vowed to myself I would not become a bride with matching "what's its". But suddenly, I found myself carried away by all the hype.There I was buying bridal magazines, and looking at cake decorations. Everyone wanted to help and we asked our children to get it all together.

Alon and I decided we would definitely use Dan and Tuvia's Lithuanian Chuppah.

I wanted to be married in our garden, amidst a flourish of home grown blooms -a simple wedding with just our children and people who were important in our lives around us. Tuvia, my sister Jinny's daughter was to be married on the same day in Cape Town, so we could not be together. Our lovely grandchildren would be our attendants. Our children would stand as our pole holders in true South African style. Dave, Alon's son would be his best man and sing us the song he'd written for the occasion. Daniel my son would lead me under the chuppah and my daughters Tirza and Alissa would accompany us. Our friends would sing *"Baruch haba,"* welcome the bride and groom, and everyone would surround us while I circled Alon seven times in traditional style.

I truly believed that many other important people would be under the Chuppah with us.

There would be angels and souls. I imagined Dorah Nurek in her tilted hat and fox fur standing with a broad smile. Donyiel and Tuvia would have loved Alon. He could have sat at the table and sung songs with Gramps. I hoped Mom and Dad would be there to see me remarried again after 34 years since my last chuppah. It would have made them feel confident despite the rugged journey of life that I had survived.

In memory of our departed spouses we asked the Rabbi to make the wedding B*rach*ot, the seven blessings of marriage, with both the silver cups that we had originally married with. This gesture held special meaning for both of us.

So often Alon told me I said things that his late wife had said. There was many a moment when I felt Alon was so like Wilf in temperament. We decided that we would be married with Mom's 50th anniversary wedding ring, the one Dad had left beside the bed for me to find when he passed away.

I hoped it would bring us some of the 57 strong years they'd had together. If we lived ten years together we'd be very lucky at our age , but now that we'd made the decision, every moment counted.

We approached Rabbi Levy who informed us that this was quite acceptable as long as Alon purchased the ring from me for a reasonable amount, and the ring would therefore be his, to contract the wedding with.

"Yeh, I'll give her ten bucks" he laughed.

"No", I reminded him, "a *reasonable* amount".

"Well, how much do you want for it" he asked, in a tight corner.

"New curtains for the lounge" I pronounced. A wise man knew when he was defeated. The deal was done.

The Wedding fayre was, as it always is at Jewish functions— important. Ours was not to be conventional or English. Joseph was an expert sushi maker and had produced umpteen platters of delicately rolled sushi, little packages in seaweed and cucumber expertly covered in sesame. This was handed around the garden on square black platters, each plate holding a rose. Alon and I made a toast with champagne. Alissa had produced a gorgeous double layered chocolate, wedding cake. Alon's children had provided a band. It was complete with a bride carrying the groom over the threshold, which caused a laugh.

We agreed that I did not want to wear my mother's diamond.

Together, with deliberation and solemnity, we stitched Gittel's diamond from Linkuva back into the Crown of the Chuppah to await Daniel's destiny, where he would find it on the occasion of his marriage.

I made my way down the aisle, accompanied by Joseph's parents as my *unterferers*, the couple accompanying me to the chuppah, as Julie had been responsible for starting all this. Alon was accompanied by the hostess who held our first dinner. My young friends, JT and Eve, Larry and Ingrid, who had traveled the long round journey of emigration to London with me, took photos and videos. The Nureks came from Johannnesburg. My fellow traveler in life's adventures Ann came from Johannesburg. Her man Ben came from Klerksdorp and he seemed to know all Alon's side. Alon's older brother arrived unexpectedly from New York to stand by his side. Alon was so pleased to have his support. The garden filled up with neighbors and special friends. They sat under the apple tree murmuring with festive expectations. The purple velvet Chuppah standing ready to receive us was my 100th canopy since I began to make them in Britain.

Charlie the dog padded very solemnly alongside me in a suitably big bow. I walked hopefully towards a happy new life in an English garden, amidst South African voices singing the blessings, and our special ex South African Rabbi smiling as he quietly counted the number of times I had circled Alon.

Birth is a beginning and death a destination.
From loneliness to love,
From joy to gratitude.
From pain to compassion,
And grief to understanding.
From Fear to faith,
From defeat to defeat,
until looking back ,or ahead ,
We see that victory lies
Not at some high place along the way,
But, in having made the journey,
stage by stage ,
A Sacred pilgrimage
Birth is a beginning.

HILARY RUDICK
is an international Textile and Fibre Artist.
producing silk textiles using Japanese Shibori
She lives in London with her husband, children and grandchildren
Her speciality is the making of wedding canopies, the Chuppah
She works from her studio in Portugal and London where her husband's
dental jackets are often unwittingly dyed along with the artwork.
She writes cookery books and a cookery column.
This is her first novel.
2005

CCNU, the chemotherapy drug became a registered drug under the name Lomustine,
25 years after it was successfully used on Wilfred.

Part proceeds from sale of this book to:
CANCERTRUST -ROYAL MARSDEN HOSPITAL